VICIOUS CRIMES

A totally captivating crime mystery

MICHAEL HAMBLING

Detective Sophie Allen Book 12

JOFFE BOOKS

Joffe Books, London
www.joffebooks.com

First published in Great Britain in 2023

This book is a work of fiction. Names, characters, businesses, organizations, places and events are either the product of the author's imagination or are used fictitiously. Any resemblance to actual persons, living or dead, events or locales is entirely coincidental. The spelling used is British English except where fidelity to the author's rendering of accent or dialect supersedes this.

Cover art by Nick Castle

ISBN: 978-1-83526-311-2

CHARACTER LIST

Wessex Regional Serious Crime Unit (WeSCU):
Detective Chief Superintendent Sophie Allen
Detective Chief Inspector Polly Nelson (Somerset)
Detective Sergeant Rae Gregson (Dorset)
Detective Sergeant Adrian 'Ade' Ahmed (Somerset)
Detective Constable Tommy Carter (Dorset)
Detective Inspector Barry Marsh (Dorset)

Local Watchet Police:
Special Constable Jackie Spring (a volunteer officer and local librarian)
Constable Sarah Levy

Other Important Characters:
Tony Fisher, Jackie Spring's boyfriend
Donny Lomax, a somewhat light-fingered farm worker
Bryn, Babs and Maddy Guthrie, a family working a farm on Exmoor
Lady Braycombe, local 'lady of the manor'
Harry Campion, Lady Braycombe's estate manager

Glossary
For convenience, a short glossary appears at the end of this book. It also lists the main ranks within the UK Police Force. You'll also find a short introduction to the area in which the novel is located.

To my two daughters-in-law, Kate and Kat

But oh! more horrible than that
Is a curse in a dead man's eye!

'The Rime of the Ancient Mariner'
Samuel Taylor Coleridge

PROLOGUE

Water, water, everywhere,
Nor any drop to drink.

'The Rime of the Ancient Mariner'
Samuel Taylor Coleridge

Water. Bloody water everywhere. And too much even for a million people to drink. It fell from the sky in torrents, gushed down gullies in the muddy banks on the uphill side of the lane, cascaded across the narrow roadway and rushed down the slope on the other side. The sound of it hammering on the roof of his old Land Rover was deafening, like a hundred drumsticks pounding on sheet iron. Jesus. Donny Lomax had lived all his life in the countryside, but he couldn't remember rain like this. The wipers on the ancient vehicle might as well not have been there, so useless were they at clearing the liquid that obscured the view through the windscreen in front of him.

He smiled wryly. Not a good night to be out in the back of beyond, up on Exmoor, but the trip had been worth it. He had two reels of thick copper cable in the back of the van, hidden under a tarpaulin. Must be worth a few hundred if he could find the right dealer, even if they were stolen. Serves the electric company right for leaving them out like that. Asking for trouble. Some lazy worker, probably. Couldn't be arsed to secure them properly before finishing work for the day. Well, their loss was his gain.

Donny rounded a tight bend on a downhill slope in the middle of a tree-lined section of the road. There was a loud thump. Christ. He'd hit something. Maybe a fox or small deer by the sound of it. He braked hard, stopped, and climbed out to have a look-see. He could hardly see any better out here in the downpour than when he was inside the cab. It really was coming down like stair rods. He walked to the rear of the van and looked back. Nothing there, as far as he could see. Whatever he'd hit, it had already gone. Couldn't have been that serious.

He failed to look in the shallow ditch at the side of the road, half full of muddy, surging water.

CHAPTER 1: AN ANCIENT MARINER?

Monday

Jackie Spring stepped out of her front porch and made her way blearily along the street. She could see the harbour ahead, the water calm in the early morning air. The town clock struck nine. Not as early as she thought then. She'd been to a live music event in the local tavern the night before, and she'd drunk rather more cider than was good for her. She'd fallen straight into bed on arriving home and had enjoyed two hours of alcohol-induced semi-coma, although this was followed by a stumbled trip to the toilet to relieve an over-pressured bladder. Then she'd been woken a couple of hours later, this time by a continuous low rumble of thunder out at sea. She'd glanced northwards through the landing window as she passed it on her second visit to the loo and watched sheet lightning flickering inside a huge cloud trapped off the South Wales coast, some twenty-five miles north. They'd had a similar deluge here in Watchet the previous night, with the river almost overflowing its banks due to the torrential rainfall.

That was the trouble with the Bristol Channel. Clouds got blown up from the Atlantic to the west and found themselves squeezed into a concentrated storm-filled mass by the two converging coastlines. Result? Thunder; lightning; rain; winds. The works. Jackie used to give thanks that she lived on the southern side of the Channel, in Watchet, on the Somerset coast. She'd always imagined that the South Wales shoreline opposite, at Barry, experienced considerably more rainfall each year. Apparently not so, according to a superior-sounding geography teacher she'd once dated. He came from Cardiff, told her rather too sniffily that rainfall statistics didn't agree with her theory, and went to the bar for another pint. He didn't last very much longer. Jackie preferred not to remain in the company of people who shattered her cosy illusions. She chose the more comfortable alternative, of living in her own small bubble in Watchet, the possible hometown of the Ancient Mariner, as immortalised in Coleridge's brooding poem, and mixing with people who were more amenable to her opinions. After all, it wasn't as though she was an unreasonable person. She liked to think of herself as broadminded and even-tempered.

She was passing the statue of the Ancient Mariner now, as she headed towards the village's tiny quayside police station, key in hand. She didn't get there.

'Um, Jackie, there's something odd in the water. Across in the outer harbour.' The speaker was Tony Fisher, a local painter and decorator. He'd obviously been waiting for her. He, too, looked only semi-awake. She tried to remember if he'd also been in the pub last night but the effort of attempting to recall her drinking companions was too much for her. She sighed and put a hand to her head.

'Tony, I haven't even unlocked the station yet. Can't it wait?'

He looked worried. 'Not really. You might want to see it. The tide'll start coming in soon. It looks a bit like . . . you know.'

She shook her head and rolled her eyes. It was more than ten years since a body, that of a woman, had been pulled from the sea off Watchet. Rumours had circulated that she'd been carried by currents all the way across from the Welsh side. Jackie had taken that theory with a pinch of salt. Surely currents and winds moved flotsam up and down the Channel, not from side to side? Added to which, it had happened well before she'd moved to Watchet and volunteered as a special constable with Somerset Police. She'd never bothered to check the truth behind the story. It was just a bit too gruesome for her. Maybe she should have read up about the case. After all, her part-time job as Watchet's librarian gave her ample opportunity. But true crime books were really not her thing. In fact, any type of crime book was far from her thing. Even though she was a volunteer police officer she'd much rather be curled up on the sofa reading a light romance or a work of historical fiction, sipping a mug of tea, her two cats asleep beside her.

She followed Tony Fisher onto the huge wall that separated the inner harbour from the outer, musing on the inaccuracy of surnames. Tony was a painter and decorator by trade. Yet Freddy Painter, who she could see ahead of her on the harbour wall, was a local fisherman. How did that happen?

Her roaming thoughts came to a juddering halt as soon as she looked over the low edging wall.

'Christ.'

It certainly looked like a body down there, slumped on a mudbank as if jettisoned by the previously incoming tide. The water was now on the turn, and here, in the Bristol Channel, the tidal range was one of the highest in the world. The water came in quickly and with real bite.

Jackie glanced around at the small knot of people who'd gathered beside them. One was the harbourmaster, his interest obviously piqued by the sight of the local special constable hurrying out onto the harbour wall.

'How do we get down to it, Phil?' she asked. 'We'll need to get it ashore before the water covers it and pushes it off to God knows where.'

Phil Murray sucked at his cheeks. 'Some kind of small pontoon that we can haul into place. Maybe duckboards across the mud.'

'How long have we got?'

'About twenty minutes. Maybe half an hour at the most.'

'Shit! Is that all? Okay, get it organised. That doesn't even give me time to get the station unlocked and some video equipment across here. I'll have to film it on my mobile. Let's move!'

Phil hurried back along the sea wall towards his office, accompanied by a worried-looking Tony Fisher. They ran down a set of quayside steps to a small motorboat and fixed a rope to a narrow pontoon, then threw some planks into the boat. Within ten minutes they were back at the scene, but this time on the water. Jackie had been filming the area around the body, trying to capture an idea of its position with respect to the harbour entrance. She shot clips from a range of locations, trying to identify the spot that gave the best illumination from the morning sunlight. Once satisfied, she quickly called her area headquarters to report the incident and summarise her decisions. She cut the call as soon as Phil's boat approached the bottom step. Time was running out.

Jackie clambered down the slippery flight, using the side railing to steady herself as best she could. 'Okay, Phil. I'll need a closer look before we make any decision to move it. It might be some kind of elaborate stunt.'

She jumped aboard and glanced down. The water had already risen several inches, just in a few minutes. It would reach the corpse, if that's what it was, any moment now and, within ten minutes, would have submerged the body. And then what would happen to it? Logic suggested that it would push the body further into the harbour. After all, the tide was incoming. But logic didn't always apply to flotsam carried by the tidal currents around here. And she could feel a breeze beginning to blow from the south. Would it push the body back out to sea?

The boat grounded on the mudbank close to the body.

'We won't need the pontoon at first,' Phil called. 'The water's getting really close. I'll just toss the duckboards onto the mud close to the body, on either side. Then it's over to you.'

'So, is it a body?' Jackie asked, trying to peer past Phil's bulky frame.

'Looks like it. Maybe someone who's fallen off a boat.'

'Don't say it, Phil. I know your sense of humour.'

The harbourmaster looked puzzled for a few seconds, then his expression cleared. 'Oh, you mean the Ancient Mariner.'

Jackie held her head in her hands. 'I said don't mention it! For pity's sake, are you stupid or something?'

Phil chuckled then looked back at the corpse. 'Once you're off the boat, I'll push the pontoon against the mud-bank. Maybe you can roll the body onto it. With a bit of luck, we might not need to get it aboard my boat. Oh, I can smell it already.'

Jackie sniffed the air as a waft of breeze blew towards them. 'Oh, God. Is that from the . . .'

She didn't complete the question. It was all she could do to stop herself from heaving her sparse stomach contents into the water.

She stepped gingerly across the boat's side onto the boards, helped by Tony Fisher. Thank God I decided on flat shoes this morning, she thought, as she crouched down and crept along the planking. How on earth was this going to work? Squelching noises sounded from the mud under the duckboard as she inched her way along it. Sea water was already beginning to lap against the body, which seemed to be clad in an old thin coat. The stink from the mud was bad enough, but the additional smells near the corpse were indescribable.

It was the incoming tide that made the task easier than Jackie had anticipated. The water helped to lift the body slightly and Jackie could use her foot to push it hard against the small floating pontoon. She then crawled across the boards onto the floating structure and grabbed a leg, hauling the corpse onto the raft as well as she could, trying to keep her eyes focussed on the lower part of the body. She really didn't want to look at that face. She knew what prolonged immersion in sea water did to a body.

'Go, go!' she yelled, as soon as she felt that both she and the corpse were reasonably secure on the pontoon. Phil slowly guided the boat towards the nearby landing platform.

Jackie looked down at her legs, encased in what had been her new pair of uniformed trousers, now soaking wet and caked in smelly mud. Flecks of muck covered the rest of her clothes, and she could feel spots of the foul stuff on her cheeks and brow, drying in the breeze.

'Fuck,' she said, under her breath. She closed her eyes.

* * *

'Fuck,' Jackie said, under her breath, for the second time in one day. This was highly unusual, because she rarely swore. On this occasion she was enraged, but she knew better than to voice her feelings any further. It was like talking to a brick wall.

'What was that, Special Constable Spring? Did you say something?'

Sergeant Alan Churchill was a stickler for protocol; he expected his area team members to follow set procedures at all times and had driven down from area headquarters to remind her of the rules she should have followed. Jackie had been forced to endure a ten-minute dressing-down in which he'd stressed the actions that she should have taken, as set down in the manual.

'I'll say it again. Suspected dead bodies are to be left *in situ* to preserve forensic integrity,' he said. 'You breached that absolute rule. You're fortunate you've not been suspended.'

She refrained from rolling her eyes at him, turned and left the tiny police station, wondering if she'd misjudged her own suitability for a voluntary role in the police. It was obvious to everyone who had watched the incident at Watchet harbour that she'd done precisely the right thing. If she hadn't acted as quickly and decisively as she had, the body would have ended up floating around in the harbour or, even worse, sucked back out to sea. What made it worse was the fact that she still hadn't had time to change out of her filthy clothes. And she was sure that she smelled like a sewer.

Her immediate boss, Constable Sarah Levy, was approaching along the quayside. Jackie nodded tentatively to her. What now? Not another dressing-down, surely?

'I just wanted to say, well done. Forensics have got a real body to work with rather than trying to chase a rogue corpse, or something that might look like a corpse, around the coast. You got it out of the water just in time, so they're pleased. The wind's strengthened and one of the tidal experts I've spoken to said it would have most likely ended up back out at sea.' She wrinkled her nose and stepped back. 'You might want to go home and clean up.'

'Yeah, I know. And thanks.'

'Someone may need to speak to you later, that's my hunch. Someone with more sense than bloody Alan Churchill. Will you be at home?'

'Yes. I'm only on duty this morning. I'm due to finish . . .' She glanced at her watch. 'Half an hour ago.'

Sarah laughed. 'Par for the course.'

Jackie passed the statue of the Ancient Mariner for the umpteenth time that morning. She could have sworn it winked at her.

CHAPTER 2: FACT FINDING

Wednesday

For the next few days, Jackie was back at work in the library, earning her keep, as she described it to anyone who asked. Did her job have a long-term future, though? Libraries in small towns and villages up and down the country were closing at an alarming rate, caught between the twin pressures of reduced funding and spiralling costs. Added to which, an ever-increasing proportion of the population were choosing the more convenient option of accessing digital information and entertainment from online sources. Maybe she needed to bite the bullet and get out before her job disappeared altogether. Was it worth considering becoming a police community support officer, the most junior full-time rank? She certainly didn't want to move away from Watchet. She'd only just got her small home the way she wanted it, and it was ideally situated, only a few minutes' walk from the quayside. Added to which, it had enough space to put up her son and daughter when they came to stay. She could even manage to house them both at the same time if it came to the crunch, although this wasn't likely. They just didn't get on well with each other.

She'd found time to write her report about the incident in the harbour and had received a positive comment from Shamema Smith, the area inspector, for its clarity and precision. She hadn't said anything about Jackie's decision-making on that memorable morning though. Jackie's interpretation was that the poor woman was caught between a rock and a hard place. If she were to say anything too positive, she'd be undermining her number two, the bumptious Alan Churchill, and that might create difficulties within the chain of command. But if she were to criticise Jackie's actions, that might well go against her own instincts that Jackie had used her initiative to good effect. Ah well, she thought. Can't win them all.

She was back on duty on Wednesday afternoon and asked if anything definite had been established about the body from the harbour. Sarah Levy summarised what she knew in a few words.

'Male. Maybe mid-fifties. Bumps and bruises, some new, some old. Nasty head wound, apparently. Recent. No positive identification yet.' She went back to completing a report about local rural crime.

'So was it foul play?' Jackie asked.

'Hmm? Oh, you mean the cause of death? Maybe. Not enough to go on yet. That's what I heard. Someone may be down to visit later, depending on what else shows up. Come on, Jackie. Do you really think our elders and betters tell me anything? Ha!'

Sarah could often come across as a bit of a cynic. Not surprising when you considered who her superior officer was. Jackie wondered who the visiting senior officer would turn out to be. Hopefully someone with a bit more originality and flair than either Alan Churchill or Shamema Smith. But how likely was that?

It was late in the afternoon when a tall auburn-haired woman pushed open the door from the quayside and stepped into the interior, glancing around her.

'Well, I've been in some unusual police stations in my time, but this one takes the biscuit.' She held out her hand to Sarah. 'DCI Polly Nelson. I think you might have been expecting me?'

'Yes, ma'am. It's probably Special Constable Jackie Spring here you've come to see.'

Polly smiled as she shook hands with Jackie. 'Shall we go walkabout? It's a wonder you don't suffer from permanent claustrophobia in here. It's like a bloody shoe box.'

'We like it, ma'am,' Jackie replied. 'It's got real character.' She was indignant. Didn't this woman recognise historic charm when she saw it?

Polly laughed and held up her hands in mock surrender. 'Okay, you win. Never let it be said that I condemn our British liking for quirkiness.'

Jackie was beginning to be won over. Someone from on high with an engaging personality and a sense of humour. Wonders would never cease. She led the detective out onto the quayside and walked her through Monday morning's events, explaining her decisions.

'Sounds good to me,' Polly finally said. 'I'd like to think I'd have done the same thing. When an emergency strikes, adaptability is the name of the game, Jackie. Do you have a kettle back at that dolls' house of a station? I'm parched. A cup of tea would work wonders.'

* * *

Polly Nelson, one of the most experienced senior detectives in Somerset, decided that it was worthwhile finding out a little more about this woman, the special constable who had been forced to make snap decisions under pressure on the morning the body had been found. As it turned out, those unusual decisions were the right ones, but she'd probably have picked up criticism from her immediate superiors. The two of them were in the tiny inner office of Watchet's police station, sitting on the only two chairs. She took another sip of tea and glanced at Jackie. Average height. Dark brown curly hair, flecked with grey. Good complexion. Clear, intelligent, deep-blue eyes. Attractive. Probably popular in this small town.

'What do you do as your main job, Jackie? I assume you have one?'

'I'm a local librarian. I moved here nearly ten years ago. It was a full-time job but that got reduced to three days each week a couple of years ago.'

'Is that when you decided to become a special constable?'

Jackie nodded. 'My children had just left home for university, so I was kicking my heels a bit. It seemed a good way to fill my spare days.'

Polly frowned. 'Doesn't earn you much money, though, if any. Can you manage on your reduced time at the library?'

'Just about. I'm not poor. When my husband died, I got some money back from the sale of our London house. I don't spend wildly. Whether I can keep going on my present income in the long term is a bit more uncertain, but I'm okay at the mo.'

'I can understand your feelings. I'm beginning to realise just how important a sense of belonging to a community is. You fit in here in Watchet, don't you?'

Jackie smiled gently, as if at her own thoughts. 'I hope so. I think so.' She hesitated for a few seconds before continuing. 'Have you found anything out about the body? Who it was?'

Polly shook her head. 'Not much. Not yet anyway. I've only just taken charge, so I'm out on a fact-finding mission. It's what we do. I'd better explain. I'm based in Somerset, but I'm seconded to WeSCU, the Wessex Serious Crimes Unit. Your body only came to our attention late yesterday after the autopsy showed the victim to have been seriously assaulted before ending up in the sea. Our guess is that the body was dumped into the water, maybe from a boat. The pathologist reckons he might have been alive when he was shoved overboard, but she's not sure yet. Further tests needed. If he was still alive, he didn't stand a chance, not with his injuries. Personally, I have my doubts. Broken arm, fractured wrist, damaged leg and the side of his head was caved in. He'd been given a real going over. Internal damage too. Bruised kidneys. Ruptured spleen. He'd have been in a real state.'

'So it was murder?' Jackie seemed aghast.

Polly nodded. 'Once that was established it ended up on our desk. The boss of WeSCU, Detective Chief Superintendent Sophie Allen, sent me down here. I'm second in the unit, you see, and I'm usually based in Taunton. Not far.'

'I'll help any way I can,' Jackie said.

Polly frowned. 'Of course you will. That's your job.'

'No, I didn't mean it that way. I mean, I know you're right. What I meant was, I'll do anything I can to help, not just as part of my duties. Sorry.'

She looked mournful, so Polly laughed. 'Good on you! I thought you might. I'm usually a good judge of character. Eyes and ears, that's what we need. Picking up tittle-tattle in the area, listening in to any local gossip that might give us somewhere to start. And special constables are often ideally placed for that. Café chat. Pub chat. You know the kind of thing.'

'How did you know? That I'm a local pub-goer?' Jackie showed her surprise.

'You don't think I'm going to reveal my sources, do you? First rule of good undercover detective work.' She laughed again. 'Anyway, to be serious, we haven't yet been able to identify the body, as I said. There aren't any real clues, and no one's been reported missing. He was a biggish bloke, maybe in an outdoor type of job. Well-worn clothes. Outdoor boots. Maybe he was a labourer or farm worker of some type. Just do some gentle asking around. But be subtle about it. Not when you're in uniform. Okay?'

Jackie raised her eyebrows. 'So you want me to work undercover? In my own town? This is Watchet, not Bristol or Taunton. Everyone knows everyone else. I bet half of them even know my shoe size.'

'Well, as long as it's that and not your bust size, I think you'll cope. The thing is, we'll have teams out doing official inquiries. I could do with someone on the ground doing a more unofficial one, a bit more under the radar, if you like. There's been no mispers reported matching his description, not yet anyway. He'd been in the sea a couple of days, according to the pathologist. That means he's now been missing for, what, four days? Yet nothing's come in from anywhere along this coast, or across on the Welsh side.'

'Is this in addition to my normal duties or instead of?'

Polly looked at her shrewdly. Clearly Jackie Spring was no one's fool, a good sign. 'We'll take you off most of your normal work, but not entirely. People need to think you're working as usual, even though you're not. Get the idea? And we'll pay you for any extra time.'

'Thanks, ma'am. And it's clever. Actually, I'm quite excited about it. Things can get a bit tedious, and I could do with getting stuck in to something different.'

'I was hoping to get an incident room here, in Watchet. But this place?' Polly looked around her at the tiny police premises and shook her head. 'I'll get the locals onto other ideas. You stay back from it, okay? You're my secret weapon. You're working for me but hidden in plain sight. The rest of the team will be here once we've got things moving. There's a DS, Rae Gregson, and a DC Tommy Carter, both from Dorset. My own DS, Adrian Ahmed, will be coming down from Taunton. And you'll doubtless meet the boss at some time, Sophie Allen.'

'I've heard of her,' Jackie said. 'I read the papers.'

'Glad you do. We need people who keep themselves up to date.' She stood up. 'Nice tea. I'll keep you posted. No discussion about this with your own colleagues. Okay?'

With that she left the tiny inner room and, after a brief nod to Sarah Levy in the outer office, left the station, feeling satisfied with the way the meeting had gone. She knew she'd gambled in her decision to bring the local special constable into the team, but Jackie had come across as someone who could be trusted to use her instincts in the right way. Only time would tell whether her decision would prove to be a good one.

* * *

Jackie went out to join Sarah.

'What was that all about?' Sarah asked.

Jackie pursed her lips. 'Just grilling me to get the facts straight.'

She collected her kit and hurried out of the station before she could be asked anything else. Below the radar work? It sounded challenging but fascinating. She could start this evening at one of the local pubs, where she was meeting a friend for a meal. No time like the present.

CHAPTER 3: QUAYSIDE TOUR

Late Wednesday

Sophie Allen was the last team member to arrive in the CID suite tucked inside Taunton police station.

'Well, here we are, together again, we happy few. Apart from Barry, that is. Oh, to be on honeymoon again. Those were the days.' She sighed dramatically. 'And there's no point in Stevie joining us yet, not until we need him. It's a long way from his base in Devizes and his wife's pregnant.'

'Do you know where Gwen and Barry are, boss? Somewhere warm and exotic?' Rae Gregson asked. She was the senior DS in the team.

'The Canaries, apparently. He got some kind of discount on a suite in an upmarket hotel. I shouldn't be telling you this, but he was originally thinking of staying here in the UK. He was muttering about Cornwall. I had to take him aside and give him a bit of a telling off. You know what he'd be like. He'd be in St Ives or Newquay or somewhere, and we'd be up here, only a couple of hours away, investigating a murder of some kind. He wouldn't be able to resist poking his head through the door to check up on how things were going, and Gwen would be incandescent. We'd have another murder on our hands.' She paused to take stock. 'Anyway, it'll be WeSCU's first big case with Polly as the SIO. From what I understand, it's been a good start so far. Over to you, Polly.'

Polly's DS, Adrian Ahmed, ran the first video clip, taken by Jackie Spring on Monday morning. It showed the location of the body, splayed out on the harbour mud.

'We think he was brought in on the overnight high tide,' Polly explained. 'Maybe the wind helped. There was a thunderstorm in the early hours, with the wind shifting in all kinds of directions. But there was one spell when it was definitely a northerly.'

'No chance of it being dumped in that spot?' Rae asked. 'Maybe from a boat in the harbour?'

Polly shook her head. 'We can't discount it completely, but it doesn't look that way.' She switched to a series of photos of the corpse, taken from different angles on Jackie's phone. 'First on the scene was the local special constable, a community volunteer, one Jackie Spring. The video and these photos are from her phone. She was quick off the mark and got the body brought ashore just before the tide reached it. If she hadn't acted as fast as she did, it would have started floating around in the harbour and could have ended up anywhere.'

The final photo in the sequence showed a mud-splattered Jackie Spring back on the quayside beside the body. 'This is her. Onto the next sequence, photos from the post-mortem. There are no distinguishing marks on the body. Very little of significance that we can use to help in identification, other than his sandy-coloured hair. He's in his fifties or thereabouts. We think he'd been in the water about two days, maybe a bit less. There's a chance he was alive before he went in, according to the experts. Unconscious at the time with severe concussion.' She raised her eyebrows somewhat cynically. 'So it was a body disposal, even if he wasn't quite dead.'

'Any mispers in the area, ma'am?' DC Tommy Carter asked.

Polly shook her head. 'None that correspond. Nor even further afield. It's a puzzle, I can tell you.'

She took a sip of water before continuing. 'We need our incident room to be local. It's that kind of place, with a pretty open distrust of strangers, even though it's a tourist area. Or maybe that's why. You know what tourists can be like with their demands, upsetting the locals.' She paused to take another sip of water. 'I think I've found a pretty good location for an incident room in the village, a community hall that's not used much. And it comes with some parking space. The area squad suggested it.'

Sophie broke in. 'Sounds great, Polly. Well done.'

Polly shrugged. 'Mainly due to the mudlark special you saw in the photo, Jackie Spring. She should be useful. I've asked her to keep her eyes and ears open for gossip. When you're down there, use the local full-time copper, Sarah Levy, for information and help. The area sergeant is based further out. He's a prat. Sucks up to senior officers but a bit too bossy to his own junior people.'

' I like your idea for this special, Jackie Spring. So we don't make direct use of her?' Rae asked.

Polly frowned. 'I'd prefer it if we didn't, not openly. She's the local librarian and knows a lot of people. She gives us a day and a half each week. I'd like to take her off her normal duties, double her time with us and give her a free role, trying to pick up on local snippets of information.'

'A bit of an unusual approach, Polly,' was Sophie's comment.

'I know. But she's far from stupid. In fact, she's a really quick thinker. I could see that as soon as I met her. She's happy to give us the extra time.'

'A secret weapon. I like it.'

'When do we start?' Rae asked.

'Tomorrow morning. Ade here is looking into accommodation for anyone who wants it. Welcome to Somerset.'

* * *

Local uniformed officers had already made a start on house-to-house enquiries when Rae arrived at the incident room in

Watchet the next morning. Its facilities were still being set up, but the county technical support team were working hard to lay out the furniture and hardware that a modern murder investigation needs.

She and Tommy greeted Polly's DS, Adrian Ahmed, as they entered the main room.

'We're just about ready,' he said. 'The boss wants a quick meeting in an hour to decide on priorities, then it's down to business.' He pointed to an open door beside a small hatch. 'The kettle's in there. Tea, coffee, milk, biscuits. The local Co-op's just down the road. We'll have half an hour or so spare before the briefing, so I thought we'd have a quick look around the harbour so you can get your bearings. Make yourself a drink first, though.'

'How long have you been with the DCI?' Rae asked.

'About two years. I think you and I have met before. Didn't our paths cross a while back, when I was new here? Weren't you involved with some historic case on a farm in the Quantocks?'

Rae realised why Ade had seemed familiar the previous afternoon. 'Of course. We had a dog team searching the woods. That's where you were.'

Ade nodded. 'We didn't chat. You seemed totally engrossed. But I did talk to your boyfriend about pub pool teams. At least, I think it was him.'

Rae laughed. 'Yeah, that sounds like Craig. A man of many talents, in fact, though I wouldn't count playing pool as one of them. I always beat him so he's kind of given up. He's switched to darts now. I pretend to be rubbish at it, so he always wins. Do you remember anyone else from our unit?'

Ade shook his head. 'Sorry. Just you and your partner.'

Rae wondered if there was more to this comment than was apparent, but she let it pass. She knew she stood out and would possibly always do so.

'I've got us all really good accommodation,' Ade went on. 'A small hotel just a couple of streets away. The manager's promised us slap-up breakfasts, so that's a bonus. No evening food though. It'll have to be pubs in the evening. Or fish and chips.'

A few minutes later they were walking through an open parking area and down towards the quayside. They'd been joined by Jackie Spring, and she pointed out the location where the body had been spotted, then other key parts of the harbour. Rae was surprised by the sheer height of the harbour walls and the obvious size of the ancient gate system, now broken and out of use.

'It's the huge tidal range here,' Jackie explained. 'Those gates to the inner harbour used to be closed as the tide went out, keeping water inside. You can guess the problem now. All these boats sink down onto the mud at low tide. They couldn't have that in bygone times when Watchet was a working port.'

She led them back to the quayside, past the tiny police station, to complete their brief tour and left them with Sarah Levy while she returned to the library.

'We'll do anything we can to help,' Sarah added. 'With local info, I mean. We're already well into the house-to-house. Nothing yet, as far as I'm aware.' She glanced at her watch. 'Better get back and join them, in fact. They'll be accusing me of slacking.'

She hurried off and the detective trio returned to the temporary station in time for the briefing.

* * *

A mud-spattered Land Rover, its windows obscured by several months' worth of accumulated dirt, had been parked at the eastern end of the harbour. The driver dropped a pair of binoculars onto the front passenger seat and started the engine. The vehicle swung out onto the road that headed south, and noisily climbed the narrow lanes inland, heading towards the vast hinterland of Exmoor. The sky was darker here, with brooding clouds hanging above the higher ground, unlike the sunnier coastal belt that stretched from Watchet westwards to Dunster and Minehead. Drizzle started to fall as the vehicle climbed higher, winding its way along a sequence of narrow lanes. The panorama was bleak, in complete contrast to the lush farming strip closer to the coast. Life was harder here.

CHAPTER 4: PUB CHAT

Thursday

Jackie was finding progress slow in her role as an undercover sleuth, using her eyes and ears when out and about in Watchet. Townspeople were happy to chat about the body pulled from the harbour but expected her to tell them all the details, not the other way round. Maybe it was to be expected. The locals wouldn't know much about it, just what they'd picked up from unofficial gossip networks. She soon realised that the events at the beginning of the week had made her a bit of a local celebrity, particularly since word had got out that she'd almost received a reprimand for the decisions she'd made that first morning. How had they found that out? She was worried that Alan Churchill would get to hear of the leak and give her another of his 'we need to talk' lectures. She could do without that!

The other problem was that, if she was to stick to her task of working undercover, she couldn't ask any questions of local townspeople in a way that might raise suspicion. It had to be seen to enter the conversation naturally, seamlessly. It was proving to be very frustrating work.

The one unexpected bonus to her fame was that it seemed to have increased footfall in the library. People she hadn't seen inside the building for months would sidle in, scan the shelves of the true crime and crime fiction sections, then come across to her desk and ask her advice on their selections. Inevitably they'd also ask her about the body in the harbour. At first it was interesting, and she enjoyed the chat, but it soon got tiresome. She still smiled and answered their questions. Maybe one of them would turn out to know more than they were letting on and make a comment that could initiate some kind of breakthrough. It hadn't happened yet, though. In fact, she realised that conversations in the library were unlikely to provide her with the leads she'd been tasked to find. In this day and age, visitors to the library were likely to be educated and socially concerned citizens, not necessarily acquaintances of the kind of thug who'd beat someone senseless and chuck the body overboard from a boat at midnight.

Jackie was in the Star Inn that evening, having a meal out with her boss and buddy, Sarah Levy. This had become a ritual of late. On the second Thursday of each month Sarah's husband stayed in with their two youngsters, leaving his wife free for an evening out. On this particular evening conversation between the two police officers was as far away from criminal matters as it could possibly be.

'I reckon he's got the hots for you, Jackie,' Sarah said. 'The clues are all there.'

Jackie, who'd been sidetracked from their conversation by the sight of a man on a neighbouring table shovelling food into his mouth faster than anyone she'd ever seen before, was temporarily confused by this comment.

'What?' she said, trying hard to remember what they'd been talking about before she'd been distracted by the gruesome sight.

'Tony Fisher. He fancies you, I'm sure of it.'

The man at the neighbouring table belched loudly. Jackie wondered if this could be made into an arrestable offence. It certainly broke the rules of civilised behaviour.

And to make matters worse, he was wearing grubby, misshapen tracksuit trousers. She glanced at the woman and three children sharing the table with him. They were a bit shabbily dressed but clean enough. And the kids seemed relatively well-behaved, absorbed with their phones. No, maybe she'd leave the man in peace. He hadn't broken any real laws, after all, just offended her own social expectations. If she did retain a few prejudices, maybe fat blokes who belched loudly and thought that grubby tracksuit bottoms were suitable clothing for a family meal out were acceptable targets.

'Are you listening to me?' Sarah said.

'Sorry. I was miles away.' Jackie looked back at her friend.

'You don't say. You've had that vacant look in your eyes since you finished your pudding.' Sarah looked past Jackie's shoulder as the door opened. 'Well, speak of the devil. Here he is.'

'Who?' Jackie asked, as she took another sip of cider.

'Tony Fisher. He's just come in,' Sarah hissed. 'I said, I reckon he fancies you.'

'Really? Me? Why on earth would he fancy me?' Jackie frowned.

'Moron,' Sarah whispered. 'I keep telling you. You're probably one of the most eligible single women in the town. You've got great legs, as well. I wish mine were as shapely as yours.' She paused and raised her hand slightly. 'He's spotted us. He'll be coming over once he's got his beer. Act naturally.'

'You're so bossy sometimes,' Jackie replied indignantly.

'I am your boss, idiot.'

'Well, I'm not about to start something with a guy who's already in a relationship.'

Sarah spluttered into her wine. 'What? Tony Fisher? He's not in a relationship.'

Jackie responded quickly. 'I've seen him around town several times recently with a busty blonde in tow. They were coming out of the curry place together last weekend.'

Her close friend rolled her eyes yet again. 'She's his sister, you cretin. She was staying with him last week while her own house in Nether Stowey got de-fumigated for dry rot or woodworm or some such thing. Don't you know anything?'

'Obviously not. And so far, in the last couple of minutes you've called me an idiot, a moron and a cretin. Doesn't that break some code of behaviour within Somerset Police? Are you allowed to call me things like that?'

'Oh, God. You are incorrigible, whatever that means. You're my best friend, Jackie. If I can't call you an idiot when you act like one, what hope is there for the world? Here he comes. Sit up and stick your bust out. That's an order.'

Jackie glanced sideways and smiled as the man in question approached their table.

'Mind if I join you?' he asked politely.

'Of course not,' Sarah replied before Jackie had time to speak. She pointed to the empty chair beside her own. 'I was just saying to Jackie that we hadn't seen you for a while, then the door opened and in you came. It must be fate.'

This time it was Jackie's turn to roll her eyes. 'Ignore her, Tony. She's being an idiot tonight. It must be the full moon.'

Tony looked confused. 'Shall I go somewhere else?'

Jackie put a hand on his arm. 'Of course not. We're just two silly women, slightly tipsy. Please ignore us when we talk rubbish.'

'Okay,' he said, still looking baffled. 'I wanted to speak to you anyway, 'cos of something I spotted at the quayside. It's probably rubbish, and I wasn't going to mention it but then I thought I'd better.' He stopped and scratched his head. 'Is it okay?'

'Of course,' Sarah replied. 'You know us coppers. Never really off duty.' She pretended to grimace.

'It was this morning. I'm repainting the front of one of the buildings on the harbour. I was up a ladder. I could see Jackie talking to a couple of other people and pointing. I guess they were detectives?'

Jackie nodded.

'Well, I think someone was watching you. It looked like a guy in an old Land Rover had a set of binoculars. He could have been looking at anything, I guess, but I thought he'd have got out to look across the harbour at the views. After all, it wasn't raining, was it? When you went back inside, he drove away up Harbour Road. I just thought it was odd.'

'The world's full of odd people doing odd things, Tony,' Sarah replied. 'You get used to it in the police, believe me. There could be any number of reasons for him looking across the harbour. It won't be anything linked to us, trust me on that.' She picked up her glass and glanced at Jackie. 'Another?' It sounded more like an order than a genuine question.

'Okay. Thanks.'

Jackie waited until Sarah was out of earshot. 'Did you see this guy in the Land Rover, Tony? You know, what he looked like?'

Tony shook his head. 'Not really. I was up a ladder. I couldn't really see his features. I think he had a cloth cap on. I caught sight of that when he drove away.'

'What about the registration?'

'Sorry. Didn't note it. It was a bit mud-spattered anyway. To be honest, I didn't think it was suspicious until after he'd gone. I only put two and two together when I realised your little group had been out there.' He took a swig of beer. 'Sarah obviously thinks I've got an overactive imagination.'

'She's much more experienced than me,' Jackie replied. 'I'm only a part-time volunteer, remember. But thanks for mentioning it. And I haven't really had a chance to thank you for Monday morning when you told me about the body. If you hadn't been so quick at telling me, it might have been too late to get it out before the tide reached it. So, I'm saying thanks now.'

She smiled at him. After all, he was a nice guy. Everyone in the town knew that.

* * *

Jackie was on the phone the next morning soon after breakfast, but a little nervously. She still wasn't too sure of this strange undercover task she'd been asked to perform. Nor was she entirely at ease with the unusually informal relationship she'd found herself in with the DCI, Polly Nelson. She spoke tentatively at first, half-expecting a reprimand, but the DCI seemed quite breezy.

'Hi, Jackie. Something to report?'

She told Polly about Tony's observations.

'Interesting,' came the response. 'Shouldn't be ignored. And your Tony didn't recognise this man, whoever he was?'

'No, sorry.'

'No apologies necessary, from either you or him. He's well known locally, I take it. I mean, with him being a painter and decorator?'

'Yes. He knows most people in the town, and they know him.'

'Useful,' came Polly's answer. 'That means the guy watching probably wasn't local. That ties in with the mud on his Land Rover and a few things we've picked up on from early forensics. We think the body you found might be country-based rather than a townie. Pesticide traces in the seams of his clothes.'

'I would have thought it would have all been washed out by the water,' Jackie said.

'So did we. Yes, it is a bit strange. It's away for forensic analysis but it all fits, doesn't it? Good work, Jackie. I knew I did the right thing bringing you on board. Keep it up.' And with that, Polly closed the call.

Jackie didn't know whether to feel elated by the DCI's recognition or disappointed by the speed with which she'd ended the conversation. Better get used to it, she told herself. After all, she was playing with the big kids now.

CHAPTER 5: PLANNING

Friday

'A farm worker of some kind?' Rae said. 'That's how it looks, surely?'

Polly agreed. 'Or a keen gardener. Anyway, Tommy has more on that, don't you, Tommy?'

Tommy hastily swallowed his mouthful of tea before he spoke. 'Yes, ma'am. We haven't had confirmation yet, but the initial tests suggest it might have been a tar wash, like Jeyes Fluid. But traces had survived the soaking his clothes got. Maybe he spilled some on himself or got sprayed somehow? Maybe the guy was a low-level farm worker or a gardener? Whoever he was, he didn't bother with following safety procedures, or he wasn't trained properly.'

Polly held her hand up. 'It's possible, I'll give you that. We all come from rural counties. We know that the vast majority of farmers are decent employers who look after their workers, if they have them. But there are still a few rogues out there. Of course, a lot of farms are now just worked by the family owners or managers.'

'Do you think he could have been some kind of itinerant seasonal worker?' Rae said.

Polly tugged at a stray lock of her auburn hair. 'Again, it's possible. But that begs the question as to why he was killed in such a brutal way. Farm work can be very seasonal, we know that. But people complete a contract, then move on. Or they get the sack if their efforts aren't up to scratch. They don't get murdered in this vicious way. There's got to be something much deeper. But, at this stage, it's not worth speculating what it is. What this all does, both the report on the clothes and this information that's come in from Jackie Spring, suggests that we ought to shift focus out of the town and into the countryside. Ade, can you show the map?'

Adrian projected a large-scale map of the region onto a screen fixed to the wall. It showed an area stretching from Minehead to Kilve in a west-east direction, and from the coastline well into Exmoor and the Quantocks on its north-south axis.

'It's tricky judging how far we should extend,' he said. 'Exmoor goes way off south and further west, and the Quantocks head a lot further south-east, but we have to set some kind of initial limits. The fact that the body ended up in the water here at Watchet probably has some significance, so we've decided to restrict ourselves to this area. That will change if we get further intel.'

'There must be loads of farms around here,' Rae said.

'There are. It's not going to be easy.'

Rae was thinking of something her usual boss, Barry Marsh, had said to her about his farming background. Was it something about the specific nature of some farming practices? Targeted shots for particular crops, that's the phrase he'd used. They'd been in a pub at the time, which was why he'd used a drink analogy.

She cleared her throat. 'Do we know what kind of things that fluid is used for? Is it a general one or one that farmers or gardeners would use in a targeted way or at a specific time of year? If we knew, it might save us a lot of time.'

Polly became very alert. 'That's good thinking, Rae. We could then target the people that are most likely to use it.' She turned to her assistant. 'Ade, can you get busy? If necessary, look for some advice from the local NFU or maybe a DEFRA office. But before you do, there's another snippet that's arrived from the pathology team and it makes interesting reading. The water in his lungs was less saline than they expected. It's possible he spent some time in fresh water, followed by a day or so out in the sea. What are your thoughts on that, please?'

'Maybe a pond or river?' Tommy said. 'Before his body was dumped out at sea.'

Ade shook his head. 'No need. He might not have been dumped from a boat or even thrown off a cliff. Wasn't there a huge rainstorm here last weekend? What if he ended up in the river somehow and was just carried down in the surge?'

Polly screwed up her eyes at the displayed map, trying to make out the fine detail. 'Where does the river join the sea? I didn't notice any outflow into the harbour.'

Ade used the mapping software on his laptop to zoom in on the harbour area of Watchet. Polly stood up and walked to the magnified wall projection for a closer look.

'Ah, now I see. It might come out just to the west of the harbour. I think I'll call my local spy and see what she thinks.'

Polly disappeared into the small room she'd taken as her office. She emerged after several minutes. 'You're right, Ade. Saturday night. There was a huge storm here and the river ran really high. It's channelled through a big culvert under Market Street and the small car park on the other side. And it does come out a hundred yards or so west of the harbour complex, not in it. She reckons that the flow that night was so strong that all kinds of stuff would have been carried out to sea. Then the tides and the sea currents could have brought it back in again the next night, and left it stranded on that mudbank in the harbour. Not what we first thought at all.'

Rae was impressed with the DCI's willingness to adapt her ideas. Maybe not quite so original in her thoughts as Sophie Allen, but impressive, nonetheless. Would she be as open to speculation as the chief, though? Well, there was only one way to find out.

'Maybe he wasn't even dumped in the river, ma'am.'

Polly was suddenly alert. 'What do you mean?'

'What if he was just wandering about in that storm, maybe hurt? He could have fallen into the river. Could he have got his injuries by hitting rocks and debris as he was carried downstream? Or is there no doubt?'

Polly scowled and consulted the post-mortem report, flicking her way through every page. She quoted from its contents, peering at the team over the top of her reading glasses.

'The injuries are consistent with a beating. Marks from a toecap on his back and sides. Finger marks in some of the bruise patterns. It looks more likely that whoever did it hoped we'd think he'd got his injuries during his passage down the river. Maybe we should concentrate at first on premises and farms near it. Though it's not a big waterway, is it? About ten or twelve miles long, according to the map. Do you think a body could be swept down it, even in the upper section?' Polly looked dubious.

'There was a lot of rain that night, boss,' Ade said. 'These rivers that take runoff from the hills get swollen very quickly when there's a heavy downpour. And Saturday night was exceptional. It was pretty bad in Taunton but down here it was absolutely awash, by all accounts.'

Polly consulted the map then thought for a few seconds. 'Okay. We'll leave the local units here in the town and check the riverside farms. Ade, you and I can do the lower section, between Washford village and here. Can you and Tommy do the top section, Rae? It's a bit longer but they're more likely to be upland farms in your section, so fewer of them. At this stage we'll just do a bit of gentle questioning. Anyone gone missing? Any strangers spotted? You know the kind of thing.' She crinkled her nose. 'Wellie boot kind of stuff but it's got to be done. No time like the present, so let's get going. Report anything interesting right away.'

* * *

They were in Rae's car and heading southwest out of Watchet before Tommy asked the inevitable question.

'What do you think, boss? Of the DCI, I mean?'

'She's good. Not as good as the chief, of course, but she's on the ball. Adaptable. Willing to listen to ideas. She doesn't give a lot away, though. I think that cheerful engaging exterior is probably just that. An exterior. She might be colder and more calculating underneath. But let's not complain. I've worked for some real bastards and right dickheads in the past, so I'm giving thanks. But I miss Barry, to be honest.'

'He's only on leave for a couple of weeks, boss.'

'Yeah, but he's gold dust in terms of the police force. I owe him and the chief so much. I wish there was some way I could show them the kind of gratitude I feel, but they're my bosses so it's difficult. The thing is, they saved my life, and they don't even know it. I was at the lowest of the low when I first joined the unit, though I didn't realise it. And that first case with them allowed me to turn a corner, and here I am. She wants me to do my inspector exams next year.'

'Don't you want to?'

Rae shrugged. 'I don't know. Really, I want to stay working for the two of them for ever. But that won't happen, will it? Barry will be going for a DCI job soon, and the chief? Well, the sky's the limit in some ways. But she doesn't want to go any further in the force, if her hints are to be believed. I reckon she's lining things up to leave in a few years and head for an academic job. She told Lydia a couple of years ago that was her aim, before I appeared on the scene.'

'You look a bit uneasy, boss.'

Rae shrugged. 'Not really. I just don't know how much I should open up with ideas and thoughts. It's early days, isn't it?'

'Any idea in particular?'

'What if he didn't come down the river? Well, not far anyway. What if he was beaten up somewhere else entirely, then driven here to Watchet and heaved into the river in the town or close to it? I just wonder if this might be a bit of a waste of time.'

'But we don't know, do we?'

Rae sighed. 'You're right, Tommy. I shouldn't be so negative. Let's just get on with it.'

They wound their way up the valley and through the village of Washford, taking the road south and climbing as they entered Exmoor proper. They could see the countryside ahead become bleaker and more desolate as they turned off the road into the first farm.

Several hours later, Rae was feeling even more negative. Nothing seemed amiss at any of the farms they'd visited. Moreover, none of the farm staff they'd spoken to had heard or seen anything unusual at any time the previous weekend. Rae, an experienced observer of body language, had felt no reason to doubt the honesty of the accounts they'd listened to. Tommy drove on the return journey while Rae spoke to Polly on the phone. She and Ade had made little progress, either. Was the team about to get bogged down in one of those infuriating cases where progress slowed to an absolute crawl and people became dispirited? After all, they still didn't know the identity of the victim, five days after his body had been recovered and probably a week after he'd been killed. This was when they needed Sophie Allen's presence. Unfortunately, she was at some kind of regional strategy meeting in Exeter and, in Rae's mind, was probably feeling just as frustrated as the members of her team. It was about time something positive happened.

They still had Jackie Spring sifting community-based information in the background, not that Rae had met her yet. Realistically, what difference could a single voluntary special constable make?

CHAPTER 6: EVIL TEMPTRESS

Jackie was in the Star Inn again, meeting another close friend for an evening meal. A 'nosh-up and natter', as they both described their semi-regular evenings out together. She and Lizzie Buchanan had been friends since their school-days. It was Jackie's sole friendship that stretched back to her childhood, so she valued her meet ups with Lizzie, the only social events that permitted her that degree of nostalgia. Reminiscing about fellow pupils, old teachers and childhood experiences could be therapeutic in small doses. They only met up sporadically, which was a good job considering the extra calories she must be ingesting from this pub alone, not counting her cider nights in the nearby tavern. The two friends tended to stick to the Star or one of the pubs in Willisford, where Lizzie lived and worked as a nurse in the local community hospital.

The two women's careers reflected their favourite school subjects as teenagers. Lizzie had loved Biology whereas Jackie had been a booklover, favouring English. Jackie was very aware, though, that her friend had a much more secure job than she did. Good nurses would always be in demand, whereas libraries in semi-rural communities seemed to be always under threat of closure. On the other hand, Lizzie obviously experienced some heartrending tragedies as part of her daily routine, whereas Jackie's stress levels rarely went much further than damaged or missing books, or budget constraints. Maybe that explained Jackie's decision to become a volunteer police officer, some kind of search for adventure. On these occasional Friday evenings, though, they could forget their workplace concerns and indulge in light-hearted chit-chat, helped along by some cider, wine or beer. Conversations in which they caught up on each other's news.

Lizzie's jaw dropped while she listened to her friend's Monday morning exploits with the body in the harbour. 'Why didn't I know?' she protested. 'I only live a few miles away. I heard a body had been found but I didn't know you were involved. That supplies a whole new level of interest.'

'I don't see why it should. What difference does it make whether it was me or someone else who got the body out? Though it made a right mess of my clothes, I can tell you. And my hair. All that filthy mud. I still think I can smell it at times.'

Lizzie shuddered and ran her fingers nervously through her own hair, recently cut short in a pageboy style. 'Of course it makes a difference when someone you know is involved. It's a bit of drama, isn't it? Helps stir up our humdrum lives a bit.'

Jackie smiled wryly. 'I take it nothing very interesting has happened to you in the last couple of weeks?'

'What, a nurse in a community hospital out here in the sticks? You must be joking.' She snorted, then frowned. 'Actually, there was something a bit odd on Monday, first thing. I had to treat a young woman with Down's syndrome who'd had pretty rough sex. She'd been bleeding. The mother wanted a quick check-up and the morning-after pill.'

Jackie was suddenly alert. 'Do you think she'd been raped?'

'I can't be sure. The injuries were fairly mild, so I gave her some specialist cream. Rape is all about consent, isn't it? Sometimes you can't tell just by a medical examination alone. All the mother said was that the girl's boyfriend had been a bit rough. The girl said next to nothing. Her mother refused to admit that the girl was Down's.'

'How old was she?' Jackie asked.

'Oh, she wasn't underage. Nineteen is what she told us. I wanted to get a doctor to look at her, but the mother wouldn't have it. I went to find someone senior to take over but when I got back to the examination room, they'd gone. Once I'd said that there didn't seem to be any serious injuries, the mother must have decided to do a runner at the first opportunity. The name she gave me was false. Didn't check out with anyone on our records.'

Jackie put down her fork. 'That does sound odd in this day and age. Were they local, do you think?'

Lizzie shrugged. 'No idea. They gave a Nether Stowey address, but it doesn't exist. The girl was almost definitely Down's.' Lizzie finished her lasagne and wiped her mouth with a napkin. 'There's not much more we can do. It came up for discussion at a management meeting but all we could do was to record the details for reference. I've come to the conclusion that the mother brought her in for a check-up just for reassurance and a pill. And when they got that, they left as quick as they could. I think my boss notified social services and the police about her just so we're covered, but there's not much can be done, what with the false name and address, not unless someone's come across her before and recognises who she is.' She finished the wine in her glass and poured another. 'Let's talk about cheerier things. How's your love life?'

'Ha! Nothing particularly cheerful there. Sarah, my mentor in the police, thinks I should hook up with Tony Fisher. She reckons he's lusting after me. Honestly, I wish she'd give it a rest. It's starting to drive me barmy.'

'But he is a nice bloke, Jackie. You've got to agree with me on that.'

Jackie sighed. 'He comes with kids in tow. I've been through all that and come out the other side, only just hanging on to my sanity. I'm not sure I want to put myself through it again. All that teenage stuff. Eugh!'

Lizzie laughed. 'You're exaggerating and you know it. His kids can't be that bad, surely? How many does he have?'

'Three. Two girls and a boy. Sixteen down to twelve.'

'Okay. I suppose it could be a bit of an emotional upheaval.' She stopped suddenly. 'Hang on! Who said anything about settling down with him? Why don't you just go for the easy option and have a fling, with both of you keeping your own places? Don't let things get too serious. Stay in charge.'

Jackie looked coolly at her friend. 'But I respect him too much for that, Lizzie. He is a really nice guy.'

'Ah, I'm beginning to understand the problem. Your sense of responsibility is just too well developed, Jackie Spring. You've always been like it.'

'Takes one to know one. Now drink up. There's a live band playing up at the tavern. I thought we could give it a whirl. We'll see about my supposed sense of social responsibility.'

'Oh, you evil temptress, you! Let's get going. I feel a party mood coming on.'

CHAPTER 7: EXMOOR

Saturday

Jackie was busy the next morning, driving to the local community hospital at Willisford to speak to a tired-looking Lizzie Buchanan again, then returning to Watchet to share a hastily arranged coffee date with Tony Fisher. She left the café and walked the few hundred yards to the police team's incident room just before noon. A silver saloon car was edging into a parking slot as Jackie turned into the open area in front of the small hall. She reached the door at the same time as the driver, a slim middle-aged woman with short honey-blonde hair, wearing a grey tailored trouser suit. Jackie realised she was being scrutinised.

'Can I help you?' the woman asked.

'I was hoping to have a quick word with the DCI in charge,' Jackie said. She realised that the woman had green eyes, unusual in someone with blonde hair. Did that mean the hair colour wasn't natural?

'She's just left for a meeting in Taunton,' came the reply. 'Can I help?'

Jackie frowned. 'It's just some information for her. I'm sure it can wait. I can pop in again later.'

'You must be Jackie Spring,' the woman said. 'I'd better introduce myself. I'm Sophie Allen.'

Jackie took a step back, realising that she was standing rather too close to the most senior police officer she'd ever been in a one-to-one conversation with.

'Sorry, ma'am. I had no idea.'

A slight smile flickered across the woman's face. 'No need to apologise. Why would you know who I am? Let's go inside and get a cuppa. I've driven all the way from Wareham and I'm parched. Chat's always better over tea or coffee, don't you find?'

The rumours and chit-chat were right, then. This woman had presence. An indefinable something that meant you realised you were in the company of someone special. It wasn't a police thing. Neither was it directly due to her seniority. It was something about the way she held herself, her personality, her level of assurance. For goodness' sake, she'd only spoken a few sentences. How could someone have that much of an effect? It was unreal. Jackie followed the woman through the outer door into a small vestibule and from there into an open room, seemingly full of desks. Several other people she'd met earlier in the week looked up. Rae Gregson, the tall, dark-haired woman, quickly made her way across the room to greet them.

'Morning, ma'am,' she said. 'The usual? Coffee?'

'Please. What will you have, Jackie?'

'Umm, tea please. Just a quick one. I don't have long.'

'We'll slip into one of the small interview rooms. You're not really here, are you?' Sophie said quietly.

'No, I suppose not. Not sure why, though. Something to do with maintaining an appearance of non-involvement.' She took the tea that was pushed her way and followed the two detectives into a small side room.

'Well, Polly can be a bit melodramatic at times. She has her reasons, I'm sure. This is DS Rae Gregson, my right-hand woman. But you've already met, haven't you? Now, what snippet have you got that's brought you in to see us?'

Jackie took a sip of tea, gathering her thoughts. This was awkward. Her contact was meant to be with Polly Nelson alone. How would her mishmash of information go down with these other people?

'The DCI told me to let her know about anything unusual I picked up on. Really, I didn't expect anything, not this soon, but last night a close friend told me about something very odd that happened on Monday.' She went on to summarise Lizzie's account of the young woman's visit to Casualty. 'I didn't see how it related though, not last night.'

She felt a little stupid, if truth be told. Here she was, talking to the region's top detective, and the information she'd brought with her sounded so thin. Could it have any relevance to the murder investigation?

'You look as though you have something more?'

'Sorry, ma'am. Yes, I do.' Once again, she felt those green eyes on her, appraising her.

'I paid a visit to the local hospital this morning and had a look at their CCTV sequence from Monday morning. There are some clear shots of the young woman and her mother. But there's also a camera scanning the entrance and part of the car park. They arrived in an old muddy Land Rover that waited in the car park for them. It looked as though the driver was a man in a cloth cap, though the details are a bit fuzzy.'

'Why is this important?'

'Because of what Tony Fisher spotted a couple of days ago. He's a local painter and was working on a building at the quayside when the DCI and the rest of the unit were here. He was sure someone was watching them from a grubby Land Rover. A man wearing a flat cap.'

Sophie Allen appeared to ponder on Jackie's news for a few seconds. 'Rae here will log the information and we'll tell Polly when she arrives. It may not be relevant, but we don't know that. It is intriguing, though, isn't it? Why would someone bringing a young woman in for that kind of check-up give totally false information like that? It really doesn't make sense unless they're trying to hide something. And then your other snippets. Very odd.' She sipped at her coffee.

'I've also been listening in to local chat about who our dead body might be. Especially if the gossip mentions people who haven't been seen for a week or so. The first possibility is a no-go because it was someone local here in Watchet. I checked it out and he was on holiday. The second sounded a good candidate but he turned up late yesterday. The third is way up on Exmoor near Braycombe. It sounds unlikely because it's way beyond the basin of our local rivers.'

'Well done. Leave that third option with us. And listen, don't do anything that would put your job at the library at risk, like cutting into your time there.'

'It won't be. In jeopardy, I mean. Apparently, I've become a bit of a local celebrity since Monday. It's been one of our busiest weeks in ages. Mystery thrillers and true crime books have been flying off the shelves.'

All three women laughed, and Jackie took another mouthful of tea, more carefully this time. It had cooled during her account of the teenager's visit to the hospital, so she finished it and put the mug on the counter. She headed for the door.

* * *

'I can see why Polly was impressed,' Sophie said, watching Jackie walk across the small car park.

'Do you think there's anything for us in that story?' Rae sounded surprised.

Sophie shrugged. 'It's unlikely but we can't ignore it. Anyway, what other potential leads do we have?' She finished her coffee. 'Take it yourself, Rae. Sensitive handling is called for. They can't live too far, can they? Otherwise, why would they have come to this area for treatment? And if the younger woman is Down's syndrome, she must be on a health register somewhere. Get onto it now. See if you can get descriptions and staff feelings about those two. With a bit of luck, we might have a clearer picture by the time Polly arrives back for the late briefing. Take Tommy with you.'

'Two of us?'

'Yes, two of you. Tommy can try to get copies of any CCTV they might have. I know what you're thinking, that it's probably a waste of time and resources, based on the over-active imaginations of a few locals. It's what Barry would be thinking, and no doubt Polly too. But they're not here and I am. Get back for our late briefing with Polly, please. At that point we make a decision as to whether it's worth pursuing further. Find out whether the girl and her mother are farming folk, and anything else about them. Okay? If you've got time, check out this possible missing person. But don't expect too much. I'll message Polly with what I've suggested.'

Rae collected Tommy and the two of them left, with Rae wondering, not for the first time, what kind of logic ruled in the chief's brain. Was logic even the right word?

Meanwhile, Sophie made her way across to Ade's desk.

'Anything else of note?' she asked.

He nodded. 'Slower than we'd like though, ma'am. It was definitely traces of Jeyes Fluid on his clothes. What they can't explain is why traces were still there after a day or two in the water. The only suggestion is that he had loads of the stuff on his clothes. It's not a major toxin, though it isn't used as much as it was. It's still widely available. Used as a general disinfectant. Drains and stuff. Some people use it as a winter wash on fruit trees and in greenhouses.'

'That's useful. I'll let the others know. It might confirm some of our other leads.'

* * *

Rae and Tommy had needed less than an hour at the hospital. Jackie Spring's friend, Lizzie, proved to be the most helpful, but they'd already been told most of her thoughts. Rae asked about the women's clothes and their accents, while Tommy tracked down the security officer in order to see the CCTV footage. He also gained one interesting snippet. The old vehicle the duo had left in turned in the uphill direction after leaving the car park. And he confirmed that it had been very dirty.

'Not any old mud, either,' the security man had added. 'Definitely farm gunk. Cattle muck, I reckon.'

The two detectives climbed back into their car and Rae glanced at the time. 'I think we've got time to do a bit of exploring,' she said. 'We'll head inland and up, a bit further than we went yesterday. We need to get a feel for the lie of the land up on the moors, and that supposed person who's gone walkabout is up there. It's just the kind of bleak place that holds secrets.'

Tommy, who was driving, grinned. 'That's a bit deep, isn't it, boss?'

'I'm a brooding romantic at heart, Tommy. Maybe I've been reading too much Coleridge since we've been here.'

'Really? I've never read much poetry.'

'Well, this is an ideal opportunity then. I'll give you a copy when we get back. The Ancient Mariner is really bleak. Full of death and suffering.'

Tommy looked mournful. 'Do I really have to?' he asked.

'Of course not. But it's there if you want it.'

They drove on, climbing up the increasingly narrow lanes, heading over the Brendon Hills and towards Exmoor. The farms thinned out, the trees becoming sparse and the landscape ever bleaker. Brooding was the right word, Rae decided. It didn't look welcoming. The land looked distrustful. It must be hard to scratch a living up here, she thought. Gone were the lush green fields of the coastal strip and, to a lesser extent, the Brendons. Here, everything looked scrawny and windswept. All the natural vegetation seemed to be hanging on by the thinnest of threads, often looking as though the next gale might uproot much of it and send it spinning to destruction. In sunshine it might look pretty but on an overcast day like today it looked depressing.

Rae switched her gaze from the view outside the car to her young colleague, watching the road ahead as it ribboned its way across the windswept moorland.

'Welcome to Exmoor,' she said. 'People have heard of Dartmoor, further south, in Devon. They tend to forget about this place.'

'I don't blame them,' Tommy replied. 'It doesn't look very welcoming up here, does it?'

CHAPTER 8: REMOTE COTTAGE

Justin Penhale was a Cornishman who lived in Devon, a circumstance that caused him to be treated with suspicion by both sets of long-term native inhabitants. He sometimes felt like a homeless outcast, a nomad even, set to be something of an outsider for the rest of his life. His Cornish family members derided him for opting to live in that soft place to the east of his natural home. His Devon neighbours wondered if there was a hidden Cornish tempestuousness to his character, something untamed linked to his origins in that hard, wild county to the west. He just felt bemused by it all. He was only in his late twenties and lived in the modern world. He really couldn't understand the origins of these deeply held prejudices, not in this day and age. Shouldn't those kinds of views have died out during his grandparents' generation?

Justin had opted to remain in Devon when he'd finished his degree at Exeter University. His father, a hard, moody man, had died after a fishing boat accident and his mother, much softer in temperament, had come to live in Exeter, not far from his own home. Her hope had been that this move would bring her closer to her own older brother, a quiet, solitary man who lived frugally and spent much of his time painting landscapes of the southwest peninsula's brooding countryside. But Justin and his mother had lost much of their contact with the artist when he'd moved to Exmoor and, now his mother was in hospital suffering from a serious chronic illness, Justin was finally trying to track him down. That's why he was here, on a rather bleak part of the moor, peering out of his car window at the lonely cottage beside the road. A badly weathered nameplate was fixed to the wall beside the door: Bynehill View.

The place looked deserted. Justin knew that his uncle Ben was a bit of a recluse, but even so. No face at any of the windows, no washing blowing on the line and, most importantly, no car sitting on the small, tarmacked parking area at the front of the house. Hadn't his mother always said that her brother was a fresh air fanatic and always had windows open, no matter the weather? Yet they were all closed, even on a dry, relatively mild day like today.

He clambered out of his car and walked to the front door. There was no answer to his rings on the bell push so he hammered loudly on the door. Still no response. He walked around the low house and tried the same set of actions at the back door, but with the same result. Silence. The rear garden had a vegetable bed, but it had that somewhat bedraggled look of a plot that hadn't been worked on for a while. The back orchard looked pretty, with signs of early blossom appearing on some plum or damson trees. There might be a logical explanation to the silence, of course. Maybe his uncle had gone on holiday. But, if he had, it would have been a first in his adult life. Apparently, Ben was a man who loathed all the trappings of tourism. That was the reason he'd opted to live all the way up here, in the middle of a semi-wilderness. He lived for his paintings, Justin's mother had explained. That and the wildlife.

Still no signs of life. Justin wandered around the house again, first looking for hidey-holes where a key might be concealed, then, when that search proved fruitless, scanning the building for an insecure window that might provide a point of entry. Was that one at the side of the property?

What appeared to be a bathroom fanlight might not have been secured fully. Or was it just a trick of the light? He continued around the house to an old garage, its wooden doors not fitting together neatly. He returned to his car and extracted a wheel brace from the boot. Using it as a lever, he quickly had the door open. A small car took up most of the room, but an old timber ladder was laid out along one wall. He hauled it out into the daylight. It didn't look very secure, but it was the only available item that would permit him to peer through the upper windows. He carried it across to the house and lodged it against the wall beside the bathroom window. The rungs on the ladder were rather more rickety than he would have liked, but they felt secure enough if he kept his feet close to the side struts. Justin climbed, slowly and carefully, testing each strut as his feet found their place. He finally found himself level with the frosted glass of the bathroom window, but his hopes were dashed. The narrow fanlight at the top had been latched securely in place. There was no point in continuing. He made his way slowly back to ground level, asking himself, what now? He sat on the front step, getting his breath back. The sun momentarily broke through the clouds and the moorland scene in front of him was transformed into something of beauty. No wonder his uncle had chosen to settle here. He heard a car draw up and looked up to see a man and a woman walking towards him.

* * *

The two detectives had passed a number of hill farms, stopping to take a brief look at each one, but without calling in on the farmers. None had raised any suspicions, although Rae was aware that anyone involved in the death of the person who'd washed up in the harbour would have taken precautions not to arouse interest locally. They were now on a lonely stretch of road, crossing one of the highest parts of Exmoor, heading towards Braycombe. The house they were looking for was somewhere along this desolate stretch of road. She suddenly leaned forward in her seat, trying to peer ahead. 'Can you slow down, Tommy? There's a bloke up a rickety ladder at that house ahead. It looks as though he might be trying to force his way in through a window.'

Tommy dutifully pulled in at a patch of rough ground, level with another car. By the time he and Rae had got out of their vehicle, the man was back at ground level, sitting on the front step of the house. He looked up as they approached.

'Police,' Rae said, flashing her warrant card. 'DS Rae Gregson. I caught sight of you up that ladder just now. Could you explain?'

'It's my uncle's place,' the man replied. 'He's a bit of a recluse. I came to visit him but there doesn't seem to be anyone in.'

'Was he expecting you?' She noted the name of the house, Bynehill View. It was the one they were looking for, where the owner hadn't been seen for some time.

The man shook his head. 'No. We don't know his phone number. To be honest, I don't even know if he's got a phone. He cut himself off from the rest of the family years ago. I've been trying to find him because my mum's seriously ill. She wants to see him before she dies. They were close as kids.'

'And you're sure he lives here?'

'Yes. But I only found out yesterday when our solicitor confirmed it. We think he moved here about five or six years ago. That's why I'm here today. I live in Exeter.'

'And what's your name, sir?'

'Justin Penhale.'

Rae nodded to Tommy, and he returned to their own vehicle to carry out a check on the car and its owner.

'Can we go walkabout, Mr Penhale? I'd like to take a look, please.'

Rae looked closely at the old house as they made their way around it. It was solidly built and sat in a slight dip in the ground that would give it some protection from the prevailing winds.

'Bleak up here,' she said.

‘Well, that would suit my uncle. He paints landscapes of the moor, as far as we know. And he’s a tough old bird, that’s what my mother used to say.’

By now they were at the rear of the house, near the orchard. Rae stopped and sniffed the air. ‘What’s that smell?’ she asked. ‘There’s a chemical whiff in the air.’

‘I think it’s something he’s sprayed on the fruit trees,’ came the reply. ‘Something like Jeyes Fluid. Isn’t it sometimes used as a late-winter wash? There wasn’t any of it in the garage but there’s an old shed behind. I haven’t looked in it yet. The door’s locked. I was hoping to find a key to the house but no luck.’

Rae followed the man towards the shed and examined the door. The padlock was relatively new, but the hasp was old and looked insecure. Tommy joined them and gave Rae a nod, indicating that the name on the vehicle database check had matched up. With Tommy’s help, and using Justin’s wheel brace as a lever, she managed to force the door open wide. It was dingy inside, but she noticed an empty plastic vessel of what looked like tar wash lying on its side in a dark corner, with a few trails of the stuff on the uneven concrete floor. Several scuff marks could be seen in the thin spillage. Garden tools were neatly hanging from wall hooks, but a few lay on the floor. She held out her arm to stop Justin from approaching.

‘Have you touched anything in here or in the garage?’

He shook his head. ‘I just grabbed the ladder from the garage. I didn’t come in here.’

She thought quickly. ‘Mr Penhale, I’m going to take it on trust that the owner is probably your uncle, as you claim. It looks as though there might have been some kind of scuffle in here. I think we need to get inside that house to check if he’s inside, injured. Are you sure there’s no key hidden anywhere?’

He shook his head. ‘I really couldn’t say. I had what I thought was a good look near the house and didn’t spot one anywhere.’

'What about the garage?'

'It's very bare. Just his car and the ladder propped against a wall. I didn't come in here. You can see that.'

Rae looked around. No row of hooks. She carefully moved to a nearby shelf where a couple of grubby plastic tubs were resting. Screws and nails? She tipped the contents out across the small bench. Several keys lay at the bottom of one of the containers. She pocketed them and carefully retraced her steps to the door, trying to avoid treading in the spilt tar wash on the floor. They then made their way back to the house and tried the keys. Rae felt the usual sense of trepidation as the second key slid home and turned. What would they find inside? If her guess was right, the place would be empty, but she couldn't be sure.

'Best if you stay outside, Mr Penhale. Leave the search to us.' Rae slipped a pair of nylon foot liners over her shoes, tugged latex gloves onto her hands and indicated to Tommy that he should do the same. They entered the hall and looked around. The downstairs rooms were large, with a spacious kitchen diner to the left of the hallway and a plainly furnished sitting room to the right. Both had good views across the moorland. To the rear of the kitchen was a walk-in larder and a small laundry space, leading to the back door. The two detectives returned to the hall and climbed the stairs. Two bedrooms led off the landing, a larger bedroom at the front and a small single room beside it. A bathroom was next, only just large enough to contain the bath, washbasin and toilet. Rae opened the fourth door and did a double take. It was a relatively spacious art studio, with windows overlooking the view at the rear of the house. Paints, brushes and other art tools lay on shelves along the longer wall, with several easels standing in front of the window. Flat tables lined the shorter wall, and paintings were kept in support frames along another. Rae walked carefully over to the paintings and started to flick through the first rack, all landscapes of moorland views. Rae thought they were good, although she knew that she was no expert. They seemed to capture the bleak beauty well. She moved to the second rack, containing only a single painting, a portrait of a young woman. Rae gasped. Surely the painting was of the young woman with Down's who'd made the unexpected clinic visit? The artist had captured her look accurately and turned it into a thing of beauty, making her look almost other-worldly.

Rae backed across to the door, pulled out her phone and called Sophie Allen. There was something very strange going on here.

CHAPTER 9: A SIMPLE SOUL

Cars lined the narrow roadway, and several forensic vans were parked directly in front of the cottage as Polly Nelson drew her car to a halt. She scowled as she hurried across to the small group outside the front porch.

'Just my luck to miss the first big breakthrough.' She looked at Sophie accusingly. 'How do you manage it? You always seem to be in the right place at the right time.'

Sophie laughed. 'It's karma, Polly. Rewarding me for my constant good behaviour, like a benevolent primary school teacher. Or maybe it's just serendipity.'

Polly harumphed. 'You and your cod philosophy. Anyway, can I ask what all the fuss is about? I picked up on some of it from that message you left but I don't think I got the whole story.'

'We've identified our body, we think. He was the resident of this cottage, one Benjamin Carlyon. There's Jeyes Fluid spilled on the floor of the shed. He uses it on his fruit trees. His nephew, Justin Penhale, is sitting in the car with Tommy. He identified our victim from a photo on my phone. But there's more. The man was a talented artist, specialising in watercolours of the moorland around here. But he also painted a portrait. And guess what? It's of a young woman who looks as though she might have Down's syndrome. And that links up to what your Jackie Spring told us this morning.'

'This is the girl who might have been raped, yes?'

Sophie nodded.

'So the murder might have been some kind of revenge? Maybe from her family? Any clue as to who she might be?'

'That's what we'll be looking for once Forensics have finished with the place. Maybe you or Ade could arrange for Mr Penhale to carry out a formal identification as soon as he's able to. Technically he's not the next of kin but his mother is too ill to make the journey up from Exeter.'

Polly looked around her. 'It's a wild spot up here, isn't it? What makes someone choose to live a solitary life in a spot like this?'

'We could speculate on that for ages and then probably get it completely wrong. Though we know he's an artist. Maybe he needed to live up here to get a true feel for the moors.' Sophie shrugged and looked at her watch. 'Well, now you're here I think I'll head off. It's a bit of a trek back to Wareham.'

* * *

Once the forensic chief had given them the go ahead, Rae and Tommy gave Polly a tour, concentrating on the shed with the tar wash spillage and the art studio.

'Those footmarks on the shed floor could be useful,' the DCI said. 'And these paintings are interesting. I'm no art expert but my guess is that the landscapes are good. And they're so varied. Moors, woods, streams. The different seasons and distinct times of day. All kinds of stuff. He obviously liked a bit of variety. So why the portrait? Do you think she might have meant something to him?'

Rae shrugged. 'It's the obvious conclusion, I guess. It's the way our thoughts were going. It's not quite as good, though, is it? As artwork, I mean.'

'Right. And where does that lead us?'

'Well, his painting is meticulous in the landscapes. It's quite fine brushwork in places, don't you think? I'd guess he was there at the scene for at least part of the process. They've got that level of detail. But don't you get the feeling that the portrait isn't quite of the same quality? And that kind of asks the question, what was its purpose?'

'You mean the landscapes have been done for commercial sale, whereas the portrait wasn't?'

Rae nodded. 'But it's just a thought. Was she someone he knew? Someone he cared for or was interested in?'

Polly frowned. 'Well, we could speculate all we like but it doesn't count for anything without some solid evidence. Where do we start?'

Rae pursed her lips. 'Locally, I suppose. But one of the forensic guys had a look at the paintings. He said there were scenes from all across Exmoor. She could be someone he met while out painting.'

'But why paint her if that's the case? It's not common, is it? Wouldn't you do one and then hand it over? He's kept them here. It's something odd. All we can do is try to trace her. If she's Down's, she's got to be on a register somewhere, it stands to reason. But if we can't trace her that way then we'll have to organise some kind of house-to-house. All the bloody way across Exmoor. Maybe not a huge number of houses or people, but a big area. Lots of half-hidden hamlets and tiny communities. Lots of people with reasons for keeping themselves to themselves.' She looked up at the fading sunlight. 'We'll start tomorrow.'

The detectives moved to their cars. Rae and Tommy set off back to Watchet, whereas Polly sat with Justin Penhale for a few minutes, arranging for him to visit the county hospital at Taunton to make a positive identification of his uncle's body. That would be a mere formality, surely?

Up on the higher ground to the west, a man who was crouching behind a clump of heather lowered his binoculars, then sat for a few minutes as if deep in thought. He slowly made his way back to a battered Land Rover parked a few hundred yards away, hidden from view on a rough track.

* * *

Within the hour, Rae and Tommy were back in Watchet, about to head to their hotel rooms.

'Pub meal tonight?' Rae asked.

'Why not?' came Tommy's reply. 'Though my mum says that you and the chief super are teaching me bad habits.'

Rae laughed. 'Listen, there are far worse habits than having food and a couple of drinks in a nice pub. I know, Tommy. I indulged in more than a few of them in my previous life.'

Tommy didn't know what to say, so he just headed for his room. He felt there was the potential for danger if any conversation they had strayed too far into Rae's back story. He'd been warned against it by Barry Marsh soon after he'd joined the unit, and he'd taken that advice seriously. He liked Rae and recognised that she was a really good detective, better than he could ever hope to be. But she had a personality that was impossible to pin down, difficult to categorise. A bit like the chief super in a way, kind of unpredictable. Whereas Barry, his usual DI, was a straight-ahead normal guy with no hidden agendas. Or so it appeared. Did that mean, though, that he was just better at hiding his thoughts and feelings?

Tommy thought back to the evening reception at Barry's wedding. That had been a bit of an eye-opener for him, although his girlfriend, Olivia, seemed to have taken it all in her stride. She was a nurse, though. He'd heard rumours of how uninhibited some student nurses could be when they had opportunities to let their hair down. He supposed it must be a similar kind of story for Rae and the chief super. Maybe they both had tensions that needed a release one way or another. Like at the wedding, when it had seemed for a while that he had strayed into a parallel universe. The feeling had begun when Sophie Allen picked up the microphone and started her own karaoke rendition of Gloria Gaynor's famous songs, 'I Am What I Am' and 'I Will Survive'. The feeling had got even stronger a few minutes later when his boss, Rae, had stripped down to her lingerie on stage while the bride's uncle had mimicked Tom Jones singing 'You Can Leave Your Hat On'. Tommy could hardly believe what was happening, even though the performance had obviously been pre-planned and well-rehearsed. But everyone roared their appreciation, even Olivia. She stood up, applauding and whooping loudly, something she'd never done before in their six-month romance. And Tommy had to admit one thing. Rae had looked stunning in her fishnets, crimson corset, matching heels and red trilby hat.

Maybe life was just too complicated to understand the oddities of human behaviour, as Olivia had suggested.

'Just go with the flow,' was what she'd said when he'd expressed his surprise a few minutes after the performances had ended.

He felt there was a coded message in there somewhere. Maybe he should work on losing some of his own inhibitions. He knew he had them. Clearly some of his work colleagues had found ways of easing the tensions of their working lives. After all, here he was, out on an investigation with his boss, Rae, and she was back to being the imaginative and super-efficient cop everyone knew her to be. Life wasn't just complicated, it was weird.

He'd come to the conclusion that he was just a simple soul with a correspondingly simple outlook on life. He looked at the time. Better get a move on. He needed to phone Olivia before getting ready to go out.

CHAPTER 10: RAGGED SCARF

Sunday

Donny Lomax wasn't a particularly imaginative person. Seemingly random things happened in life. He left it at that and didn't really consider causes and links. He didn't speculate about the reasons why events happened. After all, the world was a strange and unknown place where chance and luck ruled. Or bad luck, more likely.

He heard about the body found in the harbour down in Watchet and he didn't give it much thought. Then he heard that the cops were treating the death as suspicious, although he just shrugged at the news. This was followed by some gossip that they were poking around in the river in case the body had been washed downstream on the night of the big storm. Then came a conversation he overheard in a pub up on the moors, that the victim may have blundered into the river accidentally while staggering about already injured after an accident of some kind. He'd then drowned in the raging waters, swept about in the torrent like a cork, finally spewing out into the sea close to the harbour.

Here Donny was, lying in bed, watching the early morning light creep around the edge of the curtains, trying either to sink back into slumber or summon the enthusiasm to get up and head off to work early. But an unsettling germ of a notion had formed in his head when he'd first come awake. That bump he'd heard on the blind corner on the night of the storm. He'd hit something, hadn't he? But he hadn't seen what it was, even though he'd stopped for a look. Jesus. What if it had been this guy, the one washed up? But how could there be any kind of link? He'd been miles away from the river valley, way up on Exmoor, miles from here. Could someone have staggered that kind of distance and ended up in the torrent? Surely not. It was impossible. And he couldn't tell the cops about the night of the bump, could he? Not with three grand of stolen copper cable in the back of his van at the time of the collision. They'd be aware of the nearby theft and would start putting two and two together. Better to stay quiet about it. Even asking questions of some local folk might draw attention to himself. Some of them were a suspicious lot, wary of outsiders. He'd just have to keep listening out for the local pub gossip, maybe ask a few careful questions. Keep a bit of an eye on the cops, just in case. It wouldn't take him long to up sticks and scarper if the worst came to the worst. He didn't have any real ties here, after all. He'd just grown used to the area. But he'd only need a couple of hours to chuck his stuff into the Land Rover and head off up to Yorkshire, to his sister's place. He grimaced over his drink. That would be a last resort, only to be used if he was sure the cops were on to him. He hated his sister and her holier-than-thou attitudes.

Should he head back to that spot up on Exmoor and have a quick look? It might be a good idea. He could go after he'd finished work. The evenings were getting lighter now it was April, so he should manage a quick check in the hour or two of daylight that would remain, just for his own peace of mind. He might be a bit of a rogue, but he was no killer. He had a conscience, unlike some of the guys he knew. And if he got up now and started work on the farm early, he might be able to get away a bit sooner than usual and give himself more time.

* * *

Donny spent that day working in the top field. He was on the old tractor, sowing a crop of turnips that would be used as late-season fodder for the animals. They all liked a bit of fresh stuff to eat, a change from their usual diet of manufactured pellets. Not that he was against that kind of feedstuff. It was easy to use, and the animals liked it. But there was still something to be said for natural vegetable fodder. He was glad he worked on a farm that kept to some of the old traditions. His boss, Kevin Bright, the farm owner, was slowly changing to more sustainable methods of farming and this pleased Donny. He liked nature and wanted to do his bit to help it survive.

The so-called top field was a bit of a misnomer. At one time it probably had been the highest-lying field on the farm, but expansion several generations earlier had added several more fields to the farm's land, all of them closer to the moor's edge. A name was a name, though, and farming folk were slow to change their habits. Names stuck. Top Field was still close to the edge of Highcroft Farm, though, with only a single pasture separating it from the neighbouring property, Greymoor Farm, a smaller holding of poorer soil whose fields climbed up onto the moor. Donny often wondered how it managed to survive in these difficult times. Its animals looked scrawnier than their own and its crop yields must be lower. He didn't know much about the property and, what was even more unusual, neither did Kevin. The people who farmed Greymoor kept themselves very much to themselves, rarely mixing with the rest of the local farming community. An unofficial support network operated among the local farming families, but the Greymoor people were conspicuous by their absence. They were secretive and distant. Several possible explanations had surfaced in local gossip. That the family were members of a strict religious sect. That some of them were criminals, just out of jail. That they practised black magic, organising strange rituals on nights with a full moon. Donny took it all with a pinch of salt, though the idea of midnight satanic orgies was an appealing one. If he ever saw one of the farm workers close enough for a chat he'd have to ask about such goings-on. The idea of semi-naked people running around in the woods and having wild sex sounded attractive, in a strange way. He'd once said so to a couple of mates in the pub. They'd dissolved into gales of laughter and told him he was naive in the extreme.

'Too bloody cold up there, mate,' was their concluding comment.

Another thing that puzzled him about Greymoor Farm was the cluster of caravans beside one of the barns. He'd caught sight of them once when he'd been up on the roof of one of their own outbuildings, fixing a loose sheet of roofing. Caravans on farms sometimes meant holidaymakers, people looking for a low-cost break in summer. But tourists hadn't been spotted on the local roads in the kind of numbers that might be expected from half a dozen holiday caravans. So what were they used for? He'd rarely seen any Greymoor workers out in the fields to be able to ask. They kept themselves to themselves. Maybe next time he did catch sight of one he ought to make another effort to start a conversation. He could guess what would happen, though. As he approached the boundary, they'd move away. It had happened before.

Donny got most of the field planted by midday, completed the task after lunch, then helped with the afternoon milking. The cows seemed docile today.

'Happy cows are productive cows,' his boss said with a grin.

* * *

Donny remembered the narrow lane appearing to be scarily tight and enclosed in the darkness and rain on that stormy night, but it seemed less threatening this evening, with the sun still out. The road headed across the upper reaches of Exmoor in an east-west direction, sometimes twisting from side to side, sometimes running up and down humps, and sometimes doing both at the same time. He reached the wider dip, heavily wooded with ancient, gnarled trees, moss-covered and dank looking. This was the corner. He pulled off the road at the next suitable spot and walked back to the scene of the possible collision.

There was nothing to be seen, not on the road surface nor in the ditch that lined the lane, but he remembered with a jolt that the ditch hadn't been there that stormy night. Or more precisely, he hadn't noticed it. There had just been a continuous stream of water rushing down the side of the road. The ditch must have been so full, he hadn't spotted it. What if whatever he'd hit had fallen in? It would have remained out of sight of him and his torch. Donny walked up and down the lane, prodding the ditch with a stick but there was nothing suspicious there, just the usual contents of mud, broken debris and gravel washed in from the road surface. Whatever he'd hit had gone during the intervening week. Either that or he'd imagined the whole thing and had hit a branch blown down by the wind. If so, where was it? There were plenty of small twigs still littering the road surface but nothing large. Anyway, the sound would have been different, surely.

He stepped across the ditch and took a look at the trees beyond. They were more thinly spread than appeared from the road. A bruised deer could have easily slipped through the copse and made its way to somewhere safe. The green fronds of new-season ferns were beginning to uncurl from the dull brown mat of dead bracken, created from last year's growth. Had it just been a deer, hit with a glancing blow? He walked a few yards into the undergrowth, attracted by the hint of a colour that looked out of place. A sodden scarf in pale blue was caught up in some scrawny brambles. It looked badly entwined, so much so that it might never be disentangled from the thorns that held it in place. It didn't look as though it had been there very long, maybe a couple of weeks at the most. Could it have come from someone he'd hit? Donny began to worry again. What should he do?

In the end, he did what Donny always did when faced with a moral dilemma. He pushed the problem into a back recess of his mind and tried to forget about it. But the worry wouldn't go away, not completely.

CHAPTER 11: PICK-UP GONE WRONG

Monday, Week 2

Donny was working on the farm boundary the next day, securing some old sections of drystone walling that were in danger of collapsing. Cattle had a habit of rubbing their skin against the abrasive surfaces, probably to counter some kind of itching, and this could lead to destabilising the wall. He wasn't an experienced wall builder, but he could get by. If there were sections that showed serious problems, they'd call in a professional, but this was rarely needed. Kevin was a firm believer in the stitch-in-time principle and always dealt with problems while they were still in their infancy. He'd come across to join Donny just now, late in the morning, to inspect one section that his employee was unsure about.

'I don't think we've got time to fix it all right now, Donny,' Kevin concluded. 'Put three posts in along the length and stretch some barbed wire between them, just to keep the cattle away from the wall surface. It'll last a few weeks with a bit of luck, and we'll get it rebuilt when we've got time.'

'And the other side? Greymoor?'

Kevin shrugged. 'They've rarely put cattle in this field. They just use it for hay, don't they? Well, if it happens, it happens. Let's not worry about it.'

'What do they do, Kev? How does that farm pay its way?'

'I don't poke my nose in. The first and only time I tried to chat to Bryn Guthrie, he threatened me with his fists for asking too many questions. He's an oddball and no mistake. Everyone steers clear. But I've already told you that. Why are you asking now?'

It was Donny's turn to shrug. 'No reason.'

He didn't say that the possible collision the previous week had taken place just beyond the far boundary of Greymoor Farm, where it merged into the woods. If he mentioned it to Kevin, his boss would ask too many questions about the why, the where and the how. Better to stay quiet. But he clambered back on top of the wall once his boss had gone. They were still there, a handful of men from the neighbouring farm in the distance, all with poles, probing hedges and possible hidey-holes. They were clearly searching for something or someone. Two men were staying back, keeping an eye on the others in front of them. It looked as though they were telling the searchers what to do. One of the two leaders looked across to Highcroft, and Donny, up on the wall, pretended he was busy. Was it Guthrie himself? And what were they up to? He slid back down from the wall and got on with the job he'd been told to do, fixing up a barbed-wire section to keep the cows away from the old wall.

* * *

Donny went into Watchet that night, something he did only rarely. It was a bit of a drive to get down to the coastal strip. Even worse was the drive back at the end of the evening, often with a couple of pints of ale or cider inside of him. He knew the local traffic cops kept an eye out for drivers who were a bit the worse for wear, though most of their efforts were focussed within the tourist season or Christmas. If the worst came to the worst, he could always stay in the town and kip down in the back of the van. He kept a sleeping bag there for that very purpose, though he'd rarely needed it.

The tavern looked packed and had some loud live music on. Not his thing. Maybe that was why the Star Inn was quieter than he'd expected. He took his pint across to a small corner table and settled down to make himself comfortable. He'd only been there for a few minutes when he realised that an attractive dark-haired woman was sitting alone in the opposite corner, finishing a meal. He watched her surreptitiously, glancing across each time he lifted his beer to take a mouthful. She rose from her seat once she'd finished eating, lifted a newspaper from a rack by the bar and returned to her table to read it, sipping at a glass of cider while doing so. She occasionally exchanged a few words with the manager when he passed on his way to other tables with plates of food but, apart from that, she just sat quietly in the shadows. He couldn't make out her features clearly, though it looked as if the dark hair that touched her shoulders was curly.

Why would she be here, by herself? It would never occur to Donny that a solitary woman might well be in the pub for the same reason as him, that she had a spare hour in which she chose to relax over a drink. His immediate thoughts were, am I in with a chance? Should I make a move? He might be a few years older than her, but he looked after himself reasonably well. He was wearing clean, presentable clothes. And he had to face the fact that he was lonely. He'd been by himself since his marriage broke up some five years earlier and he missed the warmth and comfort of having a woman in his bed on a regular basis. In fact, he sometimes felt slightly desperate to fill that void.

He drained his glass and made his way to the bar for a refill but chose not to return to his previous table. Instead, he wandered across to the woman's corner, pretending to look at the artwork on the walls, efforts by local artists with price tags attached.

'Some of these paintings are good, aren't they?' he murmured while standing next to her table.

She looked up at him. 'Pardon?'

'I said, some of these are good.' He pointed to the nearest painting.

'Yes, they are.' She returned to her newspaper.

'Can I sit here? It's just that I'm on my own across there, and so are you across here. Maybe we could chat.'

He was aware of her looking at him coolly. She flipped her hand towards a free chair but said nothing. This gave Donny an opportunity to look at her ring finger, something an old friend had told him was one of the most important observations he could make of a potential new girlfriend, and something he wouldn't have thought of without a direct instruction. No rings, so he might be in with a chance. The trouble was, the woman spotted his glance and frowned.

'So, is this place your local?' he asked.

Again, a chilly look. 'Pardon?'

'Is this place your local? Do you live around here?'

She nodded, then immediately returned her attention to her paper.

'I don't. Live in Watchet, I mean. I'm up on the moor. It's airier up there.'

She raised her eyes again, but slowly. 'Really?'

'Well, I think so. Compared to some of the other places I've lived in, anyway. Exeter, Plymouth, Bristol.'

'Gosh, you're really well travelled, aren't you? What a thirst for adventure you must have.'

Donny wondered what she meant. He was trying hard to get a good conversation started but she wasn't really playing her part. Maybe she had learning difficulties or something and found it hard chatting to people. He found conversation hard enough himself. Possibly she was even worse at it.

'So where do you live, then?' he asked.

She sighed loudly and put her paper down. 'Here in Watchet.'

'You said that. Have you heard much about the body that was found washed up last week?'

At last he seemed to have her attention.

'In what respect?' she asked. He felt that she was looking at him a bit too suspiciously, but at least she was showing an interest. Maybe she knew something.

'Well, maybe someone knows who he is and where he came from,' he replied. 'I bet people are talking about it.'

She shrugged. 'Gossip probably doesn't help.'

'So, you locals don't know?'

'Don't know what?'

'Who he is. How he got there. Where he came from. That kind of stuff.'

'No. Do you?'

Donny snorted. 'Course not. I said, I'm from up on Exmoor. A bit out of touch with the news. You're bound to know more if you're local.'

She shook her hair and her curls danced on her shoulders. Donny suddenly felt very lonely and realised again that his life as a farm worker gave him few opportunities for romance. Sod it, he thought. In for a penny, in for a pound.

'Whereabouts in Watchet do you live? What street?'

'What? I don't give my address out to all and sundry.'

She looked angry. All he'd done was to ask where she lived. Had that been a bad move? He was feeling confused and muddled, something that happened often when he was in a one-to-one chat with a woman.

'Why are you pestering me like this? I didn't ask you to come across here and sit at my table.'

He realised that he'd got everything wrong. Again. 'I'm only trying to be friendly,' he protested. 'I did ask you if it was okay to sit here.'

'And I agreed in the mistaken hope that's all you wanted to do. Sit here. I should have known better. I should have guessed you'd be trying it on within a few minutes.'

'What do you mean?'

'Asking where I live,' she replied. 'You're obviously trying to pick me up. You see a woman alone in a pub and immediately think she must be available. You're a pest, Mister Not Local. And a transparently obvious one at that.'

She gathered her belongings, slid into her jacket, stood up and left.

Donny was bemused. As far as he was concerned, what he'd said was true. He was only trying to be friendly. Okay, if she'd have been up for a bit of romance, he'd have jumped at the chance, but that wasn't the main reason he'd started chatting to her, was it?

The pub manager came across, all six foot four of him. 'You do that again and I'll throw you out. You're lucky she didn't slap handcuffs on you.'

Donny's sense of confusion worsened. 'What?'

'She's the local special constable and tough enough to floor you with one punch. That's the only reason I didn't step in earlier. This is a safe space for women, and we take our role seriously. Who do you think you are? Some kind of God's gift? Get real.'

Donny finished his beer and headed for the door. Were all the people down here in the town as barmy as those two? Or was it him? He'd always had difficulties expressing his feelings, putting things into words. That's why his relationships had a habit of falling apart. Well, the few he'd managed to make last more than a week or two. He just felt happier in the company of a woman. It was as simple as that. But he couldn't put it into words and why should he be expected to? He'd never hurt anyone, not intentionally. He was quite a gentle bloke really, although he did recognise that he really, really didn't understand women.

* * *

Jackie Spring left the pub feeling distinctly irritated. She'd always hated that masculine sense of entitlement, the view that too many men had, that all and sundry were keen to hear their opinions and thoughts. No, we're not, she thought. Give us a break, please. And far too many seemed to be unaware of the difference between opinion and fact. The catalyst for these thoughts was that guy in the Star. Not that he'd tried to give her a lecture, which was a point in his favour. But what right did he have, assuming that because she was alone she must therefore be available, and coming across on the chance of a pick-up? Didn't that show the same type of arrogant presumption? The idea that he had some kind of God-given right to behave in that way?

She walked to the bridge and stood looking over the stone parapet, watching the rushing water. Had that body really been swept down here? It was hard to imagine. She caught sight of the pub door opening and the annoying man come out. Who was he and why was he so interested in the events of the previous week? She slipped across the road and into the shadows of a dark alleyway. He walked past, taking a flat cap out of his jacket pocket and placing it on his head. She waited until he'd passed, then quietly followed him. He turned up the next lane into the nearby parking lot and made his way to an old mud-spattered Land Rover. The engine started with a cough and the vehicle spluttered its way back down to the main road, where it headed west out of town.

This was all very interesting. And she now had the vehicle's registration details. She walked up to the hall that was being used as an incident room and poked her head around the door. The place wasn't as busy as during the daytime, but a small group of detectives were in the room. Polly, the SIO, looked up.

'Hello, Jackie. What brings you in to see us this late in the evening?'

Jackie described the strange encounter with the man in the pub. 'I didn't think much of it at first, ma'am,' she said. 'It was just another incident with a dickhead in a pub. It was when I watched him come out putting a cap on his head that I began to wonder. Then he got into his grubby old Land Rover and I thought, well, I could be onto something here. I've got the registration. Is it worth a look?'

'Of course. Ade, let's check it out.'

They looked over the DS's shoulder as he entered the details into the database.

'Donald Lomax. Blackstream Cottages, Laxford.'

'Where's that? Is it fairly close?'

Jackie shook her head. 'It's up on Exmoor, inland from Dunster. Maybe a half-hour drive from here.' She bit her lip. 'The Washford River rises nearby. And there are several deep pools in the area.'

'So it might fit,' Polly said. 'This alters things. It gives us another angle to work on rather than thrashing about in the dark. We think we know who the deceased is, Jackie. It looks like he was an artist who lives up on Exmoor, Benjamin Carlyon. He painted landscapes of the area, and good ones at that. And we also found a portrait in his studio. Of a young woman who looks as though she might have Down's syndrome. His nephew should be doing the ID tomorrow morning, but there's not much doubt, not from the photos we've seen.'

'Quick work, ma'am,' Jackie replied.

'We're a top team. We don't hang about. And we had your intel to get us started. Sometimes I think an investigation like this is a bit like a voracious meatgrinder. Chuck anything in. Luck, systematic legwork, forensic data, bits of gossipy information, database snippets, memories, odd behaviour. Turn the handle and hope that useful stuff comes out. It seems to be working in this case and long may it continue. The only problem is, where Carlyon lives is nowhere near the Washford River. His place is miles further on, well into Exmoor, and that's where we think he was attacked. Our next step is to trace how he got to where we found him.'

Polly spotted that Jackie was stifling a yawn.

'It's getting late,' she said. 'We all need at least some beauty sleep, even me. Keep doing what you're doing, Jackie. You're proving to be our secret weapon.'

Jackie left the incident room and walked back down the street towards the quayside. She might be tired, but a few minutes of fresh sea air wouldn't go amiss. She stopped at the statue of the Ancient Mariner, her eyes scanning the figure, as they'd done many times before. What had he really been like? Had Coleridge modelled the character on someone he knew in real life or was he entirely a creation of the poet's imagination? She really ought to do some research on the background. Everyone knew that Coleridge was taking opium when he wrote 'Kubla Khan', with its exotic descriptions. Could he have been doing the same when he imagined the horrible scenes of death and suffering described in the 'Ancient Mariner'?

Jackie shrugged and walked on. The sky was clear, and the night sky was breathtaking. She felt uplifted by what she saw; not only the stars but the view across the wide expanse of water to the Welsh coast more than twenty miles away. She could even see a few lights flickering on the distant coastline. Or was it her imagination? On impulse she took out her phone and sent a message to Tony Fisher, then stood waiting for a reply. It didn't take long to arrive. She headed off in the direction of his house. She had to jump sometime, and now seemed as good a time as any.

CHAPTER 12: PASSIONS RUNNING DEEP

Tuesday, Week 2

Polly was feeling more positive about the way the investigation was progressing. The body had been identified by the man's nephew. The forensic team had just finished its sweep of the victim's home. Everything they'd discovered so far knitted together, producing a narrative that had some consistency. But there were still a worrying number of unknowns, including the all-important perpetrator and their motive. The house had yielded no real clues. It didn't look as though Carlyon's killer had attempted to get inside. The forensic evidence had all come from the outhouse: spilled tar wash and bloodstains on the floor, along with several good shoe prints. The other problem was that the house-to-house inquiries close to Carlyon's remote cottage had yielded no useful information so far, neither in the village nor in the nearby farms. That wasn't really a surprise given the artist's reclusive nature, but it was disappointing, all the same. They were only just at the start of a long and gruelling haul, so how best to proceed?

Both of Polly's sergeants, Ade and Rae, thought that the link to the young woman with Down's syndrome was worth pursuing. Rae had taken a photo of the girl in Benjamin

Carlyon's painting and had shown it to Lizzie, the nurse at the local cottage hospital who had treated her for her injuries. Lizzie had no doubt that there was a facial similarity, but could she be certain it was the same person? The answer was no, not for sure.

The team had then compared a good-quality still image of the young woman extracted from the hospital CCTV recording with the face in the portrait. Again, the result was inconclusive. There was no doubt that it was very similar. But identical? They couldn't be sure. Nevertheless, it needed further investigation. None of Carlyon's neighbours knew of any Down's youngsters in the immediate area so she'd set Ade the difficult task of trawling through historic databases of Down's syndrome children from a decade or two earlier, hoping for a link to a child from this area of Somerset. Nothing had shown up yet.

Polly had then sent Rae and Tommy back to Exmoor, in an attempt to find out more about Carlyon's background and his relationship with others in the communities dotted about the area. If they had time, they could also check out the village where this man Donald Lomax lived, but she suggested they should keep that part of the investigation low profile. Polly herself would be visiting Exeter to speak to the dead man's nephew, Justin Penhale. She needed to flesh out the currently sparse details about his uncle's character and life. People didn't get murdered for no reason, not in her experience. Serial killers are an extremely rare phenomenon, even if they populate film and TV drama to a major extent. And this particular incidence of murder had the markings of some kind of personal feud or grudge killing. Passions could run high in some of these remote rural communities, as Polly knew well. She'd grown up in one and had seen some of the spite first hand, particularly in her late teenage years when she'd unwisely let slip one or two clues about her orientation. Relationships had changed at that point. She hoped that things would be different for a teenager in a similar situation today.

She met Justin at his home in a Victorian terrace near the university. They talked over coffee.

'I think you described your uncle as a tough old bird a few days ago. Could you elaborate?'

'That was an expression my mother used. To be honest, I never got to know him all that well, but what I did see fitted that view. He always seemed a bit complicated. Mum used to think he lived a semi-spartan existence. Apparently, he made a thing of it, being up on the moors, out in all weathers looking for ideas and scenes to paint. Yet he was surprisingly sensitive when you got to know him, and he chose to show that side of himself. This was all when he used to live in Bodmin, by the way, close to the moor there. We lost touch when he moved to Exmoor. He was a very private person. I've begun to wonder if he was driven by some kind of personal demon.'

'What do you mean?'

'I can't really explain it. I sometimes wondered if there was something troubling him, but I could never find out what it was. To be honest, I never really tried very hard. We only visited him a few times and I found him hard to get to know. He came across as very moody, almost sullen. That was when I was a teenager. It was almost as if he resented our visits, even though it was only once or twice a year. But then he could sometimes be really thoughtful.'

'Was he at all close to any neighbours of his? Did he speak of friends or love interests?'

Justin shook his head. 'No. As I said, he was a very private person. And I can't imagine him in some kind of romantic relationship. He had this rugged wild-man-of-the-moors thing going on, so I just can't picture him having a starry-eyed candlelit meal out, talking sweet nothings to someone. I never saw him in clothes that were remotely fashionable or even tidy. He was always in baggy corduroy trousers and a shapeless jumper. I do wonder if he was just presenting us with a facade, though. There must have been a more sensitive soul underneath. There had to be, considering his paintings. They show a lot of delicacy. That's what I think, anyway.'

'A bit of a mixed-up loner, then?' Polly prompted. 'Possibly hidden passions that ran deep?'

A shrug. 'Maybe. But I don't really know. Mum and I lived too far away when I was a teenager. And at that age, why would I want to get close to an irritable uncle who chose to live a solitary life miles away? Looking back, it was all a bit sad, I suppose. He didn't do much to encourage me to get to know him, so I didn't bother.' He paused for a few moments and looked Polly in the eye. 'I suppose your hidden passions idea might have some truth. He could have been hiding something, but it was never talked about. I can tell you one thing, though. He wasn't stupid. He knew an awful lot about the local moors and their wildlife.'

'And you still don't know who the young woman in that painting was?'

Justin shook his head. 'No. And finding it was a bit of a shock. I mean, he never painted portraits. Never. He was dismissive of portraits on the few times we chatted to him about his painting. I have no idea who she is. She must have meant something to him, it's obvious. I can't explain it.'

'His finances looked okay, as far as we can see. He just about made ends meet, didn't he?'

Justin agreed. 'I had a meeting with someone at his bank yesterday. I can't get full access until after probate, but he was doing okay. He lived comfortably, though that was partly because he was so frugal.' He smiled. 'I've never used that word before. It was something the bank person said to describe his spending.'

'He'd paid off his mortgage for Bynehill View?'

A shake of the head. 'I don't think he had one. Though where he got the cash from, I don't know. He just had to find money for his fuel bills, water and council tax. He didn't seem to have a mobile phone, just the landline.'

'Maybe there's a signal strength problem up there. Someone from my team said the signal was intermittent when she tried to call me. If so, a mobile might not have been worth the expense.' Polly flicked through her notebook.

'I think that's about it, Mr Penhale. But if anything else does occur to you, please contact us right away. By the way, have you contacted your uncle's solicitor again? I just wondered if next of kin has been established yet?'

'Yesterday afternoon. And it's my mother, as far as we know. In practice, that means me. I wonder about that young woman in the paintings, though. What if she's got a link somehow?' He frowned. 'We never knew why he upped sticks from Cornwall and moved to Exmoor. That's when he cut ties for some reason, but we never got an opportunity to ask him. I just wonder if it was something to do with that young woman he painted. Or do you think I'm reading too much into it?'

It was Polly's turn to shrug. 'Who's to say? We're trying to identify her as a line of inquiry, but it might prove impossible. And there's always the chance that she only existed in his mind. So don't hold out too much hope. I need to ask you where you were last weekend.'

Justin pondered for a short while. 'I was here most of the time. I was out with my partner on the Friday evening for a meal. It was her birthday and she'd managed to talk her ex-husband into taking their two children for the first half of the weekend. I spent Saturday with her, too. Sunday, we collected the kids just before lunch and then took them to the local park in the afternoon. I came back here in the evening after the kids had gone to bed. I think it was quite late.'

'Your partner?'

'Her name's Ali, Alison James. She works at the same place as me, Williams Engineering. I'm an electronic systems designer, she works in the office. Do you want her contact details?'

Polly nodded and noted the information. She then gathered her things together and left.

CHAPTER 13: MOORLAND CONVERSATIONS

It didn't take Tommy and Rae long to reach the small village of Laxford, a few miles inland from Dunster. Tommy took the car into a suitable parking space and switched off the engine.

'How do we play this, boss?' he said.

'Carefully,' was the reply to his question. 'We can't afford to give the game away, that we're interested in Donald Lomax. It's all very tenuous if you ask me, but I can see why Polly wants to check out the link. Let's go for a walkabout to get the lie of the land. Then we'll chat to a few people, maybe to gauge their feelings about rural crime rates. We need to be cautious about mentioning the body in the harbour. Maybe wait until someone starts talking about it. Ditto Lomax and the girl with Down's.'

'What happens if we get challenged? We've got our Dorset warrant cards and our WeSCU IDs. They'll give the game away, surely?'

Rae looked at him. 'Tommy, you're too much of a worrier. We'll stick together. I'll blag my way through any difficulties.'

As it happened, there weren't any difficulties. They strolled around the village for twenty minutes, spotted Donald Lomax's home in Blackwater Cottages, then decided to visit the hamlet's only café for a mid-morning coffee and, with a bit of luck, to listen in to some of the local gossip.

In fact, the small café was very quiet, with only three other customers. They looked to be tourists. Rae managed to get a few words out of the waitress when she came across to take their order.

'On holiday here, are you?' the waitress asked when she brought their coffees across.

Rae shook her head. 'We're working for a few days down in Watchet. We're police detectives.' She nodded towards Tommy and smiled. 'I'm his boss.'

'Well. Good for you. I like it when a woman's the boss,' came the reply. She looked at Tommy. 'Does she treat you well?'

Tommy grinned. 'Yeah. She's good.'

'Wish I'd managed to do something more with my life. I was a lazy nuisance at school, though. Wasted most of my time. It's not clever, is it? Despite what we thought at the time.'

Rae took over. 'You enjoy your work, though, don't you? You get to chat to people. You must know all the gossip in the area. What's going on. Stuff like that.'

The waitress raised her eyebrows in a rather melodramatic way. 'Sounds good when you put it like that. But it's a quiet backwater, really. The whole area's stuck in a bit of a time warp.' She suddenly frowned. 'Well, apart from that body washed up down in Watchet last week. That's got people talking. Is that what you're here for?'

'Yes. We're following up the idea that it could have been washed down the river from somewhere up this way during a storm. Is that likely?'

The waitress frowned. 'We've heard that too. Most of us up here can't see it. There're too many places it would get stuck, even if the river's running high. It's not much more than a stream, really, this far up. Wider down in Watchet though.'

'That's the general consensus, is it?'

The waitress nodded her head. 'Even from the farming people. And others that know the river better than most.'

'What do most people do for a living?'

'Not a lot, to be honest. Farm work, forestry. Jane Aston has a pottery business. There's someone recently moved in who does knitwear. Then there's the retired folk. Why they'd want to retire to a place as dead as this is anyone's guess. About a quarter of the homes are holiday lets. That doesn't help.'

'And you're not aware of anyone who's gone missing?'

She shook her head. 'No. That's what we've all been asking.'

The bell tinkled as the door opened and a small group came in. The waitress moved away to take their order, so Rae and Tommy finished their drinks and left.

'I noticed the pottery. It's close to Donald Lomax's place. Let's have a look.'

* * *

A middle-aged woman looked up when they opened the door. Rae made a beeline for some brightly coloured sets of bowls and dishes.

'These are lovely,' she said as the woman approached. 'Are you the owner, Jane Aston?'

'I am, yes. These are my own designs.'

'They're gorgeous. I sometimes think that country potteries produce stuff that's a bit too rustic-looking, with muted colours. These are really vibrant.' Rae looked at the price tags and shuddered slightly. She'd been looking for something like this as a possible housewarming present for Tommy and Olivia, who were planning to move in together, but could she afford the price? It would need thinking about. She turned back to the proprietor.

'We're police, looking into the body that was washed up in Watchet last week. Are you aware of the case?'

'Of course.' Jane looked at them suspiciously.

'We're following up on the idea that the body was washed down the river in that big storm. It's possible that it came from right up here. Are you aware of anyone who seems to have disappeared?'

'No. And I'm not the person to ask about whether it's possible something like that could make it all the way down to the coast. Why don't you ask someone who knows the river?'

'We've already checked with the Environment Agency people. But local knowledge is always useful. Who would you suggest?'

The suspicious look was still there. 'Some of the locals go fishing in it. They might know.'

'Any names?'

'Phil Langham. He's a local farmer just down the valley a bit. His farm butts up against the river. Then there's Donny Lomax. He lives next door, though he doesn't work around here. He works on a farm way up on the moor, somewhere near Braycombe, so we don't see a lot of him. He fishes in the river. I heard that you've got an identity for the body.' She was looking at Rae shrewdly.

'Possibly. But the question remains how he got there. Anyway, thanks for your help. And I did mean what I said about your work. I may be back for a closer look.'

They called in at Phil Langham's farm to ask his opinion about a body being washed all the way down the river on the night of the big storm. He was a big, ruddy-faced, friendly man, the epitome of a west-country farmer. He shook his head.

'Ah, that body at Watchet, eh? Can't see it happening from all the way up 'ere. I was out for a while that night, checking on one of my ewes. She was lambing, in distress. The river was high, that's for sure. But carrying a body all the way down to Watchet? Nah. It's not a big river. Too many narrow stretches, then wider. Too many places it would get snagged or wash up. You can't even get a bit o' wood to carry all the way down, even if the river's high. My kids tried it once, a couple of years ago when the river was high. It didn't get more than a few hundred yards. If that body went all the way down from up here, then I'm a Dutchman. And I ain't one o' they!'

Rae decided it was time to head for their more important destination, Braycombe, the nearest village to Benjamin Carlyon's lonely cottage. They could call in briefly at his house then spend the middle part of the day in the village, sussing out the local gossip and asking a few questions. They'd then come back to Laxford late in the afternoon in the hope of being able to speak to Donald Lomax.

The two detectives were now repeating the drive they'd made several days earlier, when they'd happened to arrive at Carlyon's lonely cottage as his nephew was trying to break in. They called in at the house, now vacated by the forensic team that had spent several days combing through the contents, to little avail, apparently.

They took another look at the upstairs studio with its collection of paintings. Rae wanted a longer look at the portrait of the young woman, hoping to fix the facial features into her brain. Good paintings could sometimes tell you more than photographs. A talented artist would try to capture aspects of the subject's personality in the artwork. Had that happened here? She was unsure. There was certainly a vulnerability in the way the young woman was portrayed, along with a kind of other worldliness. Had Carlyon been trying to capture some of the ethereal beauty that Down's had bestowed on her? The head and shoulders portrait showed her with pale ginger hair, pink lips and a pale complexion. She had a pink rose fixed in her hair, was wearing a pale pink blouse and had a gold locket around her neck. The backdrop was of a garden with smudges of green and pink to represent shrubs of some type. Possibly rose bushes? It was impossible to tell. Was the scene real or had Carlyon painted it from memory? Or was the background just a figment of the artist's imagination, created for effect? Another thought struck Rae. It might have been based upon a photo. Worth looking into?

She must remember to ask the forensic and CSI people about any they'd found.

Rae and Tommy left the house and walked around to the rear garden area, with its small orchard of fruit trees. There were signs of spring growth on their branches, green buds just starting to appear on the tips, with the beginnings of some red colour where blossom would be coming into flower very soon. Rae stopped and put a hand on Tommy's arm.

'Apple blossom,' she said. 'That was the pink in the background of the painting. Maybe she was here.'

'How can you tell?' he replied. 'It was just smudges of colour, wasn't it? It could have been anything.'

'You're right on a factual level, Tommy. But this spot will be a mass of colour in a couple of weeks. What if she was here, posing for the painting or getting a photo taken in May last year? That would fit.' She turned to face him. 'That makes it more likely that she's local. We'll need to let the boss know when we get back.'

They took quick looks inside the outhouse and garage but spotted nothing new. Why would they? The forensic team would have gone through both with a fine-tooth comb.

They returned to their car, turned and drove back along the narrow lane, heading a few miles further east, into the village. It lay in a small valley, but the local stream didn't drain northwards, to the Somerset coast. It was one of the small tributaries of the mighty River Exe, taking its water south for many miles towards the English Channel, just one component of the network of streams, ditches and ponds that emptied their waters into one of the west's most famous and iconic rivers. Not that you'd know that fact up here, of course. Here, it was just another small waterway that had gouged out a path for itself over uncounted millennia, creating a sheltered location for a small community, partly protected from the occasionally wild weather of the high moorland.

'Same as before, boss?' Tommy asked as they climbed out of the car.

'Yeah, unless you have a better idea. I'm always open to suggestions, Tommy.'

Her fellow detective gave her his usual sheepish look. 'Not really,' he murmured.

'Well, this place is a bit bigger than the last. It's got a village shop and an actual pub, so let's visit them in that order. And we can be a bit more open about why we're here this time. They'll all know about Carlyon by now.'

They made their way across the road to the local mini-market, probably the only shop for many miles around. The bell tinkled as they entered and they took a moment to let their eyes adjust to the rather gloomy interior, with its shelves packed high with goods. Food, drink, household goods, hardware, magazines, gardening materials; the shop seemed to stock everything. Rae glanced at a freezer filled with meat of various types. Goodness! It even had joints of venison. But should that really be a surprise? This was Exmoor, after all. Everything looked well organised and neatly stacked. A customer had just left the till, so Rae approached with Tommy following close behind. A middle-aged man looked up inquiringly.

'Georges Lacoste?' Rae asked. She'd spotted the name above the door as they'd entered.

The man nodded.

'We're police,' Rae said. 'I'm DS Rae Gregson, this is DC Tommy Carter. We're with the Wessex Serious Crimes Unit. You may have heard that the body washed up in Watchet harbour a couple of weeks ago has been identified as Benjamin Carlyon, who lived along the road a couple of miles. We're trying to flesh out his life. Do you have a few minutes to talk to us?'

The man's welcoming smile had faded to a frown. 'Sure. Give me a moment and I'll get someone across to take over from me here. I'm the shop owner.' He spoke with a French accent. He even looked slightly Gallic, with a visual similarity to Eric Cantona in his prime.

They were soon in a small office to the rear of the shop.

'I was shocked when I heard the news,' he said. 'Yesterday, wasn't it? Though we suspected it after some of the locals saw all the activity along at his house a few days ago. It didn't come as any surprise when we heard the news on local radio.'

'Was Mr Carlyon a customer here?' Rae asked.

'Yes, a good one. The sensible people are. They know if they don't use us, we'll be forced to close. And that would mean the end of the community here. The pub wouldn't last long if we closed. Ben didn't buy much, he lived by himself, after all. But we used to see him once a week for his main shop, then maybe a couple of times for odds and ends.'

'How well did he fit in with the local community?'

Georges pursed his lips. 'Hard one. He was a loner and didn't mix much, but he wasn't the bad-tempered man some may claim. He liked his privacy and he liked to control his time. There are some who complained that he didn't put much into the community but that's not true. He offered some of his paintings as prizes at local events. But he didn't get involved personally. He kept himself to himself.'

Rae realised this was a similar picture as the one Carlyon's nephew had painted of his uncle. Some consistency there, then.

'Did he have any local enemies? People who might have born a grudge?'

The shopkeeper shook his head. 'I don't think so. He wasn't unpleasant, just very solitary.'

'Drink?' Rae asked.

'Not really. He liked good wine. We used to have discussions about it. Vouvray. Côtes du Rhône. They were his favourites. And not the cheapest, either. He preferred, how do you say it, quality over quantity. He also bought a bottle of scotch occasionally. But again, not cheap stuff. Glengoyne was his first choice.'

Rae cast her mind back to the contents of the kitchen cupboards in Carlyon's house. Yes, Glengoyne. She remembered it. 'What did you think when you first heard the news that it was him, the body at Watchet?'

Georges shook his head. 'We were expecting it. He hadn't been seen for days, and then the police were crawling all over his house. It was no surprise. But the fact it might not be an accident was a shock. We all thought, that can't be true. Why would someone kill him? No one knows.'

Rae checked that Tommy was noting the information. She wanted him ready for the next question.

'Mr Lacoste, are you aware of any young women in the area who have Down's syndrome?'

Georges rubbed his head. 'Down's syndrome?' He looked puzzled.

'That's right. You know what it is?'

'I think so. Is it when a baby is born with an extra chromosome?'

'That's it.' She waited.

'I don't know. None of our regular customers, from here in the village. Let me think. Don't they often need a carer looking after them? I can't think of anyone like that. We might see some in the summer, with tourist families staying in the area.' He thought for a while longer then shook his head.

Rae thanked him and the two detectives left the shop, though not before Rae had bought a bag of pasties.

'They may not be true Cornish pasties from up here in Somerset, but I love them all, wherever they come from. And I spotted a rosette pinned to the wall. They've won a prize at a local show. They'll make a change from supermarket sandwiches for a snack in the incident room.'

CHAPTER 14: EXMOOR VILLAGE

The local pub, the Stag, was unusually modern for a village such as this. Rae had expected an old, oak-beamed establishment, one with a low roof, possibly with the same kind of thatch as some of the nearby cottages. But, in fact, the building was red-brick with a tiled roof, probably dating to the mid-twentieth century. It wasn't a complete anachronism, though. The landlord had worked hard to ensure it fitted the ambience of the village, with roses growing around the porch and windows, along with lower baskets hanging from the walls. Though at this time of year they only contained springtime blooms of pansies and small bulbs. It was clean, neat and well balanced.

The same could be said of the interior. The owners hadn't followed one of the recent trends of fantasy history. There weren't any brass-like fittings pinned to the walls, nor false beams made of plastic or cleverly disguised plywood. Again, it was neat and tasteful. Rae liked it.

She chose a table and sent Tommy across to the bar for drinks and to collect a couple of menus. Soft drinks, of course. And lunch would be light snacks. Sophie Allen might be an ale-drinking-steak-pie fanatic but she, Rae Gregson, wasn't planning to follow her down that particular route. The toasted paninis looked inviting.

They sipped their fruit juices.

'How do you think things have gone so far this morning, boss?' Tommy asked.

Rae shrugged. 'Okay, I suppose. But it's difficult to be sure. How do we know what small snippet of information is going to be the one that opens the case up? All we can do is gather stuff, examine it, look for openings and try to spot inconsistencies. It's what the chief super says. Killers usually make mistakes. We've got to be on the lookout for them. The slip-ups. The things they've overlooked or forgotten to hide. But this is a bit of a weird one, I have to say. To be honest, I miss Barry. He's so level-headed and down to earth. Polly's really good but she's too much like the chief super, coming up with occasional zany ideas. Barry balances her out. Polly doesn't do that to the same extent.'

'He'll be back soon, though, won't he?'

Rae took another mouthful of apple juice. 'The boss won't bring him down here though, not with Polly already in charge, not unless he's really needed for some reason. That was her plan for WeSCU, to use one or the other of them on a case, not both. Use Barry if it's in the east or south of our patch, and Polly if it's in the west or north. I just hope we don't lose Barry completely.'

Tommy looked shocked. 'What? Why would we?'

Rae looked him in the eye. 'Several reasons. Kevin McGreedie, across in Bournemouth, will be retiring soon and that would be a sensible move for Barry, what with Gwen working in Southampton. They could move a bit further east, with less of a commute for both of them. And Kevin's number two is Lydia. She worked with Barry a lot in the past and they kind of overlap in the way he does with Sophie Allen. And I'm not sure how well he gets on with Polly. If the chief super decides to retire in a couple of years, Polly is likely to take over running WeSCU. How would he feel about that?'

Tommy looked confused. 'I don't ever think of all this political stuff. I never think it's got any relevance for me.'

'Well, maybe that's the sensible angle to take. There's nothing we can do about it, so why worry?'

Rae glanced across the pub as the barman approached with their food. At the same time two men came in and made their way to the bar, examining the ale selection available from the three hand pumps.

'It's my birthday,' the more authoritative of them said. 'So it's my treat. We've got about an hour before we need to be back for the afternoon milking. That's enough time for a couple of pints and a good nosh.' He turned to the barman. 'What do you recommend today, Paul? Anything particularly good?'

'I'd go for the lamb casserole. Cindy's made it fresh this morning. The smell's been making my stomach rumble.'

'Okay. I'll go with that. What about you, Donny?'

Rae came alert. Could the second man possibly be Donny Lomax? It was a possibility, surely. He only lived a few doors away. And hadn't the potter, Jane Aston, said that he worked on a farm up this way? She flicked through her notebook, looking for the description they'd been given. Middle-aged, medium height, dark hair flecked with grey and thinning on top. Possibly wearing a flat cap. It all corresponded to the second man standing at the bar, but such a description could apply to a sizeable proportion of the male population. Really, it was only the name, Donny, that singled him out. How common was it? More importantly, should she go across for a chat right now or was it better to observe and listen for a while? She opted for the latter. Earwigging on the conversations of others was one of her favourite pastimes.

The two men came across to sit at a nearby table. At the same time, their own food arrived, a Stilton, celery and cranberry panini for her and a ham, cheese and onion one for Tommy. Tommy started to chat about the investigation, but Rae quickly silenced him with a finger to her lips. She tried to indicate her wish to listen in to the conversation being conducted behind her by flicking her eyes, but she wasn't sure that Tommy understood. He looked puzzled. In the end, she wrote a short note of explanation on her phone, *His name's Donny*, then passed the screen across the table to her colleague. At that, Tommy clammed up.

The two detectives finished their lunch and the more substantial food for the two men arrived. Rae was still unsure how to proceed, but in the end decided merely to watch and listen. There was no certainty of how Lomax, if that's who he was, would react if she were to introduce herself and Tommy as detectives, out to question him. That was best left until later, when they could speak to him on his own.

She discovered that the other man's name was Kevin and that he was Donny's employer on a farm situated only a mile or two away. Much of their chat was about the farm and Kevin's plans for the next couple of weeks. Late sowings, animal health, vet visits, and the strange goings-on at the neighbouring farm seemed to dominate their conversation. Donny was convinced he'd seen people out searching the fields. His boss replied that the people who farmed there weren't worth worrying about, that they were best left well alone. He refused to elaborate any further, even though Donny pressed him. Rae was disappointed. She enjoyed intrigue.

She and Tommy chatted about their respective relationships and how he and Olivia saw their future panning out. Rae explained how, if she and Craig ever settled down together on a permanent basis, something that was far from certain, any children would have to be adopted. The conversation was very much one of marking time while the hour ticked away.

Finally, the farming duo got up to leave. Rae and Tommy waited for a minute then also left, heading for their car, parked almost opposite. She followed a Range Rover once it pulled out from the pub's car park, heading further west towards the county boundary with Devon. They didn't get very far before the vehicle in front turned off down a short farm track.

'Highcroft Farm,' Tommy called out.

Rae slowed and they had a close look as they passed by. They then drove a little further along the quiet lane. The fields belonging to Highcroft Farm looked neat, tidy and well organised. This was in marked comparison to the neighbouring farm, the last before cultivated fields gave way to open moorland.

'Greymoor,' Tommy said. 'It looks a bit more run down, doesn't it? Do you think this was the farm they were talking about?'

'Could be. We'll go a bit further, then come back. We'll keep an eye out for this Donny, then follow him back to Laxford. If our guess is right, he'll be in an old, battered Land Rover.'

CHAPTER 15: THE GIRL WITH DOWN'S

Adrian Ahmed was a Somerset man born and bred and had lived most of his life in the county town of Taunton. He'd only recently gained his promotion to detective sergeant and started working full-time for Polly Nelson in WeSCU. He'd worked with her on several earlier cases and had come to admire both her tenacity and her rather confrontational methods. Sometimes he wished some of her barely suppressed irritability towards people would rub off on him. His nature was more conciliatory, maybe too much so. As a mixed-race child growing up in a community that was overwhelmingly white, he'd endured more than a few incidents of bullying. He'd always preferred to adopt a softly-softly approach to dealing with these situations, opting to avoid confrontation whenever possible. It had usually worked. Aggressive teenagers had left him alone after a while when he'd refused to rise to their challenges, moving off to look for more volatile prey. But he still remembered the burning resentment that he'd felt, along with the sense of injustice, and he'd turned it into something positive by joining the police. He suspected that, somehow, Polly had also been through some similarly hard times. That would explain why she was so independent, so much of an original thinker. But she was hard to get to know. She rarely relaxed, rarely let down her guard, and he felt that it had been hard work gaining her trust. She was very different from the chief super, Sophie Allen, someone who seemed able to put people at their ease instantly. He felt a little envious of the two Dorset detectives working the case with him, particularly Rae Gregson, the DS. She seemed so relaxed and confident in her relationship with her boss. She appeared to have an innate ability to come up with ideas and the confidence to speak up about them. She seemed totally at ease in her role, and it was clear that the chief super valued her, both as a detective and a person. Ade was still in the early stages of his relationship with Polly and was yet to gain that degree of mutual trust. He suspected that it would be harder for him, anyway. It wasn't just the fact that he and Polly had the gender divide to cross, it was also the fact that he'd come to suspect that Polly, underneath, was quietly brittle. He recognised it because he was the same. With him, it was due to the mixed-race thing. But what was it with her? He hadn't been able to come to any firm conclusions. Time would tell.

Ade switched his attention back to his computer screen. You'd think that it would be easy to track someone with Down's syndrome. Wouldn't most parents sign up for the support on offer from health authorities, councils and charities? There was even a local charity for Somerset and its neighbouring counties, specifically set up for the purpose. The staff at the various organisations were all understandably reticent to release information at first, but, once he'd explained the nature of the investigation, they promised to check their records. None had produced a definite identification, although Ade hadn't expected that would happen. He'd ended up with a list of three possible candidates, although none of them sounded promising. If parents decided to drop off the radar of the support network, it was easy to do so. But why would anyone want to opt out? It was mystifying. Surely if you had a child with Down's, you'd opt to remain inside the support system for as long as possible. And even when the youngster turned eighteen, they'd still want to remain in touch, wouldn't they? Apparently, though, that wasn't always the case. Some families moved away. Some Down's people, once eighteen, craved their independence and experienced wanderlust, the same as other people.

The support staff Ade had spoken to had emphasised the importance of using acceptable language. They'd explained that Down's was a syndrome not an illness, and that Down's people made up about one in a thousand of the population. Maybe he, Ade, needed to explain this to the rest of the team at the next briefing to ensure that none of them caused offence when talking to Down's people. Meanwhile he'd head off to visit the families of the three young women on his list. Not that he held out any great hopes. The brief details he'd been told about them didn't really match the individual they were seeking. He looked up as he heard footsteps approaching.

* * *

Sophie Allen, the chief superintendent in charge of WeSCU, wasn't feeling relaxed and confident, despite what Ade thought. She was keyed-up to a greater extent than in many of her recent cases, hadn't been sleeping well and was feeling emotionally fragile. Moreover, she knew why. It was the possibility that a Down's person had been sexually assaulted in one of the strange threads connected to this current investigation.

Fifteen years earlier she'd lost a child during the late stages of pregnancy, a boy who would have been a precious gift to her and Martin; a boy, Andrew, who would have been Down's. Only a few other people knew the full details. Their two daughters, Hannah and Jade; her mother, Susan; and their close friend, Benny Goodall, now Dorset's senior pathologist. These five people were the only ones to know the full depths of the anguish that Sophie had experienced at the loss of her son. She and Martin had come to embrace the knowledge that Andrew would be a Down's child. Even the two girls, still in their primary school years, had come to realise the important role they would need to play once their little brother was born. And then the emotional catastrophe of the miscarriage had occurred. It had been bad enough for the other family members. For Sophie herself it had been a time of intense distress that she would never forget.

Her boss at the time, Archie Campbell, had wondered why she and Martin had decided to up sticks and move from the West Midlands to Dorset, ending up in a possible backwater for an up-and-coming police detective with Sophie's level of talent and commitment. She'd never told him the real reason, that she'd felt empty and burned out after the loss of her son and needed a complete change to bring her life back together. And now, here she was, with those old emotional wounds niggling at her psyche again, those familiar feelings of despondency and despair that she'd thought she'd worked through more than a decade earlier.

Martin must have spotted a change in her. Normally he'd say something gently teasing over breakfast, but not in the last couple of days. Instead, he'd asked her if she was okay. She felt that she needed to get a grip. Maybe another trip to Watchet was in order. Leave the stress of planning and administrative work for a while and get across to see how Polly and the team were getting on. She'd probably end up irritating Polly, who was very experienced and entirely capable of heading up a major investigation without any help, but so be it. If there was a Down's person involved as a victim, she needed to be involved, even if it was just a gesture to her own lost son. She'd go mad if she sat here dwelling on it for very much longer.

She arrived at the Watchet incident room late in the morning. Local officers were coming and going but the only WeSCU team member there was Ade, hunched in front of his computer screen. He looked up as she approached.

'Morning, ma'am,' he said, as he turned in his chair. 'Everyone else is out, following things up. I'm pursuing the Down's angle.'

'Yes, Polly told me on the phone. Made any progress?' She was looking at the screen rather than at him.

'I've only got three to check out with a visit. But I'm not hopeful about any of them. It's the farm angle. The statements from the nurse and the hospital staff seemed to emphasise that the girl and her mother were from a farming background and that they might be poor. No one, not even these three, fit that description, not around here.'

'But you still think it's worth visiting them?'

'Yes. But not with any great hope of finding our person is one of them. I thought that local Down's people and their families might be able to help. They could have come into contact with her at some time. Or they might remember something.'

Sophie was impressed. 'Good thinking,' she said. 'How would you feel about me tagging along with you? Be honest now. I won't be offended if you tell me to get lost. Well, I will if you put it as bluntly as that, but you know what I mean.' She smiled at her own joke.

'No problem, ma'am. I've been stuck here all morning, so a bit of company would be good.'

'Even if it is the boss,' Sophie added.

He smiled back. Rather nervously, she thought.

'Polly and I have both got a text message from Rae, up on Exmoor. She's had another look at the portrait that Carlyon painted of a young woman who might be Down's. She wonders if the girl was painted in the orchard at the back of his house. Either that or had a photo taken there. That lends support to the idea she's local.'

'It all helps, ma'am,' he replied.

'My thoughts exactly.'

* * *

The first stop was a family home in Minehead, the largest of the area's coastal resorts, to visit a nineteen-year-old person with Down's, along with her mother. The mother,

Penny Brash, had been a prominent organiser of social support activities for Down's children when her own daughter, Anne, was small. The group she'd set up was based in a local community centre, and she was happy to reminisce about it in her conversation with Ade and Sophie, although nothing substantial came out of the chat.

Ade extracted his mobile phone and showed Penny and Anne photos of the painting that Benjamin Carlyon had completed of the mysterious young woman. They studied the images closely but, in the end, shook their heads.

'She has a resemblance to a number of people,' Penny said. 'But not closely to any single one of them. They'd all be on record anyway. Not sure we can help.'

She looked at her daughter, who was also shaking her head. Adrian thanked them and said that he might be back in touch if he felt the need for more information.

'Nice people,' Sophie said to him as the two detectives made their way back to the car. 'They were keen to help. Did you pick up on that too?'

'Yes. The mother has a record of helping with the local Down's network. I got the impression she was the type to get things done, quietly and without any fuss. Nice girl too.'

The second visit, also in Minehead, proved to be of no use. The family in question had clearly moved away from the address that Ade had on record, but none of the neighbours seemed to know where. They drove to the final address, in West Quantoxhead, this time to visit the home of a teenage boy, Neil Pover. His father greeted them at the door and seemed keen to give what help he could.

'Not that it'll be much,' he said. 'I used to take Neil to some of the support group meetings years ago but I didn't really get involved.' He looked at the phone images but shook his head. 'Nah. She doesn't ring any bells. Sorry. It's Neil you need to see. He's got a good memory. You'll find him along in the village shop. He's got a job there, helping out. He loves it.'

They found Neil filling shelves with breakfast cereals and asked if he could give them a few minutes. He was a good-looking boy with a helpful manner. The shop manager raised no objection, so Neil led them through to a small office at the back of the shop. He took a look at the pictures and frowned. He shook his head.

'Didn't come to the group,' he told them. 'But I saw her, I think. Only once or twice.' He kept looking at the images on Ade's phone. 'Maddy, that was her name. Don't know anything else.'

'Do you know where she lived, Neil? Could it have been somewhere local?' This was Sophie now asking the questions. She watched the boy closely. What was he? About eighteen or thereabouts? He had dark hair and a habit of tugging at his left ear.

'On a farm somewhere. That's why we never saw her much. Up on the moor. That's all I remember.'

They thanked him and left him to get on with his work.

'Well, that was really useful, Ade. Two things. We're more sure she exists, and we've got a possible name for her. Maddy. A good outcome, I think.'

CHAPTER 16: GOOD WORK

Donny Lomax spent most of the afternoon back in the top field, completing the temporary repairs on the boundary wall. He'd been unhappy with leaving the unsteady section of the wall with no support on the Greymoor side, so he'd suggested to his boss that a few timber posts wouldn't go amiss, particularly if they were put in butting up against the wobbly part.

He was across in the Greymoor field now, complete with digging tools, three posts, some odd bits of timber and a sledgehammer. He'd hoped to be able to use the ram fitted to the rear of one of the tractors, a much easier way of forcing posts into the ground, but he was unable to manoeuvre the tractor into a suitable position to stretch it across the wall. Back to good old muscle power. He'd collected together some fallen stones that had escaped from the wall and was making good progress on the posts when he became aware that he was being observed. A man was standing a few yards away, calmly watching what he was doing.

'Good work,' the onlooker said. He was wearing rather threadbare and grubby overalls under a ragged woolly sweater.

'Thanks,' Donny replied. 'Just want to make sure this wall stays up until early summer. We don't want to lose any of our animals.'

'Good work,' the man said again in a strangely flat voice.

Donny glanced up, curious. 'What's your name?' he asked.

'Gordon. Good work,' came the reply.

'Do you work on Greymoor Farm?' Donny asked.

'Yeah. I do good work,' Gordon replied.

Donny finished his repairs and started gathering his tools together, ready to sling them over the wall.

'Well, that's me finished. Were you all searching for something yesterday? I saw you across in that further field.'

'Billy. He does good work.'

'Right. Has he gone missing or something?'

The man nodded. He looked as though he might be about to add a few more words of explanation but they were disturbed by a shout.

'Gordon! Come back right now!' Another man could be seen at the lower end of the field, standing by an open gate. Gordon turned and walked downhill to join this other figure.

Donny watched them as they crossed into a lower field and made their way towards the distant farm buildings. Curious.

* * *

It was nearly five o'clock before Donny pulled up outside his cottage in Laxford. He climbed out of his old Land Rover, yawned and stretched. Time for a shower and a mug of tea. At least he didn't have to cook a meal for himself tonight. The casserole Kevin had bought him at the pub would keep him going for another hour or two yet. Even then, he'd probably only need a quick sandwich and a beer. There was a football match on the telly tonight, something else to look forward to.

He'd reached his front door when he became aware of two people approaching him, a man and a woman.

The woman spoke. She had a deep voice. 'Donny Lomax? We're police officers. We wonder if we could have a couple of minutes of your time. Apparently, you're a bit of an expert on the Washford River.'

Donny tried hard not to panic. Hadn't he seen them in the pub at lunchtime? Had they been following him?

'Don't worry,' the woman added. 'No need to look so anxious. You're not in any trouble. Your neighbour Jane Aston in the pottery said you'd be the person to ask about the river. We want to know whether it would be possible for something like a body to be washed all the way down to Watchet, if the river was high enough.'

Donny tried hard to relax. That was one of the questions he'd been asking himself for the past week or more. If whatever he'd collided with had been a person, and if they'd managed to stagger the nearly ten miles across the fields to this area, could the river have carried them all the way down to the sea, some twelve miles away? No, it was beyond possibility.

He looked at the woman and shook his head.

'Nah. It's just not possible. Too many narrow, rocky sections where a body would get stuck. A dead deer got washed in during a storm a few years ago. It didn't even get a mile.'

The woman looked convinced. 'Right. That's the same as Phil Langham said. Thanks for your time.'

They turned and walked back a few yards towards a car parked beyond the Land Rover. The woman turned and spoke before getting in.

'If you do think of anything, Mr Lomax, be sure to get in touch.'

Donny nodded and went into his house. It wasn't a beer he needed now. It was a double scotch. Maybe two of them. At least they hadn't mentioned the stolen copper cable, still hidden in the old shed in his garden. The problem was, now might not be the time to get rid of it. The cops might well be watching all the local scrapyards. He'd need to do a bit of thinking about the best way of cashing it in. He knew a couple of people who might give him some advice about it. Maybe some phone calls were in order.

* * *

'He was surprisingly nervous,' Rae commented as Tommy drove the car away. 'He didn't comment on why we were asking. Unlike the other one, the local farmer, Phil.'

'But some people are like that, boss. Tell them you're a detective and they go to pieces. It doesn't always mean anything.'

'Yes, you're right. But then we also have this other snippet, don't we? That he might have been at the quayside last week, watching the forensic team.'

'To be honest, don't we have to be careful with that report? Half the farm workers up here drive old grubby Land Rovers. Those things keep going for decades. Sometimes the owners die before their vehicles. It could have been anyone. And wouldn't you want to watch a forensic team at work? It's a bit of a backwater around here, isn't it? It must be the most exciting thing that's happened for years.'

'Good point.'

Rae looked at Tommy carefully. There was no doubt about it. He was becoming more assertive, more confident in his own judgement. About time, she thought. For some time now she and her usual boss, Barry Marsh, had thought that Tommy had the makings of a good detective but that his low levels of self-confidence let him down. It was good to see him speaking up and arguing a point.

CHAPTER 17: CURRY

Jackie Spring was in Watchet's only Indian restaurant, sharing a curry with Tony Fisher. Lamb shashlik for her, chicken Madras for him, although occasionally they both leaned forward and speared a morsel from the opposingly placed serving dishes. Jackie wondered if this was a sign of the increased level of intimacy between them, although they hadn't slept together yet. It was only a matter of time, though, wasn't it? She'd been introduced to his three teenage children at the weekend and had breathed a sigh of relief when they'd seemed to accept her so readily. Of course, they'd learned to tolerate their mother's boyfriends at an early age. Maybe, to them, she seemed normal by comparison. Or boringly orthodox. And she had to be honest. They seemed really nice youngsters and had spent some time actually talking to her rather than keeping their noses fixed to their phones. They'd obviously been well brought up. She could grow to like them if she was given a chance, and Tony seemed prepared to give her that chance. He was already talking about them spending a weekend with Jackie and him. Would he want to be sleeping with her by then, though? How should she play this slightly tricky situation? Sarah's advice had been simple. Seduce him with some well-planned feminine wiles. A sexy dress, a bit of cleavage on display (or maybe more than a bit), some sensuous perfume and romantic music. Jackie didn't feel entirely comfortable with this approach, though. And maybe a curry wasn't the ideal type of food to eat before a possible night of physical passion. That Madras Tony was eating was rather hot. Her dress did have quite a plunging neckline though, and she'd spotted Tony's gaze flickering over her exposed cleavage a couple of times. She took another mouthful of lager.

Her mind wandered back to the investigation, still ongoing and still largely unresolved. They might well know who the dead man was, but the case seemed to be going nowhere in terms of any further evidence. How had he got into the harbour? Why had he been killed? Was Donny Lomax really involved or was it all just conjecture?

'Tony, you know that guy you spotted last week watching the forensic team at work around the harbour, do you think he could have been in his forties?'

Tony swallowed the last piece of chicken. 'Older, I'd have thought. Can't be sure though. I was up a ladder and only saw him for a few seconds. Why?'

Jackie crinkled her eyes. 'Well, I've been trying to narrow down the options. There was a guy in the Star yesterday evening. Flat cap, drove an old Land Rover. Seemed a bit odd. In fact, he tried to pick me up.'

Tony shook his head. 'I know about that. The pub manager told me. No, that was Donny Lomax from up in Laxford. It wasn't him. I've known him for years.'

'Ah.' Jackie was feeling stupid. She'd never thought to ask Tony about the onlooker before now and had jumped to a convenient conclusion about the man's possible identity. Had she pushed the course of the investigation onto a side track because of her own animosity to someone who had merely annoyed her in a pub? Maybe she wasn't cut out for this undercover detective lark after all.

'Did he really annoy you?' Tony asked.

Jackie tried to bring herself back to the here and now. She nodded. 'Yes, he was a right pain in the neck.'

Tony grimaced. 'That's typical of Donny. He opens his mouth and straightaway puts his foot into it. He's harmless, really. An idiot, but a harmless one.'

'How do you know him?'

'His family lived down here in Watchet when he was young. He was a friend of my brother for a while.' He glanced at the empty plates and dishes that covered the table. 'Do you fancy dessert?'

Jackie shook her head. Maybe it was now or never time, despite the fact they'd had curry to eat. 'Do you fancy coffee back at mine rather than here?' She kept her eyes wide.

Tony nodded. 'Sure.' He gave her a slightly nervous smile.

* * *

A sliver of sunlight had made its way through a narrow gap in the curtains and crept its way across the pillow. It had reached Jackie's left eye and caused her to stir from her slumber. She opened the eye in question, then the other. Something wasn't quite right. She moved her hand across her stomach and realised what it was. She was naked. Her eyes widened and she slowly turned her head to the left to check that side of the bed. Sure enough, there was Tony, still asleep.

Her stomach gurgled gently, and she realised that she really needed the toilet. She rose quietly, slipped on a robe and made her way across the landing to the bathroom. She sat on the loo a little longer than necessary, thinking things through. Mugs of tea, she thought, always a good catalyst for conversation. She rose, washed her hands and crept down the stairs to the kitchen. Within five minutes she was halfway up the stairs, tea in hand, when she heard the loo flush. Ah, he was awake. She'd better get back to bed before him in case he panicked and started to get dressed. She deposited the mugs on the bedside tables, slipped out of her wrap and was sliding back under the duvet when Tony appeared, looking slightly sheepish as he carefully manoeuvred his way around the bed.

'I made us tea,' she said brightly, flapping her hand at the mugs as if he wouldn't recognise them for what they were.

'Um, great,' he replied as he joined her, though he opted to maintain a slight gap between their bodies.

What was the point of maintaining this rather shy awkwardness, Jackie thought. It was ludicrous. She sat up, exposing her breasts.

'Tony, last night was just the best time I've had for ages. Thank you.'

She leaned across and kissed him on the lips.

'That's exactly what I feel too,' he replied. 'Life really can't get much better, can it?'

She shook her head happily, her dark curls bobbing around her shoulders. 'No.'

She grabbed his hand and guided it to her right breast, then sank down onto the pillow, sighing gently. Their teas were only lukewarm when they finally got around to drinking them.

* * *

Later that morning Jackie sent a short text message to the DCI, asking for a quick chat. A prompt reply winged its way back, with Polly deciding that a short walk along the harbourside was in order.

'A bit of fresh air and exercise. Always good to get the old brain cells working again,' she explained when they met. 'Has something happened?'

Jackie felt awkward but ploughed on with her explanation for the meet-up request. 'I'm worried that I've led you on a wild goose chase, ma'am. It's Donny Lomax. I thought he was up to no good and might well have been the man watching the forensic team working here last week. But Tony, the guy who spotted him, is adamant that it wasn't Donny. Tony's my boyfriend, by the way.'

Polly frowned. 'Thanks for telling me. I don't think it alters things all that much, to be honest. Two of my team spoke to Mr Lomax yesterday, as it happens, but purportedly about something else. He didn't raise any obvious alarm bells with them, though they thought he seemed nervous, so he remains a person of interest. Apparently, the problem for us is that all the local river experts agree on one thing. That the body couldn't have been carried all the way down the full length of that river, not even if it was running high. So we're switching our attention to more local spots where it could have been pushed in. Any ideas?'

Jackie took only a few seconds to come up with a suggestion. 'The derelict paper mill. It's just on the southern edge of the town and the river runs down the west side. It's a huge eyesore once you're on site. Though you don't see much from the outside because of all the trees and wild shrubs that have grown up there. It's been empty for ages.'

'That fits in with what we think. I've sent a team up there to check for any signs that might still be there. It's meant to be kept locked up and secure though. How would someone get a vehicle in?'

Jackie shrugged. 'It's all very ramshackle. Someone could find a way in if they really wanted to.'

CHAPTER 18: SECOND BODY

Wednesday, Week 2

Polly and Rae stood inside the expanse of neglected waste-land and looked around them. The place was derelict, the buildings falling apart, and the flat expanse of land broken up with scrawny shrubs and assorted weeds pushing through the surface. The river ran down the west side of the area. To the north, the old paper mill buildings were in ruins.

Polly wondered at first why this old industrial site hadn't been developed in some way. Surely land was at a premium. But then she realised that there might be practical reasons. Maybe the ground was toxic in some way and needed time for the residues to leach out. And there was the proximity of the river, of course. It would overflow right across this flat area when it was in flood, and weren't those incidents becoming more common in these times of climate change?

'It's a bit ugly, isn't it?' she heard Rae say, mirroring her thoughts exactly. 'Surely something could be done to tidy it up?'

Polly shrugged. 'Ours is not to reason why. What concerns me is the ease of getting in here, and the fact that people have, judging by the tyre tracks. What do you think?'

They walked across to the river.

'Absolutely, ma'am,' Rae replied. 'It'd be so easy to chuck a body into the river here. And it's less than a mile down to the harbour, with a clear run if the water was high enough. It gets my vote.'

'I could kick myself. Why weren't we told about this place? Who checked it? Can you remember?'

'The local team did the town. The sergeant organised it. What was his name? Churchill?'

'Ah, that'll probably be the problem, his name. So many of them develop a Churchill complex once they get into a position of authority.' Polly sighed. 'Well, it's probably too late for Forensics now. I'll get them to give it a once-over, just in case, though.' She walked to the riverbank and peered at the fast-flowing water. 'I feel really bad at the slow progress. What will Sophie Allen be thinking, Rae? You know her much better than me. Is my job in jeopardy?'

'Not from her. In fact, my bet is that she'll be having the same thoughts as you, that her job might be on the line. She's full of insecurities, though she rarely shows it. I've heard there are rumblings back in Dorset. We were in Wiltshire just a few weeks ago, for the last big case, and now we're getting bogged down across here in Somerset. I suppose it was always on the cards for the early months, that each county wants to be sure it's getting its fair share of WeSCU time. But we can't predict where the cases will crop up, can we? People don't commit murder to order, in a nice tidy way that's easy for us to solve and in predictable places. Anyway, we always end up with the tricky cases that no one else wants. Even back in the Dorset days, we'd often find that simple murders wouldn't reach us. Local squads would run them. They'd only offload the difficult cases onto us.'

Polly looked shocked. 'Are you sure?'

'Not really. I'm probably talking rubbish.' She turned to face Polly. 'I am happy to be working for you, ma'am. I've always worked for Barry Marsh before. He's great and he's been so supportive. But he's a bloke, and so's Tommy. I always take some of the more extreme supposed gender differences with a pinch of salt but I'm beginning to wonder. It's odd.'

Polly laughed. 'Well, I shouldn't really say it, but you're the expert, aren't you?'

'I suppose you're right. I've always questioned all the usual behavioural assumptions in the past, but I really do prefer working for other women. Even mixing with other women. There's always something that niggles me with men. It's hard to define but it's there, even the really good ones, like Barry. Maybe it's just things from my own distant past, reflecting back at me.'

Polly looked at her watch. 'Better get things organised. I'll sort the order for Forensics. Can you do some detailed checking of this place?' She turned away but slowed when her phone rang.

'Hi, Ade,' she said, still walking.

She suddenly stopped, a look of shock on her face. 'What?'

A few seconds of silence were followed with another, 'What?'

She looked at Rae. 'Complete change of plans. Another body's been found, up in the woods near Braycombe. Isn't that where you were yesterday?'

Rae nodded. 'We did some interviews. It's the nearest village to where Carlyon lived, about three miles from his house. What on earth is going on up there?'

'Well, the body's been there for some time, according to Ade. Maybe even since around the time that Carlyon was killed. He and Tommy are hotfooting it up there right now. We need to join them. You drive, I'll arrange a quick forensic check of this place while we're on the road.'

They hurried across to the car. 'This could be what we need, ma'am,' Rae said. 'I know it sounds a bit callous but the chief super always says that a second body doubles the chances of getting to the bottom of things.'

'Yes, but it doubles the workload, doesn't it? And we're stretched enough at the moment.'

Rae chose to remain silent.

* * *

Polly and Rae arrived only a minute or two before Ade and Tommy. The nearest access point from the road was off a narrow lane that twisted its way north from the village of Braycombe. It passed a small electricity substation, dropped into a narrow dip, turned several tight bends and then dipped again into a heavily wooded area. Two squad cars were parked, partly on the narrow verge. Even so, they almost blocked the lane. Polly told one of the uniformed officers to head back to the village and close the road. By the time forensic vans had arrived, it would be all but impossible for anyone to drive by.

Another officer pointed out the direction they were to follow through the trees. The two detectives noticed a ragged blue scarf hanging from a low growing branch, as if it had been plucked from someone's neck. The body wasn't much further on, lying in a shallow ditch and partly hidden by leaves that had blown over it. It didn't look as though anyone had attempted to camouflage or cover it.

'Who found it?' Polly asked of the uniformed constable who was standing guard.

'A couple of ramblers. They're just across in that clearing, sitting on a log. We thought you'd want them to wait for a few words, ma'am. But they're keen to get going. They want to reach the village before evening.'

'Well, we can drop them off if necessary. Let's go, Ade.' She looked at Rae. 'You and Tommy have a good look round. See if there's anything obvious. We'll then wait for the forensic team. I don't think we'll need much time with the walkers if they are who they say they are.'

She and Ade made their way the few yards to a nearby clearing where the two walkers and a uniformed constable were sitting on a fallen log. The detectives joined them. The couple looked to be in their sixties, both kitted out in good-quality walking gear. Each had a backpack at their feet.

'DCI Polly Nelson,' she said to them. 'This is DS Adrian Ahmed. We're with the local serious crimes unit. Can you tell me how you came to discover the body?'

It was the woman who spoke first. 'We're on our way to Watchet, hoping to get there by evening. We've got a room booked for the night. We think we were on the wrong footpath and ended up wandering about in the woods.'

The man nodded. His voice sounded more strained than his partner's. 'Once we came down from the moor, we should have taken a path through one of the farms, but it had been blocked off. The neighbouring farm had put in a permissive path to use but when it came out onto a lane, we went straight across instead of backtracking along the lane a bit. We realised we'd made a mistake about a couple of hundred yards into the woods. We were trying to find our way back to our planned route when we saw the body just lying in that ditch. It hadn't been hidden or anything. It was pretty obvious. We haven't touched it. We just called 999 right away.'

'You did the right thing. You'll be delayed, I'm afraid. But the upside is that I'll get someone to give you a lift to Watchet. As long as you don't mind arriving at your hotel in a police squad car.'

CHAPTER 19: STOLEN COPPER

Donny Lomax was feeling pleased but tense. He now had a legitimate reason to visit the neighbouring farm, Greymoor. Well, maybe legitimate was the wrong word to use, since it involved the stolen copper cable. One of his phone contacts had told him that the farm's tenant, Bryn Guthrie, could help to make shady stuff disappear. He'd be willing to contact Guthrie to provide an introduction. So here Donny was, at the agreed time, directly after he'd finished work for the afternoon, parking his Land Rover next to a similar vehicle, even older and grubbier than his.

Two middle-aged men approached as Donny was climbing out of the cab. The more thickset of the duo stood a few yards away, eyeing Donny suspiciously, while the thinner, bonier individual came closer.

'I'm Donny,' Lomax explained. 'Are you Bryn? I've been told you can help me with some spare copper cable I have.'

'No. Harry,' came the reply. He flicked his wrist. Did that mean the other man, still standing in the shadows, was Guthrie? This Harry character scanned him up and down, then indicated that Donny should follow him into a ramshackle outbuilding across the yard. The inside was dark and shadowy, but Donny could spot that it was an untidy cornucopia of varied materials.

'It needs to be moved on quick, don't it?' the man said. 'That's what I was told.'

'I guess so,' Donny replied. He was a newcomer to this kind of business and was regretting his rash decision to lift the seemingly abandoned coils of copper that he'd spotted lying on the verge beside the small transformer station.

'Fifty per cent,' the man growled. 'That's our cut. Take it or leave it. We're taking all the risk.'

Donny didn't feel like arguing. He just wanted to get rid of the stolen metal. 'Sounds okay.'

'Have you got it in your van?'

Donny shook his head. 'I thought it was too risky. I can bring it over tonight, if that's okay.'

The man looked at him menacingly. 'Okay. At eight. Don't be late. Don't bring anyone with you. And don't even think of pissing us about. You'll regret it. Understand?'

All this time the stockier man stood in the shadows near the doorway.

'Yeah.' Donny thought it better not to argue.

'How much is there?'

'Two reels. About a hundred kilos each reel.'

Donny watched the hard face of the man standing opposite as he did his mental calculation.

'Six quid a kilo. Twelve hundred in total. Six hundred for you. Cash. You come in tonight. Drive right in here. Chuck the cable out. Take your money and go. No questions, no argument. Okay?'

'Fine.'

Donny was feeling intimidated by the man's manner. He decided not to ask about the search that he'd witnessed a few days earlier, or his short conversation with the oddly behaved farmhand, Gordon. It was obvious that this wasn't the time or place. Maybe there would never be a good time or place, not with these prickly individuals.

He walked back to his vehicle, parked at the side of the yard. At the same time, the house door opened and a young woman appeared, carrying a tray with what appeared to be large casserole dishes on it. She carefully placed them on a trolley that already had some plates on a lower shelf, then proceeded to turn out of the yard and walk away up one of the tracks. Donny thought it would be unwise to linger. The rather too confrontational Harry and the other man, possibly the farmer, Bryn, were both still eyeing him suspiciously. He started the engine and drove the Land Rover out into the lane. He opted to turn south rather than heading directly home. He'd never been along that stretch of road. If the map was right, it curved around in a loop and would finally deliver him back to his own place, albeit via a rather longer route. It would, though, give him an opportunity to see parts of Greymoor from the other side. He quickly pulled into a passing place and realised he was on a hillside, looking both down and across to the farmyard he'd just left. A small cluster of rundown caravans were tucked in behind the farm buildings and close up against a line of trees, woodsmoke coming from one or two of their chimneys. He remembered that he'd spotted them once when working up high on the neighbouring farm. He looked closer. The girl was coming out of one of the caravans, carrying what looked to be an empty dish. Could this be where Gordon, the farmhand he'd spoken to, lived? And had the missing man, Billy, also lived here? The whole set-up seemed strange.

Donny engaged the gearstick and slowly pulled back out onto the road.

* * *

The evening arrangement went smoothly at first. Donny arrived exactly at eight o'clock, drove into the yard and from there into the old barn, and climbed down from the cab of his vehicle. He opened the rear doors and started to haul the coils of copper out onto the floor. He could see the stockier man, possibly Bryn Guthrie, watching from the doorway again. The taller man, Harry, finally stepped forward as the last coil of copper landed on the concrete floor. He looked at the metal and took an envelope from his pocket, handing it to Donny.

'Nice farm,' Donny said. 'Who helps you work it?'

Harry's eyes narrowed. 'What's it to you?'

'No reason. Just trying to be friendly.'

'Well, don't bother. Just take your money and get out. You're that Lomax bloke who works on the next farm. We'd never have agreed to this deal if we'd known you worked that close.'

'Is it a problem?' Donny asked.

'You been asking nosy questions to one of my workers. Don't. Not anymore. Clear?'

Donny shrugged. 'No need to get narky. I meant no harm.'

The man fixed him with a cold stare. 'We don't wanna see you again. Not for anything. You got your cash. Now piss off.'

Donny shrugged and climbed back into his Land Rover. As he looked across the yard, he spotted the young woman again, watching from the back step of the house. An older woman had just stepped through the open door behind her and was pulling the younger woman back inside. There was something unusual about her and the way she held herself. Was she the farmer's daughter? If so, that could be why the men were so aggressive. They felt the need to be protective of their family and workers. But why did they feel that way? Maybe it was just that life was hard up here on the edge of the high moor. But you'd think that would lead to a greater community feeling. Everyone else around here felt that way. Why were these people so different? Odd.

As soon as Donny edged his vehicle out into the yard, the stocky man closed the barn doors behind him, then turned towards the farmhouse.

'Get inside, Maddy,' he shouted.

Donny drove out onto the lane and headed north, downhill towards the coast. The money was already burning a hole in his pocket. Maybe a major celebration was in order for the weekend but right now an evening in the pub seemed a good option, the one down in Watchet. It would be a bit livelier than the ones up here in these godforsaken villages. Maybe he'd succeed in landing a woman for the night, particularly now he had a bit of cash spare. And, if push came to shove, he could always kip down in the back of his van.

CHAPTER 20: SPRINGTIME

'Excuse me. I just want to apologise for making a fool of myself that evening earlier in the week. I didn't realise you were already taken.'

Jackie raised her eyes from the food in front of her, glanced at Tony, then turned her head sideways to look at the person who'd just spoken. She and Tony were back in the pub, tucking in to a sharing platter of cold meats and salad. Neither had heard or seen the approach of the man who now stood beside the table. She sighed and rolled her eyes at Tony. He grimaced in return.

'Mr Lomax,' she said. 'You have a most unfortunate way with words. What exactly do you mean when you describe me as being *taken*?'

'Well, you have a bloke already. That's all I meant.' Donny looked and sounded puzzled at her comment, just like before.

She sighed, even more melodramatically. 'Two things. Early last week, I wasn't *taken*, as you so indelicately put it. I wasn't seeing Tony then, but I am now. I take it that you aren't having much success in the romance stakes, Mr Lomax. I'm not surprised. Because, secondly, that word *taken* seems to turn women into objects, rather like something on a supermarket shelf. You seem to see any woman in terms of her availability, *taken* or *not taken*. I thought I'd made clear how insulting that can appear to a woman last time we met. Clearly it didn't get through.'

Tony was watching from across the table. He seemed to be trying hard not to laugh.

Jackie continued. 'Now, Tony tells me that you're a fairly decent guy underneath that rather-too-arrogant masculine exterior. So, you get the benefit of the doubt. But you've got to drop the idea that all women are always on the lookout for a guy to hook up with. And that, if they don't have one, they'll happily let themselves be swept up by any chancer with a patronising superiority complex. Get my drift?'

Tony finished chewing. 'She's a hard one, Donny. But she's absolutely right. You can be a right moron at times. You go at things like a bull in a china shop.'

Donny still looked bemused. 'Can I get you both a drink? As a sort of apology?'

Tony looked across the table at Jackie.

'Okay, thanks,' she said. 'Mine's a pint of IPA. And you can sit with us if you drop the macho rubbish. That's if you haven't managed to find some other poor woman to patronise by then.'

Donny returned with the drinks a few minutes later.

'A couple of detectives asked me about the river yesterday,' he said, as he deposited the brimming glasses on the tabletop. 'They were up in my neck of the woods, in Laxford. They wondered if a body could be washed all the way down from there to the harbour here. You're a special constable, aren't you?'

'That's right. But I'm not involved much with that investigation.'

Tony joined in. 'When we came in, we heard someone saying another body's been found up in the woods. Just today.'

'What?'

Jackie thought the effect on Donny was as if a bolt of electricity had shot up his spine. He lurched upright from his previously slouched position and spilled some of his beer.

'Yes,' she said. 'It was the two walkers across in the corner over there. They stumbled on it this morning. They were talking about it before you came in.'

'Whereabouts? I mean, where did they find this body?'

'Near Braycombe. Don't go asking them about it, though. My guess is they'd prefer to forget it. Most people would. Horrible.'

Curious, she thought. He's turned really pale.

* * *

Donny had intended an evening of celebration. Have a few drinks, meet a nice woman, hopefully be invited to stay the night, all possibilities now he had some cash to spare. Not now though. He finished his pint as quickly as he could without drawing too much attention to himself, then quietly left the pub, found his vehicle and drove the winding road back to his home in Laxford, taking the route slowly and carefully. He couldn't afford to have another collision, not with everything that had happened during the past couple of weeks.

Once he was safely home, he poured himself another beer, sipping it while sitting in his most comfortable chair and thinking things through. Should he own up? Should he tell the cops about that bump on the road the previous week? He didn't really have an issue with that part of the story. It was the stolen copper that was the real problem. Surely they'd have been told about its loss from outside the substation on that same night? He'd now managed to get rid of it, of course, but that presented a new problem. That Guthrie bloke clearly wasn't someone to meddle with, judging by his attitude. If he, Donny, landed him in trouble he'd probably come looking for revenge, bringing a couple of cronies and a baseball bat with him. Maybe it was better to forget about the whole business and let things quieten down for a while. Most important would be to steer clear of that woman, Jackie Spring or whatever her name was. Whenever he talked to her, he always felt as though she was gently pushing him into some kind of trap. Dangerous. Best avoided.

He dozed off in his chair, halfway through his second bottle of Tribute ale, but was plagued by dreams of Jackie Spring, standing by the side of a narrow road during a rainstorm as he tried to drive past her. She was wagging a finger at him and saying, 'You bad person! Untruthful! You're hiding something. I'm coming for you!'

He woke with a start, looking around at the familiar surroundings of his home. The TV was still burbling away in the corner. He yawned, stretched and glanced at the time. Less than twenty minutes had passed. She was getting to him, that woman, with her condescending attitude. He was beginning to wish that he could get back at her somehow. He really didn't like being humiliated, particularly by a woman.

* * *

On their short walk home, Jackie asked Tony how well he knew Donny Lomax.

'You said he was an idiot but a pretty harmless one. But I just get this feeling that he might be involved somehow. He went as white as a sheet when he heard about that body being found.'

Tony scratched his head. 'I know. I saw it too. I've never seen him like that before. He's always a bit brash and full of himself. Odd, really.'

'How come you know him? He lives up in Laxford, doesn't he?'

'He lived down in the town as a youngster. He was a friend of Gary's, my brother. Look, he was a bit of a tearaway as a lad. My mum banned him from the house when she caught him pinching some cakes she'd just baked for a party. It wouldn't surprise me if he wasn't still a bit light-fingered. But that's a whole lot different from assault and murder, isn't it?'

Jackie screwed up her face. 'That's one view, I'll give you that. Technically you're right. But there's a pattern to crimes, and serious thugs can often start with petty theft in childhood. For most kids who get involved, it's a phase and they quickly come through it. But for a few, it leads to much worse stuff.'

They reached Jackie's house. 'Coming in?' she asked.

Tony gave her a shy smile. He was such a lovely man, she thought. A bit different from her first husband, but that was okay, wasn't it? Simon had been an accountant who'd spent much of his spare time fly fishing for trout in the local streams and rivers. He'd also been a lovely bloke, right up until he'd keeled over and died from an undiagnosed heart defect some ten years earlier. Jackie had been heartbroken, shaken to her very core. It had taken five long years for her to regain some sense of normality in her life. It felt kind of therapeutic, dating a man who was younger than her and who came with teenagers in tow. Her own daughter and son had both finished university and were in the early stages of their own careers, living well away from Somerset. Am I just a lonely, ageing woman with an empty nest? she thought. Looking for love and a second chance?

She gave Tony a bright smile. 'It's springtime,' she said, and watched him quizzically. 'It's a joke,' she added. 'Come on, Tony. Keep up!'

* * *

Jackie was at work in the library the next morning. She'd just finished registering a batch of new books that had arrived late the previous day when the main door opened and a familiar figure slowly approached the desk, looking apprehensive.

'Mr Lomax,' she said. 'I didn't realise you were a library member.'

'I'm not,' he said hesitantly.

'So how can we help you?'

He looked as if he wanted to run back out into the street.

'I need to own up about something,' he said.

'Have you come across a stolen library book or something?' Jackie said.

He shook his head. 'It's about that body, the one found in the woods. See, the night of the big storm, I think I could've hit something on the back lane up near Braycombe. In the Land Rover, I mean.'

Jackie held up her hand. 'I'm on library duty, Mr Lomax. This really isn't for me. Why don't you report it properly?'

'Yeah, but who to? See, that Sergeant what's-his-name. Churchill? He's got it in for me. I don't want to see 'im.'

'The incident room is only a couple of hundred yards away, in the old community hall. There's bound to be a proper detective there. They'll tell you whether your information is relevant or not. Okay?'

She watched as Donny Lomax turned and walked out. She'd better check with them later in case he ignored her suggestion.

CHAPTER 21: CAKE

Thursday, Week 2

Driving into Watchet on a morning when the sun is shining is a lovely experience. The road winds down the hill with the wide expanse of the Bristol Channel ahead, its ruffled waters glittering in the light. These thoughts flickered through Sophie Allen's head as she navigated the narrow streets on her way to the temporary incident room. The air was fresh and salty, the old buildings seemed to glow and she felt happy, glad to see the back of the latest initiative she'd been asked to review by the Home Office. The trouble was, once you'd done a good job for the politicos in Whitehall, they never left you alone. Maybe the wise move would have been to only make a half-arsed attempt on her first job for them, then she might not have been asked again. She knew it wasn't in her nature, though. And this latest one had been right up her street, with her academic background in law and criminology. She'd been able to spot the flaws in the proposals right away. The difficult job had been to phrase her review of the plan in words that would get the alterations that were needed without upsetting the original authors too much. It had been a bloody pain, but worthwhile. And now here she was, looking forward to two days by the sea. Shame that there was a murder and a suspicious death to deal with.

She could guess how Polly, as the SIO, was feeling. Utterly frustrated. Her earlier jobs in a major crimes unit in Bristol and Bath would have involved murders and serious assaults. But most of them would have been crimes of passion or acts of wild violence, with clues scattered around willy-nilly no matter how careful the perpetrator had tried to be. This current case was proving to be one of the trickiest Sophie had come across. In some ways she was glad she was no longer the SIO. In WeSCU that role would fall to either Polly or Barry, depending upon the location, with a few other factors coming into play. Like this one, with Barry still away on honeymoon. Sophie wondered how things would pan out in the long term. Barry had spent so long as her number two. In WeSCU he was number three in the hierarchy. How did he really feel about that? On the surface he'd been fine about it, but she guessed that he'd never tell her his real feelings. Opening up in that way just wasn't Barry's style.

Sophie clattered her way in through the narrow doors of the main room.

'Is it coffee break time yet? I've got cake!' she announced, loudly. 'My local bakery in Wareham was just opening when I passed. You can't miss an opportunity like that, can you?'

She glanced around at everybody as they made their way across the room. She'd been right. There was a tinge of anxiety in Polly's eyes and her skin lacked its usual glow. Sophie took the opportunity to draw her deputy to one side.

'I hear there's another body,' she said quietly. 'Could it be connected?'

Polly shrugged. 'Impossible to say at the moment. But it looks as though it's been lying there in the woods for a couple of weeks. That was about the same time as Carlyon was killed. This one's a middle-aged male with severe injuries to his right side. It's got the looks of being hit by a car. But that's just guesswork at this stage. The autopsy is tomorrow morning.'

'Any identification?'

Polly shook her head. 'No, not one bit. And no one's been reported missing. We wouldn't have connected them, the two bodies, but this one was found only a couple of miles from Carlyon's house, on the other side of the village, Braycombe. One of the lanes twists down a slope into a heavily wooded area. The two walkers stumbled on the body a couple of hundred yards off the road.'

'So what are your thoughts?'

Polly shrugged. 'Hit by a car. Serious injuries. When he came to, he was disoriented and went further into the woods where he collapsed and died. That's the logical sequence. But we really need to wait for the post-mortem results.'

They both looked up as the door from the car park was pushed open and a solitary male figure came in, somewhat tentatively.

'Um, are you detectives?' he asked.

Rae moved forward quickly. 'Mr Lomax,' she said. 'What brings you here?'

Simultaneously, Polly's phone beeped, indicating the arrival of a message. She glanced at the screen. Jackie Spring. *Donny Lomax coming in to see you. Odd story. Linked to the body in the woods.*

'It's a bit tricky,' the man replied. 'It's about that body the walkers found.'

Polly looked at him carefully for a few seconds, then turned to Rae. 'The interview room is free. Take Mr Lomax there.'

'Help yourself to a cake, Mr Lomax,' Sophie added. She watched with interest as he selected the largest one on the plate.

'Coffee?' she added.

He nodded, albeit rather nervously, so Rae spooned instant granules into two mugs, added hot water and milk, then led him through to the tiny room. He settled himself into a chair.

'Tell me about it,' she said.

Rae thought he looked very apprehensive as he spoke. 'It were that night, the one with the big storm. It was absolutely peeing it down and I couldn't see proper, like. I heard a bit of a crump and felt my van judder a bit. I got out and had a look but there weren't anything about. I thought it was maybe a deer or summat. The thing is, I was back along that road a couple of days ago and I seen there was a ditch. It must've been full of water back that night. And it were dark as hell. What if I hit summat and it fell into the ditch? I wouldn't have seen it. But that body what's been found. Could it have been him?'

Rae frowned. 'Why didn't you report it earlier?'

'Well, 'cos I didn't know what it was. And I checked, like I said, but saw nothing, except for a blue scarf hanging from a bush. But I bin worried about it, I s'pose. It was when I heard about that body found in the woods yesterday. It could've been it.'

Rae was puzzled. 'How fast were you going?'

'Not very, though it was just after a downhill bit, then round the corner. That's where it was. But the van was a bit heavy. I had farming stuff in the back. It would have given a bit of a smack to whatever it was. That's if it were a deer or a person.'

Rae watched him drop his eyes as he added these last snippets of information. 'Any marks on your vehicle?'

'Nope. I checked when I got back home. Anyways, like I said, it was raining cats and dogs. Never seen anything like it. It took most of the mud off.'

She thought carefully. 'I think it'd be better to fill in an incident form with the details. Let's do it now.'

She fished one out of a drawer while he finished his coffee, then passed the paper across the table, along with a pen.

'Use your own words, Mr Lomax. I don't want to make any suggestions because that could be construed as putting words into your mouth. Do you want me to stay or go? Shall I give you five minutes or so?'

He chewed the end of the pen. Maybe chuck that one away once he's finished, Rae thought.

'Give me a few minutes.'

She left him alone in the incident room and returned to the working area. Sophie and Polly looked at her quizzically.

'I don't know what to make of him,' she said. 'He hit something on the road that night. And it was in the right place, close to where the body was found. He went back a few days ago to check and saw that blue scarf. But he's really nervous about something.'

'Maybe the fact that he might have killed somebody?' Polly suggested.

'Could be. He's a bit of an odd bloke, to be honest.'

'That's what Jackie Spring says. Apparently, she's had a couple of run-ins with him in a local pub. He tried to pick her up. She says he's a bit of a Neanderthal.'

'Keep an open mind, please,' Sophie added. 'He might be everything you've said, but that doesn't make him guilty of anything serious. I can't see why he'd come in voluntarily to make a statement about hitting something or someone that night if he's a killer. I know they often like to get involved in searches and the like, hanging around in the background to keep an eye on developments. But this is different, coming in this morning to own up to something like this. It's a bit like walking into the lion's den and then going a good bit further, by sticking your head in the lion's mouth. I'd say, well done him for calling in. A lot wouldn't.'

Rae gave him a few more minutes then went back into the interview room to check on his progress with the statement. He was just finishing. She scanned over what he'd written. It looked acceptable, and they could always interview him again if something needed checking.

'That's a weight off my mind,' he said. 'Do you know who it is? The body?'

Rae shook her head. 'Not confirmed yet. That's all I can say. Better if you keep this to yourself for the time being, Mr Lomax.'

She saw him off the premises and watched as the old Land Rover drove away. She then rejoined the other detectives.

'Surely that body has to be someone fairly local?' she said. 'Why would anyone else be out on a night like that?'

'Exactly what we were saying,' Polly replied. 'But the same thing applies. Why would someone local be out in the lane in pouring rain and storm force winds?'

Sophie watched her colleagues before adding the obvious. 'Come to that, why was Mr Lomax out? Did he say?'

Rae shook her head. 'Moving agricultural stuff. But he was a bit vague. He works on a farm nearby.'

'Maybe it needs checking. You did say he was a bit uneasy about something.'

CHAPTER 22: AUTOPSY

Rae volunteered to accompany Ade to the post-mortem examination.

'I must be mad,' she said to him as they drove to Taunton. 'I hate the bloody things. And this one will be worse than most, with the body having lain in those woods for a couple of weeks.'

'Then why did you decide to come along? It wasn't as though you had to.' Ade was looking straight ahead, concentrating on his driving. The road to Somerset's county town twisted and turned as it headed southeast alongside the Quantock Hills.

Rae shrugged. 'No idea. I have these mad moments sometimes. I've got a small pot of Benny's gunk to stick in our noses. He's Dorset's senior pathologist and says he's never got used to the smells. At least I've managed to avoid fainting up to now, though I've come close a couple of times.'

'Can we change the subject, please? You're making me worried.'

Rae laughed. 'Of course, though one last thing. Peppermint tea is good for afterwards. It's another of his tips. Helps to clean out the palette and nose. By the way, I've been recommended a good vegan café in Taunton, if we feel like lunch later. I wouldn't mind giving it a try.'

Ade nodded his agreement. 'What's your background, by the way?' he asked.

Rae wondered if this question was some kind of trap. *Take it at face value*, she told herself.

'I started in Wiltshire, in Salisbury. That's just after I graduated. But I decided early on that I wanted to be a detective rather than a beat copper. I made the switch as soon as I could. Several years there, then I transferred to Dorset and joined Sophie Allen's unit. I wasn't getting anywhere in Wiltshire because of friction with a senior officer. I'd read about the chief super's work in Dorset and decided that's what I wanted. I was really lucky. I applied at just the right time, when a vacancy just appeared. I'd also done extra training courses in behavioural psychology. Apparently, that tipped the balance in my favour.' Better to shift the conversation away from herself before she said too much. 'What about you?'

Ade spoke slowly, obviously concentrating on his driving. 'I'm like a lot of people from BAME backgrounds. We're encouraged to join the police to make a difference. That's what the glossy slogans say. But then you join up and you find the reality isn't really like that. The official line is that the force is keen to change, keen on inclusivity. But there's still some resistance from the rank and file. A few of them are anti-everything. Blacks, Asians, gays, even women still. Look at these recent cases of almost systematic misogyny. It must worry you.'

Rae thought carefully. 'I think it's changing. I'm a member of the equality and diversity panel in Dorset Police. We've registered a few complaints and made a series of proposals. They seem to have been taken seriously, but maybe only time will tell whether it's just a paper exercise or not. And I know that some of the guys will only pay lip service to going along with things. There are some who'll never have their views shifted, no matter what happens. I guess it's a generational thing.'

'Same in Somerset,' Ade said. 'Except for Bristol, the whole of the southwest is overwhelmingly white. The only time a lot of these people see anyone ethnic is when they're out getting a curry or a Chinese takeaway. Or they're in hospital for some reason. An awful lot of the junior staff and cleaners are BAME.'

'So it's almost always people who are serving them in some way?'

'Exactly. White middle-aged males are still top dogs.'

'With their lazy heteronormative assumptions. Unable and unwilling to see things from a different perspective. Having said that, my usual boss, Barry Marsh, isn't a bit like that. He's one of the genuinely good guys.'

'In that case, maybe there's hope yet.'

They fell into near silence for the rest of the drive.

The post-mortem examination wasn't quite as unpleasant as Rae and Ade had feared. The weather had been chilly but largely dry for the previous couple of weeks and insect life was still struggling to escape its winter dormancy. The same was true for microbial activity, kept partly at bay by the relatively low temperatures the area had experienced recently. The pathologist made a point of explaining this fact.

'A month later and things would be a lot more unpleasant,' Helen Cook said.

There were no injuries that screamed murder at them. No stab or gunshot wounds, no major blunt force trauma injuries to the head. The body showed hip and internal injuries consistent with being hit by a moving vehicle, followed by death from blood loss and exposure, along with some bruising.

'He might have lost consciousness for a short while because of his head injury,' Helen explained. 'But there probably wasn't any significant brain damage.'

'So do you think he came to afterwards and felt disoriented?' Ade asked.

She shrugged. 'Maybe. I suppose it's likely.'

'It was pitch black and pouring with rain,' Rae said. 'The wind would have been howling. Isn't it likely that he stumbled off, hoping to find shelter, but ended up heading the wrong way?'

'I couldn't possibly comment on that,' Helen said. 'Conjecture isn't in my remit.'

'But he was losing blood?'

'Both from the hip wound and internally,' she explained. 'I expect he was in shock as well.'

Rae glanced at Ade. 'Stumbled into the woods, then fell again. Poor bloke.'

Helen cleared her throat. 'What I can tell you is that he wasn't in good general health. There are signs of poor nutrition, and his teeth are not in good condition. My guess is that he wasn't a particularly well man, anyway.'

Ade frowned. 'That matches some of the initial forensic comments. His clothes were threadbare, and his shoes worn through. Could he have been a vagrant of some type?'

Helen shook her head, wearily. 'Again, I can't comment. It's a really tragic end, though.' She paused. 'There are some injuries, mainly bruising, that are inconsistent with being hit by a car.'

Rae came alert. 'What do you mean?'

'Around the face, for one. A couple that look like fist marks, the kind I see after someone's been in a punch-up.'

'Right.'

'And can you see this one near the kidneys?' Helen pointed to a mark on the victim's back. 'That's the result of a kick. Well, either that or I'm losing my touch.'

* * *

'Are you a vegetarian, Rae?'

The two detective sergeants were sitting at a window table in a small vegetarian café in Taunton, plates of food in front of them.

'No. I just like tasty food of all types. You're usually based in Taunton. Haven't you ever been to this place?'

Ade shook his head, unable to speak because of the forkful of quiche that he'd just put in his mouth. He finished swallowing most of it.

'No. Don't understand why, though. This is really good.'

'I was here a couple of years ago, on that case where we first met, the one on the Quantock Hills. Craig, my boyfriend, brought me here one lunchtime. He's a curry addict. He'd heard that the curried bean pasty was the best in the region and wanted to try it.' She took a bite. 'I'm surprised you gave it a miss. It's still as good as it was.'

'Well, maybe I'll learn one day. I'm always suspicious of Europeans making curry-based stuff. Maybe I'm prejudiced against the idea. Or completely out of touch.'

'The latter, I expect. It's been a trend for some years now, hasn't it? Fusion food. Borrowing ideas from a range of cultures. Sometimes it works, sometimes it doesn't. In this case it works spectacularly well. I could get addicted to this.'

They were drinking coffee when Ade's phone rang. He listened carefully, then slipped it back into his pocket.

'We'd better get off. That was the boss. Something unexpected has shown up in the DNA samples found at Carlyon's house last week.'

They paid the bill and started to put their coats on.

'Are you going to share what she said with me?' Rae asked.

Ade shook his head. 'Can't. That's all she said. Didn't want to discuss it over the phone.'

They collected the car and started the half-hour drive back to Watchet. Rae was intrigued. What now?

CHAPTER 23: DNA

As soon as Rae walked into the incident room, she noticed the difference in the atmosphere. Somehow it seemed more tense, more focussed. Maybe it was just her imagination, she thought.

The two detectives joined the others around a table in a corner of the hall. Polly wasted no time in getting started.

'The DNA results have come in and they've provided us with a set of puzzles,' she said. 'But at least they give us something to concentrate on. I'll go through the summary findings, then you can chip in with your thoughts. Does that seem okay?'

She looked around at the nodding heads.

'Good. There are three profiles that are of interest separate to Carlyon's, and they all give us something to think about. First one. This sample was in the outhouse where we think Carlyon was killed. That profile didn't show up on any samples from the house. It's from a male. It was on a rag that was found in a corner of the shed. It had Carlyon's blood on it but also skin cells from someone else. The forensic people suggest the killer might have used it to wipe his hands. That DNA shows no familial link to Carlyon himself.'

Polly paused to take a sip of water.

'Profile two was from Carlyon's studio, upstairs in the house, taken from the armrest of one of the chairs and also from the frame of the portrait. It's a female with Down's. It shows the extra chromosome twenty-one. So the subject of those paintings must have been inside the house at some point, but there are only those two samples, both found in the studio. Was she there to have a quick look at the portrait? We don't know for sure, but a logical scenario is that she sat in the chair then went across and touched the painting. I've asked for expert advice on the fact that so little of her DNA was found. The consensus view is that her visit was brief and only on one occasion. That can't count as a hard fact though.' She paused for a few seconds. 'But the really interesting fact about this one is that there's a very close match to Carlyon himself. It looks like he was her father.'

Polly took another sip of water and looked around at the attentive faces of the unit members. They were hanging on her every word. Apart from Sophie Allen, that is. She already knew the details and the ramifications.

'Then there's the third sample, also found in the studio. It's another female. This one was found on a paper tissue at the bottom of a waste basket in the studio. She blew her nose several times then threw the tissue away. It shows a very close match to the girl. It looks as though she was the mother.'

The group fell silent as the facts sank in. Sometimes the reports from DNA analysis had this effect on a team of detectives. The results would often clarify the paths that should be followed up. But occasionally they would open up hitherto unsuspected lines of inquiry. This set looked to be the latter. A probable killer. A mother. And a girl with Down's.

Polly cleared her throat. 'There is something else. That third DNA profile. It has a match on the database. There was an art theft from an exhibition here in Watchet some twenty years ago, with several valuable paintings stolen. DNA samples were taken from the gallery staff for elimination purposes. Most were deleted shortly afterwards by request from the staff, but this one wasn't. The name was Barbara Rogers, one of the cleaners. She seems to have vanished shortly afterwards and there's no trace of her anywhere in this area or anywhere else in Somerset.'

'Was she involved in the theft?' Tommy asked.

'That's the strange thing,' Polly said. 'I phoned an old colleague about it. He remembered the case and said there was absolutely no evidence of her involvement. The thief was caught, charged and served whatever sentence he was given, though my contact couldn't tell me any further details. It's possible Barbara was involved in some low-level way but there was no reason to suspect her at the time. That's what he said. It certainly needs looking into, though.'

Polly glanced across the table to Sophie Allen. She was smiling. 'Good stuff, Polly,' she said.

'Where was this art gallery?' Rae asked. 'It can't be the current one down by the harbourside because it's only been open a few years. Did that community hub on the quayside host art displays?'

Polly shrugged. 'Don't know. But I know exactly where that particular exhibition was running. This very hall we're sitting in. It was a community display centre back then, often hired for exhibitions of all types.'

'Shame we can't dust it for residual fingerprints,' Rae replied, smiling broadly. 'But twenty years is a long time.'

'Well, there is one other intriguing snippet,' Polly added. 'One of the artists whose work was on display was Benjamin Carlyon. He was a member of a Cornwall art collective that put their work on tour across the region.'

'Did he have anything stolen in the theft?' Tommy asked.

'No. It wasn't anyone from the collective whose work was taken. It was a couple of more valuable pieces on loan from a local collector. They got them back, though.'

* * *

Rae and Tommy were allocated the task of tracing Barbara Rogers, the cleaner at the defunct art exhibition, a search with two obvious routes. Barbara's job at this very hall, some twenty years earlier, might provide a starting point. Rae was already planning how best to get started. Surely some local people would remember her? If they were lucky, someone might have kept in contact and be able to supply an address or phone number. The other avenue would be accessible databases and social media. There must be records of her somewhere, on some system or other, though she knew well enough from previous cases that some people had turned the act of disappearing without trace into a fine art. Jackie Spring, Polly's local secret weapon and volunteer special constable, might be able to help.

Rae checked with the DCI, then contacted Jackie with a text message which was quickly answered. An hour later, she and Tommy waited on the quayside for the librarian to finish work for the day. It wasn't an unpleasant wait. The sun was shining, coming in low from the west, causing the incoming waves to shimmer as they swept in from the Channel. Once Jackie arrived, the trio moved to a nearby bench.

'This is lovely,' Rae said. 'Shame that we can't really enjoy it the way we'd like to. Too much to do.'

'It kind of seeps into your soul,' Jackie answered. 'You don't realise it until you're away from the place. That's when you feel the tug, pulling you back. I expect other people who live in small coastal towns like Watchet feel it too, wherever they are. When I was a lot younger, I lived in a village in Brittany for six months. It had the same pull. Anyway, how can I help?'

'We're beginning to get somewhere, Jackie. The mother of the Down's girl's name was Barbara Rogers, or it was twenty years ago. At that time, she worked as a cleaner in the local community exhibition hall, the one we're using as our incident room. We haven't found much new about the girl, except for the confirmation that she is a Down's person, confirmed by her DNA profile. Oh, and that she's Carlyon's daughter. That also showed up.'

'And you describe that as *not much*? Sounds pretty big to me.'

'Well, that depends on your perspective. It's the same as much of the other stuff. Fascinating because of the personal dynamics, but no immediate breakthrough in terms of the case. More digging required.'

'And you think I might be able to help?'

'Local knowledge, Jackie. It's often the key.'

Jackie thought for a while, her brown curls moving slightly in the sea breeze.

'Twenty years is a long time ago,' she finally said. 'It pre-dates me moving to Watchet by a good few years. There are a couple of Rogersfamilies in the town but I'm not sure any of them had a Barbara. She was a cleaner at the hall, you say. That might help. It was council owned, so there ought to be a record of employees somewhere. I can't tell you if it was the town or the county council. You might need to check both. All I can say is, good luck with that! But I can ask around for you, if you want. It'll bring me out into the open though, once I start a bit of probing about someone.'

Rae shrugged. 'We're prepared for it. The DCI thinks we've moved beyond that secret stage, so she's happy with you being a bit higher profile. I wanted to tap your brains about something else, too. Polly and I had a look at that derelict paper mill. The wasteland beside the river. We've had a forensic team up there and they found some suspicious tyre tracks and signs that the lock on the gate had been tampered with. Have you picked up on anything being said locally about it?'

Jackie shook her head. 'No. And the locals are a gossipy lot, believe me. Either whoever dumped the body has kept totally quiet about what they were up to, or they're not local to the town. But that wouldn't surprise me. It's this girl, the one who's Down's. She's definitely not from Watchet, Willington or Washford because I've been checking. They're the three fairly sizeable towns in this area. She's either from one of the bigger places east or west of here, or she's from inland somewhere. One of the smaller villages or maybe a farm. I'm stumped, to be honest.'

'Well, that's a relief,' Rae said.

Jackie looked puzzled. 'What do you mean?'

'You found the same as us. I thought we were losing our touch.'

'Hah. Maybe you are. I'm not the world's best investigator, you know. I've had no training of any kind.'

'Well, Polly seems to think a lot of you. And she really is a good detective. And the boss, Sophie Allen, agrees with her. I can live a bit easier now. Only a bit, mind.'

Again, Jackie looked at her. 'Explain, please?'

'I'm an obsessive, Jackie. I always think I should be doing better than I am. It's probably a recipe for a disastrously unhappy life.' Rae turned to Tommy. 'By the way, you didn't hear that last bit, Tommy. Okay?'

He nodded, looking confused. 'Sure, boss.'

Jackie frowned. 'You know what my gut instinct is? They're from one of the small villages up on Exmoor. That, or they're hidden away on a remote farm, keeping themselves to themselves. I can't see why someone from Bridgwater or Taunton would come to our local cottage hospital for treatment. They'd go to one of the big hospitals, wouldn't they? No, they're from somewhere around here but they're keeping themselves hidden, for whatever reason.'

'They might have something to hide? Something else?' Rae suggested.

'I would reckon so. It's not just the recent events, the one's you're investigating. Benjamin Carlyon's murder and the death of this unidentified man in the woods. They've been keeping themselves to themselves for a lot longer than that. Maybe for the twenty years since she worked in the hall.'

Rae's voice dropped to little more than a whisper. 'So what you're saying is, there's something else been going on. Have I got your drift?'

'Exactly. Possibly something very shady. Something a lot worse than art theft and suspicious paintings. But who am I to speculate? I'm no detective.'

Rae looked at her thoughtfully. 'Maybe that gives you an edge. You know, coming at it from a different angle. It's worth considering, for sure. Where should we start though?' She paused momentarily as she spotted the surprise on Jackie's face. 'Don't worry. That was a rhetorical question, Jackie. Me thinking out loud so there's no need to answer. Though something else has just occurred to me. Were there any other crimes reported at around the same time as the day of that big storm? Even low-level local ones?'

'Don't know. Leave it with me.'

They watched Jackie head off, then set off on the short walk back to the incident room. She'd given them plenty to think about.

'Tommy, when we get back, get on to the local mispers unit again. I know they've already been contacted but they might need a none-too-gentle reminder about urgency. We need to know who that body in the woods is. They should have found out something by now, surely. Check with Polly first, though. I'll have another go at this Barbara Rogers person.'

'Maybe she's dead, boss.'

'That means a death certificate would have been issued, and that's not happened. Not locally, anyway. So she's still alive, moved away or changed her name. Let's get busy.'

CHAPTER 24: ART THEFT

Ade had worked on two art thefts earlier in his career, which was why Polly had suggested he should take charge of this new angle, though those investigations had been in Bath, not this rural backwater. He wouldn't describe himself as any kind of art expert, though. He just happened to have been attached to the CID unit tasked with solving the crimes, neither of which had been the work of particularly high-level thieves. In one, the painting involved had been stolen to order, masterminded by a distant family member who had felt aggrieved at not being left her favourite painting by a wealthy great aunt who had died. The second had been an insurance fraud. In neither had he needed any art knowledge whatsoever. Probably a good job, because he had none. His wife, Luckie, knew more about art than him, something that had proved useful at the time. He had to admit that his involvement had some kind of beneficial effect, though. Since those cases, Luckie had found it easier to talk him into visiting art galleries during their infrequent weekend breaks away in London. He could now tell a Rembrandt from a Van Gogh, but maybe that wasn't something he should boast too loudly about.

The art theft in Watchet some two decades earlier had been widely reported in the local press. Several paintings had been taken, including a Gainsborough, on loan from a local landowning family. Insider knowledge had been suspected, which was why DNA samples had been taken from staff with access to the hall. In fact, those profiles hadn't been needed. The thief appeared to be an opportunist who'd gained access when a fire door had been left ajar after a member of staff had popped outside for an unauthorised fag break. The thief hadn't shown much discrimination in his choice of what to take. The paintings he'd stolen from the main part of the exhibition were low-level pieces of work by local artists, with rather inflated price tags. The Gainsborough he'd taken was in a small room by itself and, of course, had no price tag. The nature of the theft suggested that the thief might have had no idea of its value and no idea of how to get rid of it. He'd left it outside the local police station several days later, carefully wrapped in a supermarket carrier bag, one that carried several of his fingerprints. It hadn't taken the local police long to apprehend him.

The staff member who'd so carelessly left the fire door open was Barbara Rogers. She'd left her job soon afterwards, never to be heard of again. Ade wondered whether she'd really been sacked. Maybe in reality, she'd resigned of her own free will but under coercion from her bosses. The theft must have been highly embarrassing for the exhibition organisers. Maybe they'd brought pressure to bear on Barbara. Possibly they were leaned on themselves by the loaned painting's legitimate owner.

Had Carlyon met Barbara during the few weeks the exhibition was running? Maybe that was when they struck up a rapport and followed it up with a full-blown relationship, resulting in the birth of the girl a year or two later.

Ade sipped at his mug of tea as another thought came into his head. Carlyon was a talented artist. He specialised in landscapes. Was it just possible that the theft hadn't been opportunistic after all, but a carefully planned sequence by not one but two, or even three, perpetrators working together? The young man who'd owned up to the actual theft had shown so much remorse at his trial and had stressed the atypical nature of his behaviour so strongly, that he'd escaped with a suspended sentence and a fine. After all, the valuable painting had been quickly restored to its rightful owners. Everyone was happy.

Or had the original really been restored to its previous home? Maybe he needed to check on Carlyon's background as an artist to find out if the man had the necessary skills to be a forger of fine art. If the Gainsborough left outside the police station all those years ago was, in fact, a convincing copy, and if that fact had only recently come to light, then the artist's very recent murder might have an entirely different motive than the options the unit had been considering up to now. Could they have been barking up the wrong tree entirely with their focus on the young woman with Down's? Maybe the real nub of the story lay elsewhere.

He needed to talk this over with someone. He went to find Polly.

* * *

WeSCU's two most senior detectives sat in silence for a while after Ade left to follow up on his discovery, both of them deep in thought.

'Does this affect us, do you think?' Polly finally said.

'Of course it does,' Sophie replied, almost snappily. 'It's either linked or it isn't, but we have to follow it up, just to check. It might provide us with the motive we've been looking for since that pesky body was discovered in the harbour.'

'You sound a bit peeved.'

'Old age creeping up on me, I expect,' Sophie sighed. 'We nearly missed it, Polly.'

'Don't you think I know that? Thank God for Ade and his lateral thinking. We might have kept on grafting away here in Watchet, going round and round in ever decreasing circles, disappearing into a hole of our own making.'

'Well, we'll find out soon. Send him to Penzance to do some digging down there. Someone will have memories of him as a young artist and should be able to confirm whether Carlyon had the right skill set to be an art forger. It's a real can of worms though.'

Polly looked puzzled. 'What do you mean?'

'Art forgers rarely work alone. There has to be someone else, someone willing to buy it. Either that or . . .'

Polly waited but no further explanation came. 'Or what?' she finally said.

'Insurance scam. Owner involvement.'

'Oh. That could be tricky after all this time. Who did Ade say the owner of that Gainsborough was?'

Sophie's lip twitched before she spoke. 'Lady Braycombe. It was Lord and Lady Braycombe when the theft occurred twenty years ago, but the old guy died in a shooting accident a few years later. I think she's been by herself since then.'

Polly was puzzled. 'You seem to know all the details,' she said.

'The family used to own some land in Dorset, including a couple of farms managed by tenants. They were forced off the land. Then it was all sold. The story hit the local press. It was about the time we first moved there.' Another short pause. 'I don't think some of the locals ever forgave that family, Lady Braycombe in particular. Would you be happy for me to follow up this angle with the Braycombe family? I want to see what kind of person she is. Someone who could turf two families out of their homes and livelihoods. I want to see what makes her tick.'

'I couldn't say no, could I? You're the boss.'

'Polly, surely I've said on enough occasions that it's you or Barry who make the operational decisions when we're on a case? If you decided to send someone else, I'd accept it.'

Polly rolled her eyes. 'As if.'

CHAPTER 25: PENZANCE

Friday, Week 2

Ade set off early the next morning for Penzance. He'd wondered about driving along the north coast road that ran along the Bristol Channel through north Somerset and into Devon, then hugged the Atlantic coast as it approached Cornwall. The estimated arrival time to reach the tip of Cornwall made him think again. It might be picturesque, but it was also slow. So he made the decision to head south, inland across Exmoor then pick up the fast main road that stretched down the spine of the peninsula, dual-carriageway-based to beyond Newquay. He could do the trip in almost half the time. No contest when time was one of the main factors.

The road was quiet, permitting him to come up with a plan while he bowled along at a steady seventy. Penzance was his first, and main, destination. Benjamin Carlyon had lived there until he was thirty, using the rugged coastal landscapes as a basis for much of his work. He'd been a member of an art collective, and Ade had a couple of names of fellow members who might be able to supply some background. The key here would be to draw these people out into talking through their memories of Carlyon and his influences without giving away too much information himself. He couldn't afford to let slip the suspicion that Carlyon might have tried his hand at art forgery.

If he had time, Ade also intended to visit a few members of the art community in St Ives, that sparkling town on the north Cornwall coast that had been home to many of the country's top artists for years.

He reached Penzance mid-morning and grabbed a coffee before heading to the harbour area. He'd spent an hour the previous evening on the web looking for galleries owned or run by artists. The first turned out to be of no use at all, despite having been open for more than twenty years. The current owner was more of a businessperson than an artist and didn't seem remotely interested in what Ade asked. He left feeling slightly despondent and turned the street corner to the second gallery he'd identified. The owner, a Suzi Poldaire, had started out on a painting career at about the same time as Carlyon. With a bit of luck, she might tell him all he needed to know.

Ade opened the low door from the street and walked inside to the sound of the tinkle of small brass bells above the entry. Two sets of eyes turned to look at him, then resumed the conversation that he'd interrupted.

That must be Suzi, he decided. Tight, curly hair and big glasses. The photo on her website had obviously been taken years earlier. The frizz had been a golden blonde back then, but the glasses were similar. She was wrapping a painting of some type for the man standing opposite her, across a counter, securing the bubble wrap with sticky tape.

Ade took the opportunity to wander around the room, looking at the artwork on display. Bright colours in thick paint, giving the impression of coastal scenes, but conveyed in swirls and loops. He looked at the stickers beside each item, and almost gasped at the prices before he remembered what his wife, Luckie, had told him the evening before. Good art doesn't come cheap. And these were good, no doubt about it. Full of vibrancy and shapes that represented movement. He continued to move around the room and found himself facing some work by a different artist. These were more traditional, closer to photographs in appearance. With a slight sense of shock, he realised that he preferred the liveliness of Suzi's own work. Maybe Luckie's efforts to educate him in good art had finally begun to pay off.

He was disturbed by the owner, coming to ask him if he needed any help. The customer was just leaving, opening the door to the tinkle of bells again.

'I think your work is great,' he said. 'But sadly, that's not why I'm here. DS Ade Ahmed, Wessex Serious Crimes Unit.' He held out his warrant card. 'I'm here as part of an investigation into a suspicious death, up in Watchet. You may have seen it reported in the news?'

The woman eyed him suspiciously. 'I don't think so. Why do you want to see me? I've never been up that way.'

'Oh, don't worry. I'm here trying to get background information about the victim. His name was Benjamin Carlyon and he was an artist. Originally from around these parts.'

Suzi put her hand on a chair back as if to steady herself.

'Surely not,' she said. 'Not Ben. And a suspicious death?'

'I'm afraid so. Did you know him?'

She sat down on the seat she'd touched and indicated to Ade that he should do the same, pointing to a nearby chair. He pulled it across.

'I knew him well many years ago. When I first took on this little place, I displayed some of his work. He did some striking landscapes, kind of dark and brooding.'

'That sounds right.' Ade was thinking back to the paintings he'd seen in Carlyon's studio when he'd helped with the close search of the house. 'He was murdered a couple of weeks ago.'

'Why would anyone kill an artist?' she asked. 'Did he somehow get himself into trouble? He had a bit of a temper on him. I do remember that.'

'We don't know the full story, which is why I'm here, trying to fill in the background. Had he visited down this way recently?'

She shook her head. 'No. I haven't seen him since he upped sticks and left, ages ago. What, twenty, twenty-five years ago? I don't even know where he went.'

'As far as we know, he moved around a bit, then settled in Bodmin for a while. Recently he's been painting scenes on Exmoor. He finally settled there, near a small village up on the moor.'

'By himself?'

Ade nodded. 'We think so. His family say he was a bit solitary.'

'I used to love him, you know. We had a bit of a thing going for a while, but I couldn't cope with his occasional bleak moods. He used to get really morose when he'd drunk too much. I needed a bit more lightness in my life, so we parted company.'

Ade tried to put the next question as delicately as he could. 'Did he have any favourite artists of his own?'

Suzi looked as though she was about to answer. She opened her mouth as if to speak, then abruptly closed it again and looked at Ade through narrowed eyes. 'Why do you want to know that?'

He shrugged. 'Just background.'

She shook her head. 'I can't see how it's relevant. No. You're digging for something, aren't you?'

'Not really, no,' he lied.

She seemed to clam up at that point and looked at her watch. 'I need to get on. If that's all I can help you with, officer, then I'll leave you to browse a bit more.'

'Can I take a card? My partner is a bit of an art collector. I think she'd like your stuff.'

Suzi gave him a thin smile as she pushed a small contact card across the table. He pocketed it and left.

The third gallery proved to be of no more help than the first. Time to grab some lunch then head the few miles north to St Ives. He'd passed a café claiming to sell the best Cornish pasties in the town. Once he'd found a sheltered sunny spot overlooking the harbour and taken a few bites, he couldn't disagree with the claim. It was simply delicious. He'd wondered about opting for the curried vegetable pasty but now decided he'd made the right choice. Sunshine, sea air, the cacophony created by the gulls wheeling above the harbour water: it was a perfect scene. Ade felt content and thought back over his talk with Suzi Poldaire. Why had she reacted so strongly to his final question? It was almost as if she knew that the query was probing possible art fraud. Did that mean she already knew that Carlyon had been thinking of copying recognised works of art? After all, she'd lived with the man for a while when they were younger so might know if he'd planned to go down that route.

The drive to St Ives was delayed by roadworks so Ade had lost some of his sense of *bonhomie* by the time he arrived. Even so, he was looking forward to the short visit. He'd heard so much of the special atmosphere the resort had, the clarity of the air and the area's laid-back approach to life. The view of the bay and harbour took his breath away, just as Luckie had said it would. A rogue thought crept into his head. What could be better than living in a place like this? There was bound to be a downside, though. Was it possible for someone on a meagre detective sergeant's salary to even contemplate buying a property here? Get real, Adrian, he told himself.

He parked his car and walked down into the town. Curio shop after curio shop; café after café; art gallery after art gallery. Where should he start? He had an address ready, one that he'd researched the evening before. Not a gallery but a private residence for Paul Brooker, someone who'd known Carlyon as a student.

Ade was invited into a small courtyard garden, sheltered from the wind, where a couple of chairs were set around a rickety table.

'He's been found dead, you say,' the man said as they settled into their seats. 'Unbelievable, really. I mean, well, what is happening in this country? Violence, rape, fraud. It seems never-ending. What happened to the hippy ideals of my younger days?'

Ade didn't know how to respond to that particular question, so he ignored it and posed one of his own. 'Did you know him well?'

'We shared digs when we were at art college. Just for a year, though. I was lucky and struck up a relationship with the young woman who became my first wife. I moved in with her, so Ben had to find someone else to share with.'

'What was he like?'

'Decent enough bloke. Short of cash, but weren't we all? Quiet, in a brooding sort of way. Kept himself to himself.'

'How good was he? At art, I mean.'

'Very good. His technique was one of the best on the course. Really proficient and detailed.'

Time for the key question. 'Did he have any favourite artists?'

'Of course. We all did. Van Gogh. Even Picasso. But he had an odd one too. Gainsborough. We used to rib him about it, but he ignored us. Quite right, too. It's obvious when you're older and a good bit wiser. Gainsborough's a genius. I suppose it was all the portraits of aristos from his day. It kind of ran against what we believed in. We were a bit naive and idealistic, I suppose.'

'Did he experiment with the techniques of these people?'

'Listen, you can learn a lot from these famous artists. But you can't do what they did. They were geniuses. We weren't and still aren't. I mean, they're out of reach, aren't they?' Paul's eyes narrowed. 'Do you mean, did he copy them?'

'Not really. Just learn their techniques. See how they did things.'

Paul shrugged. 'Not Van Gogh or Picasso. He spent a lot of time studying the Gainsboroughs, though. Mainly the landscapes. He was a quick painter, old Gainsborough. Deft touch. Ben wanted that same feel.'

Ade nodded his head slowly and sipped at the fruit juice that his host had poured for him. He'd got the information he came here for. Time to politely end the conversation and get away.

CHAPTER 26: BACK STORIES

Polly, meanwhile, was in Exeter once again to talk to Carlyon's nephew, Justin Penhale. She visited him at his place of work, a small engineering company situated on an industrial estate to the west of the city. He led her to a small office rather than speaking to her in the larger, and rather busy, engineering design room where he spent most of his time.

'It's a team affair,' Justin explained. 'Modern design for the systems we work on isn't just the work of a single person, so it makes sense for us to be together in the same room. That way we see everything that's going on. Adapt and survive. That's the name of the game in our commercially competitive line of work. And it has to be done quickly.'

'Sounds fascinating,' Polly said. In truth, she just wanted to get this interview over and done with, then get back to Watchet to start pulling all these new strands together.

'How can I help?' Justin asked.

'A few things, really. Do you remember your uncle ever talking about including his work in an exhibition in Watchet in the past?'

Justin shook his head. 'Not really. When are we talking about?'

'Possibly twenty years ago or thereabouts.'

'You're hoping for a lot from me, aren't you? I was still at primary school in Cornwall. I was into football and playing on the beach. I can't say I was aware that Uncle Ben was even an artist, let alone doing exhibitions, not when I was that young. So the answer's no.'

'Okay, thanks. I had to ask. Secondly, did he ever talk about his own favourite artists? Ones that influenced him?'

Justin sat back in his seat and stroked his forehead. 'We had a few conversations about styles of art when I was a teenager. He was a bit critical of some modern abstract painters, but not all of them. He used to say, *talent is talent and will show through*. He liked Monet but he also liked Gainsborough. If you forced me, I'd say they were his favourites. I could be wrong, though.'

Polly smiled. 'No, that's good enough for me. Has anything else occurred to you since we talked last?'

He frowned. 'Not really. I did hear about the other body being found a few miles away. Is it connected?'

'We're keeping an open mind. That one looks to be an accidental death, though. What do you think drew your uncle to the Watchet area? Did he ever say?'

Justin shrugged. 'Not really. I assumed it was the easy access to the moor for his landscapes. But then, he could get that on Bodmin and Dartmoor, couldn't he?'

'I've heard that Exmoor has its own unique beauty, along with real gems like Dunster. Then the Quantock Hills are nearby.'

'I wouldn't know. Sorry. I'm not really into landscapes or history.'

Polly couldn't help but smile gently at his slightly forlorn look. He seemed a genuinely nice guy. Maybe she'd underestimated how much he'd been affected by the death of his uncle.

'Do you know where he studied art?'

Justin shook his head and ran his fingers through his hair. 'Sorry. It's crazy, isn't it? I know so little about him and now it's all too late. Mum would have known but her Alzheimer's is so bad she struggles with remembering anything. Sorry.' He stopped speaking suddenly and frowned. 'No, I may be wrong. He once mentioned Loughborough, that he was there for a few years and developed a taste for Melton Mowbray pies and Stilton. Does it have an art school?'

Polly shrugged. 'I don't know but we can find out. I'll pass that on.'

She turned aside while she sent a short text message to Rae, then returned her attention to Justin.

'Have you had a chance to check the details of any will yet? Who inherits?'

'That's the astonishing thing. Someone called Maddy Carlyon. It's all a bit odd. Apparently, she was added only a month or two ago. But we don't know of anyone by that name. Our solicitors are starting a search for her soon. They may need to hire some kind of private investigator.'

'We think that he had a daughter, Mr Penhale. That's the last item I wanted to talk to you about. We found traces of her DNA in your uncle's studio, upstairs in his house. She has Down's syndrome and probably lives somewhere in the Exmoor area. But we didn't know her name and there don't appear to be any Carlyons living locally. Nor can we find any trace of anyone with that surname in our area of Somerset, not on any register of any kind. If we come across anyone, we'll let you know.'

'So I have a cousin I didn't know about? And she visited him?'

Polly nodded as she rose to leave. 'We're assuming she's the subject of that portrait. We also suspected that her name was Maddy. So, that confirms it.'

* * *

Rae Gregson had the frustrating job of researching Carlyon's art college background. Nothing had shown up in the material found at the dead man's house that would have indicated where he studied for his art qualifications. Maybe she needed to pay another visit, search through yet more dusty cupboards and musty hidey-holes. Surely there'd be a graduation certificate somewhere?

Her thoughts were interrupted by the chirruping of her phone to indicate an incoming message. She glanced at the screen. The message was from Polly and consisted of one word. *Loughborough*. Saved. She almost punched the air with relief but then realised that the real work started now. She and Tommy would have to spend much of the morning on the phones, trying to prise information out of the college about a student who'd been there nearly three decades earlier. It would be intensely frustrating. She asked Tommy to get them coffee then started to prepare a list of possible departments to contact and questions to ask.

They were each on their second coffee when Tommy suddenly sat bolt upright and gripped his pen tight rather than spinning it between his fingers. He scribbled a few notes on the pad in front of him, replaced the receiver and turned to Rae with a look of glee on his face.

'That was one of the secretaries at the art college. She's been in that role for yonks. She says that Carlyon was an external examiner until a few years ago. He'd visit to help with final assessments. He also gave occasional lectures to the student art society on . . . guess who?'

'Don't tell me. Gainsborough.'

'Got it in one, boss!'

Rae was looking pensive. She scratched her nose and took another mouthful of coffee. 'It's all beginning to add up, isn't it? Not that it proves anything, but there's a consistency here, don't you think? Polly just sent another text to say that Gainsborough was one of his favourite artists, according to his nephew. It's beginning to fit.'

'The other thing, boss, is that I've been checking the dates on the back of Carlyon's paintings. He'd sign them on the front and stick a date on the back. There are a couple from about twelve years ago. That was before he bought that house up on the moor. But they're scenes from around

Braycombe, I'm sure of it. There's one of the old stone bridge on the back road. He must have been here for a few days. Maybe that was when he decided to look for a place to move into.'

Rae was looking thoughtful. 'Good stuff, Tommy. We'll make a top-notch detective of you yet.' She stopped, thinking deeply. 'I wonder if he spotted people from his past on that visit? Interesting, eh?'

* * *

Something was niggling away in Jackie Spring's mind. She was sure that it was something to do with that pest of a person, Donny Lomax. But what, exactly? She was putting returned books back on the shelf in the library and found herself facing the section on weather and climate. The book she had in her hand was on unusual weather phenomena. She slid it into its rightful place on the shelf. That was it! Lomax had appeared almost shifty when he'd reported the possible collision on the back lane near Braycombe. Yet, as far as she knew, all the evidence supported the view that the second death was the result of a tragic accident. So why was he so uneasy? Possibly he was worried that some charge might yet be brought against him for the death, but that was highly unlikely.

Unless, of course, he was worried about something else that had happened, unrelated to the collision. And there it was, staring her in the face in the books on storms of various types. Why had he been out that night? He'd said it was late, nearly midnight. That fitted with what she'd remembered about the storm. The heavy rain and lashing winds hadn't arrived until well past eleven. Sensible people would have been safely indoors by then, not out on a moorland lane that was partly flooded. Lomax must have had a good reason to be there.

She waited until her lunch break, then hurried down to the little police station on the quay. Sarah Levy, her friend and police boss, looked up as Jackie almost crashed through the door.

'Careful, Jackie. We've only just had that door repainted. I don't imagine it's due to be done again until next century, so we need to cherish it.'

Jackie didn't even smile. 'Petty crimes, thefts or burglaries. The night of the big storm. Anything reported?'

Sarah turned to her computer screen and logged into the relevant set of records, Jackie peering over her shoulder. The search results settled into a very short list with only two items on it. Sarah read them out.

'A pet dog went missing from a house in Willisford. The owner claims it was stolen but we think it probably got washed into the river and drowned. A load of copper was stolen from outside an electricity substation up near Braycombe. That's it.'

'How much was the copper worth?'

'About a thousand. Maybe a bit more.'

Jackie scowled, somewhat melodramatically. 'That's it, I bet. That's what he was doing up there that night. That's why he gets cagey when he talks about what happened!'

Sarah looked puzzled. 'Who?'

'Who do you think? Bloody Donny Lomax!'

CHAPTER 27: THE MANOR HOUSE

Braycombe House was situated a mile south of the village of the same name and was set in a small area of parkland. The house was larger than Sophie had expected and looked to be in good order, judging by the pristine paintwork and the beautifully kept flower beds. It also looked as if much of the brickwork and pointing had been worked on in recent years, something rare in manor houses of this type, in Sophie's experience anyway.

She swung her car into an empty area beside the front door, next to a well-tended rose bed. The upkeep costs for the house and estate must be enormous. She rang the doorbell and listened for a corresponding chiming sound inside. Was that a slight ring? It was hard to tell. Something must have sounded because she heard the noise of a lock being turned followed by a squeak as the hinges operated. A short, black-clad woman with wispy hair showing under a cap peered out.

'Yes?' she asked.

'Detective Chief Superintendent Sophie Allen. Is Lady Braycombe in?'

'Well, yes. You'd better come in. I'll call her. Is she expecting you? She didn't mention it.' Her voice sounded tired.

'No. I've come on the off chance. But it is important.'

Sophie was left standing in a wood-panelled hallway with doors on three of its sides. The woman had gone through the one on the left, leaving it ajar. Sophie could hear the low sound of voices but couldn't make out what was being said. Finally, the woman came back.

'Lady Braycombe can see you in the drawing room. Follow me, please.'

She opened the same door a little wider and stepped inside again but this time moved to one side. A tall, slender woman with immaculately coiffured blonde hair was standing beside an open fireplace, a log fire burning brightly in the hearth. She was younger than Sophie had anticipated. She wondered if she'd watched too many TV dramas where the lady of the manor was invariably a snootily destructive geriatric with a walking stick who fired off venomous comments to all and sundry. Sophie felt the woman's eyes upon her, a cautious gaze studying her carefully. The detective didn't move immediately into the room, though. Instead, she turned to the wispy-haired woman standing at the door.

'Thank you. What's your name?' She spoke quietly.

The woman looked surprised, as if she wasn't used to being noticed by visitors to the house. 'Babs Guthrie. I'm the housekeeper.' Her voice was little more than a whisper. She turned back to the hallway and closed the door behind her.

Something was niggling away in the back of Sophie's mind like an irritating itch but, whatever it was, it wouldn't come into focus. She brushed the thought aside and walked forward to the good-looking woman standing beside the fireplace. She was there for effect, Sophie thought. This large, high-ceilinged room must be expensive to heat but it was pleasantly warm, as the large hall had been. Lady Braycombe was still watching her carefully, weighing her up, probably. She'd be wondering what was behind the visit, scrolling through her memory, trying to identify a possible cause. She was wearing a fashionable cashmere top, peach-coloured trousers and tan shoes. She looked relaxed yet elegant.

'Good morning,' she said, her voice quiet and measured. 'Babs said you were a chief superintendent, is that right?'

'Yes. Sophie Allen. Though I'm not normally based here in Somerset. I head up the Wessex Serious Crimes Unit.'

The woman stepped forward and held out her hand. Sophie took it and shook it gently. The skin was dry and cool, the fingers thin but with soft skin. Even so, Sophie guessed that the woman was tense under the slightly haughty exterior.

'Well, good for you. What do you want to see me about? Is it something quick or do we need a rather longer conversation?'

Sophie pursed her lips. 'It's about events more than a decade ago. More like two decades, in fact.'

'Hmm. We'll sit then. I'll ring for coffee.' She pressed a button on the wall and indicated for Sophie to sit in one of the three chairs set around the fireplace. The housekeeper, Babs, appeared so swiftly that Sophie guessed she'd been waiting for the signal.

'Coffee for two, Babs. And have one yourself.'

'Certainly, ma'am.'

Sophie settled herself into one of the chairs, thinking that much of the furniture looked stylish. The chairs appeared to have been recently reupholstered, fitting in with her general observations about the state of the old house. And its main occupant.

She decided to take the initiative. 'Twenty years ago, you loaned a painting to an art exhibition in Watchet. A Gainsborough. I understand it was stolen. Would you tell me about it, please?'

Lady Braycombe frowned. 'Are you from some kind of specialist art team within the police?'

Sophie kept her answer short. 'No. I run a murder unit. It spans three counties. Somerset, Wiltshire,' she paused. 'And Dorset.'

She noticed the surprise on the woman's face at the remark about murder, and the second slight flicker at the mention of Dorset. Lady Braycombe ran a knuckle along her lower lip as she gathered her thoughts.

'Yes, you have the basic facts. I don't see how I can expand on what you already know.'

'How did it come to be on display at the exhibition? All the other artwork was from local artists, as far as we know, and was for sale. Nothing else remotely matched the value of that painting. So why was it there?'

The woman cleared her throat. 'It was when my husband was still alive. He dabbled in art and was patron of a local art appreciation group. When he heard about the exhibition, he offered the Gainsborough as a centrepiece in order to attract more visitors. That would mean more sales for his artist *acquaintances*.'

Sophie noticed that she hadn't used the word friends, choosing a more formal alternative. And the way she'd articulated the word 'acquaintances' made clear her personal feelings about the other artists. 'Go on.'

'It appeared to work. I seem to remember him saying that sales were good. Although the commercial aspects were rather dwarfed by the theft. The painting was recovered, though.'

The two women looked up as the door opened and the housekeeper appeared, carrying an ornate tray. Two rather delicate cups of coffee were deposited on the small tables beside their chairs.

'That will be all, Babs,' Lady Braycombe said.

Sophie took a sip and fought the urge to grimace. Economy-standard instant, probably from the local supermarket. Maybe even powdered rather than granules. Was everything for show, then?

'And the details of the recovery?'

'Well, that should be on record with your people, shouldn't it? My understanding was that the thief probably didn't realise what he'd stolen and took fright. He left it outside the town's police station a few days later, wrapped in a plastic bag of some kind. I'd only just made a start on the insurance claim forms so I felt able to abandon them, thankfully.'

'The thief was still charged, though, despite returning the paintings he'd stolen.'

'Of course. But we're not vindictive people, Chief Superintendent. We did all we could to influence the magistrate to take a lenient line. Fortunately, he did and delivered a suspended sentence.'

'So everyone was happy?' Sophie said.

The woman shrugged. 'You could put it like that, I suppose. Really, I fail to see why that episode from twenty years ago is of such interest today, and to such a senior officer as yourself.'

'One of the artists who took part in that exhibition was Benjamin Carlyon. His was the body found washed up in Watchet harbour two weeks ago. In recent years he lived a few miles from here. He was murdered and his body dumped into the river near Watchet the night of the big storm. Does that help to explain things?'

Lady Braycombe's face displayed surprise but Sophie was aware that her eyes changed little, instead maintaining the distant, cautious look they'd shown since the interview started. Sophie guessed that the woman was already aware of Carlyon's death, maybe from coverage in the press. In that case, why feign surprise?

'That's all quite shocking. But I fail to see the connection to me or events from twenty years ago.'

'In a murder inquiry, we follow up every possible avenue. And we do so until we are convinced that the lead is a dud one.' Sophie paused for a few seconds. 'May I see the painting in question? The Gainsborough?'

This time the look of surprise was genuine, and it took a short while for the woman to regain her composure. Finally, she said, 'Of course. It's in a locked room upstairs, but on display. It was always George's pride and joy.'

Sophie took another sip of coffee for courtesy's sake, then followed Lady Braycombe out of the room and up the stairway. She was asked to wait while the woman went into a small room for a few minutes. When she came out, she had a key in her hand which she used to unlock another nearby door. She switched on the lights.

There, on the far wall, was a small landscape, undoubtedly in the style of Gainsborough. Sophie was no art expert but thought it looked beautiful. That wasn't the point, of course. It wasn't its beauty that was in dispute in her mind. It was the painting's authenticity.

'Did you get it checked after it was recovered?' she asked.

'What? What do you mean?'

'Did you call in a Gainsborough expert to examine and verify it, considering that it had just been stolen?'

Lady Braycombe stood, mouth narrowed in anger. 'What are you saying?' she finally said.

'Benjamin Carlyon was a skilled artist. Gainsborough was one of his own favourites. What I'm saying is, did you check that the returned painting, this one in front of us, wasn't a clever forgery?'

Lady Braycombe put a hand to her head. 'George did all that. He was the art lover, not me.'

'You were more the business half of your partnership? Is that what you mean? After all, you said that it was you who started filling in the insurance forms for the painting.'

'I suppose so, yes. George had no head for business. He was more interested in this estate, not that he was particularly good at running it. Along with the paintings, of course.'

'What was your original area of work, Lady Braycombe? Before you married your husband.'

'I worked in finance and insurance. That's how we met; through some insurance I was organising for him.'

Sophie chose not to continue with this particular aspect of the conversation. There was a lot here that needed further thought and some detailed checking.

'Do many people ask to have a look at the painting?'

'A few, yes. It's probably the most valuable thing I possess, other than the house and the estate. I don't really know what to do with it.'

Sophie turned and walked out of the room. Even more to think about, if the painting's future was in doubt.

Lady Braycombe locked the room and pocketed the key, then led Sophie down the stairs.

'Are you aware of any young women with Down's syndrome who live locally?' the detective asked.

Again, a flash of surprise crossed the woman's face. 'No. Why do you ask?'

'It's possible there's a connection to the murder we're investigating. Do you own some of the local farms, Lady Braycombe? I understand a few of the farmers around here are tenants rather than owning their farms.'

'Yes, several. But even so, it's a struggle to keep the finances balanced. Landowners are the new poor, you know.' She sounded bitter.

Sophie turned as she reached the bottom of the stairway. 'There's something else I'd like to ask you. Did you also used to own farms in Dorset?'

The woman gave her a guarded look. 'We did years ago, but I was forced to sell several properties when George died, to settle the claim for inheritance tax.'

'Did you offer them to the tenants as a first option? That seems the fair thing to do.'

'I can't remember. I probably did. Why's that important to you? What on earth does it have to do with this business over the dead body in Watchet?'

'Probably nothing. I'm just curious, that's all. One of us may need to see you again, Lady Braycombe.'

The older woman scowled. 'I want my lawyer here next time.'

'As you wish.'

Sophie smiled to herself as she walked out to her car. Lady Braycombe had given away more than she probably realised. And the needling about the farms she'd sold years earlier had obviously riled the woman. She'd had spots of high colour in her cheeks as she'd shown Sophie to the door. Anger. But she'd been unable to express it fully for fear of letting something important slip. The woman clearly had some secrets she wanted to keep hidden. But what were they and how did they relate to the investigation?

* * *

The early evening briefing was one of the busiest the team had held in recent times. Every single unit member had something to report: suspicions confirmed, new leads to investigate, facts to corroborate. They'd made huge progress in the investigation, and all in a single day. Polly felt the need to bring the team back down to earth.

'I know we've made significant progress today, and it does make me more optimistic that we'll solve this thing, but we're not necessarily much further forward in terms of hard facts. And we're still left facing two entirely different motives for Carlyon's murder. Was it to do with the Down's girl, Maddy? Or was it connected somehow with that art theft? We're dealing with a recent death but with motives that seem to stretch back two decades. A lot of the evidence is historic. Some potential witnesses are dead or have moved away to God knows where. We stay focussed and build on what we've achieved today.' She turned to Sophie, who would be heading back to Dorset at the end of the meeting. 'Anything to add, Sophie?'

'I think it's beginning to unravel. If we keep picking at the loose ends, things will start to give. There appear to be two strands. Tracing Maddy, the Down's girl, and her mother, Barbara, for one. And following up on the art theft, the other. But don't discount the possibility that they're connected somehow. And someone needs to check out Jackie Spring's thoughts, that the girl, and possibly her mother, have been living in the shadows for years, somewhere up on the moor. A farm, or a smallholding. Why not use Jackie herself for it? She and the local bobby, her boss, seem to make a good team and wouldn't draw too much attention to themselves. Why not let them loose on that part?'

Polly looked satisfied. 'Sounds good.' She was about to add more but stopped when she saw a sudden frown appear on Sophie's face. 'What is it?'

'Lady Braycombe's housekeeper. I've just realised. Her name is Babs. She's a Barbara and she's from the right area, up on the moor. And she's about the right age. Shit. Why didn't I spot it while I was there?'

CHAPTER 28: CHECKING THE FACTS

Saturday, Week 2

It was sunny on Exmoor, although the coastal strip had been in cloud when Sarah Levy and Jackie Spring had set out in the squad car from Watchet. Jackie was driving. Sarah, her boss and close friend, was feeling tired after being kept awake for several hours during the night by a child with earache.

'Penicillin, that's the stuff,' Jackie told her as she took the car round another bend on the uphill drive. 'If Keith gets her to the doctor promptly, then spoons a dose inside her right away, she'll probably be back to normal by the time you get home at the end of your shift. You worry too much.'

'Isn't that what all parents do?' Sarah said. 'We can't help worrying, can we? Keith's worse than me.'

'Yeah, well, Keith breaks the gender mould, doesn't he. Actually, I like the sound of a partner who does his fair share of worrying. I think Tony might be the same.'

Sarah turned in her seat and looked at her. 'Well, that's a turn-up. You're referring to Tony as your partner now, are you? Fast work, you hussy.'

'What? You were encouraging me only a week or so ago. Now you're calling me a hussy. Some friend you are!' She stopped the car outside Donny Lomax's house in Laxford. 'Here we are. I hope he doesn't faint when he sees me. I've given him a right rollicking the last couple of times we've met.'

There was no answer to their ringing of the doorbell or rapping on the door. Jackie walked around the side of the house to see if he was in the back garden, but it was deserted. She returned to the car with Sarah.

'He's probably at work,' Sarah said. 'According to the info I was sent he works on Highcroft Farm, a few miles west of Braycombe. So that'll be our next port of call, I suppose.' She glanced at the map. 'It's quite close to where that copper was stolen. Should we take a look? Details are really scarce on the crime report.'

'Why not? I've always thought he was up to no good. I'm not saying he's a killer, mind. I'm not sure he's got that in him, but I wouldn't be surprised if he turns out to be a bit of a shady character in other ways.'

She pulled the car back onto the road and headed west through Braycombe towards Highcroft Farm, though she turned off down a narrow lane before reaching the farm.

'The substation's along here somewhere.'

It didn't take long for them to find the spot. The fenced enclosure was set back from the road beyond a wide grass verge. A power company van was parked in front of the grassy strip, so Jackie pulled in beyond it. A worker was loading tools into the back of the van as if he was clearing up after a work session. He looked up as the two uniformed officers climbed out of their car.

'Good morning,' Sarah said. 'Is this the place where several coils of copper wire went missing a couple of weeks ago?'

'Yeah, that was here,' the man replied. 'Got into trouble big time for that.'

'How did it happen?'

'Convenience theft. I had an apprentice with me. Useless arsehole. I asked him to put everything back in the van or lock it inside the compound. The lazy sod couldn't be bothered to do it properly but never told me.'

'Lost his job, did he?'

'Yeah. It was the last straw as far as I was concerned. Useless in every way. Someone must have spotted the copper lying there, ripe for the taking.'

'About a thousand pounds' worth, that's what we've been told. That right?'

The man grimaced. 'Guess so. The cocky young bugger wanted me to cover for him, but he'd pissed me off on too many occasions. I mean, there are limits.'

'Had it been left there for long?'

He shook his head. 'Nah. That same day, late afternoon. I came looking for it the next day but it had vanished. The boss was not best pleased.'

'I can imagine. We'll keep our eyes peeled and our ears open. If we hear anything we'll keep you posted. That's the best we can do.'

The man shrugged. 'Okay.'

Jackie spoke. 'What was your apprentice's name?'

'Wayne Lacey. He's from Bridgwater. The boss back at the depot gave him a right grilling but we don't think it was deliberate. He's just so bloody empty-headed. No good for this job. You can't afford to be slapdash with fifty-thousand-volt equipment.'

The two cops drove off, continuing along the lane rather than turning.

'It's along here somewhere,' Jackie said. 'The spot where Lomax said he hit something.'

The road dipped into a wooded area, then turned several sharp corners.

'This must be it.'

She slowed and they took a close look as they passed through the basin. The woods on either side looked dark and gloomy.

'I can see how it happened,' Sarah said. 'The water would have been draining down here and washing across the road. But I take your point exactly, Jackie. Why would he have been out at that time of night in that weather?' She studied the map. 'This is a back lane to the farm he works on. It's not the direct route but if he came along here on his way home from work and spotted those coils of copper, well, that might explain it.'

They continued along the narrow lane until its junction with a wider road, then carried on uphill. They soon reached Highcroft Farm and pulled into the farmyard. A worried-looking woman came out of the farmhouse to greet them.

'I was at the window and saw you drive in. I hope it's nothing serious. I'm Hilary Bright.'

'Not at all,' Sarah replied. 'I'm PC Sarah Levy and this is Special Constable Jackie Spring. We wondered if Donny Lomax was working this morning.'

'He's up in the top field with Kevin, my husband. I think they're working on a boundary fence.' She looked at their car. 'I don't think you can make it up there in that car. Give me a moment and I'll drive you up in the runaround.' She pointed to an old SUV parked at the side of the yard. 'I've got a flask of coffee ready for them. I'll just check on the kids. They're watching telly.'

Within a couple of minutes they were inside a rather more robust vehicle than their squad car, bouncing their way up a track towards a low ridgetop, while talking about life on the farm. They finally clambered out of the mud-flecked vehicle and approached the two men who'd been working on the fence, now standing looking at them. Hilary passed the flask to her husband, explaining that the two police officers wanted to speak to Donny. She and her husband stood back, sipping coffee and watching discreetly.

Sarah and Jackie walked a few yards away, indicating that Donny should follow them. Sarah then turned to face him.

'Good morning, Mr Lomax. I hope you don't mind us disturbing you at work, but we have several important questions about that stormy night when you say you were out on the road.'

'Couldn't it wait?' he asked angrily. 'It's a bit much coming here like this. I'd have come in if you'd wanted.'

'Well, we were up here anyway on other business. We're investigating a load of copper that was stolen that night. Did you see anything suspicious?'

They watched a series of expressions cross his face. 'No,' he finally said.

'You see, the copper was taken from outside the substation. It's only, what, a quarter mile from where you reported hitting something on the road.'

'Well, it wasn't a load of copper I hit,' he replied, angrily.

Sarah gave him a thin smile. 'Mr Lomax, we weren't implying it was, as you well know. Did you take that copper?'

'No, I bloody didn't,' he said loudly. He looked around, as if in protestation at such a ludicrous suggestion. 'Why would I?'

'Valuable stuff, copper,' Sarah suggested. 'Easy to sell on, if you know the right people.'

'Well, I don't,' he said. His flickering eyes said differently, though. They had fear in them.

'Here's the thing, you see,' Sarah said, calmly. 'The electricians finished quite late for a Friday. About seven or thereabouts. The weather was already deteriorating when they left. You and Mr Bright worked late that day, securing things against the coming storm, according to Mrs Bright. The main road was temporarily closed because of an RTA, so you'd have gone home that way. Do you see what I'm getting at here, Mr Lomax?'

Jackie, who was watching him closely, noticed the flickering uncertainty in his eyes and spoke. 'Now's the time to tell us if you were involved. Before it escalates any further.'

He shook his head. 'No. It weren't me.' He moved away, back towards the fence he'd been working on.

Jackie noticed a man standing on the other side of the farm boundary, watching what was going on. He was wearing threadbare clothes and had a slightly vacant expression on his face. He saw Jackie looking at him.

'He does good work,' the man said. 'I do good work too. That's why I get good food. 'Cos of my good work.'

'Glad to hear it,' she replied. 'What's your name?'

'Gordon,' came the reply. 'Have you found Billy yet?'

'Who's Billy?' she asked.

The man must have become aware that everyone was watching him. He started shifting his balance awkwardly from one foot to the other.

'Billy does good work. But he's gone. He's got lost somewhere.'

The man suddenly turned and walked away, down the hill.

'What farm's that?' Sarah asked of Hilary.

'Greymoor. Not that we could tell you much about them. They keep themselves to themselves.'

CHAPTER 29: ATTEMPTED INTIMIDATION

'Shall we check it out?' Sarah asked, as the two uniformed constables climbed back into their squad car.

'Why not?' came the reply from her junior colleague. 'We've got an unidentified dead body and an apparently missing man called Billy. I'd say it was worth a nosy visit, but you're the boss.'

Jackie turned out of the yard and took the car about a mile further west to a farm that was in a less sheltered position, closer to the edge of the moor, then into the yard. She looked around her. The immediate surroundings were markedly less tidy than the farm they'd just left. Greymoor's yard was surrounded by old buildings, all looking as though they could do with a good clean and tidy. Dogs began to bark from somewhere beyond the farm buildings as they heard the duo's voices. A few bits of litter swirled around in some of the corners, though a pretty flower bed was situated near the main door of the farmhouse, with daffodils and crocuses blooming brightly.

'Well, someone tries to do their bit,' she said to Sarah.

The door to the house opened and a thickset middle-aged man came down the steps towards them. He stopped and waited, arms folded defensively in front of him, and eyes narrowed, watching the two officers approach.

'Good morning,' Sarah said.

'What do you want?' came the response.

'Checking on the local farms. We've just come from your neighbours at Highcroft.'

The man nodded slowly but said nothing. Jackie, standing back a little, saw a slight movement from one of the upper floor windows. She could just make out the vague shape of a face, but it lacked any detail. Could it be a woman? It was hard to be sure.

'Have any of your workers gone missing recently?' Sarah asked. 'A body was found in the nearby woods last week. We've been having problems getting it identified.'

'No,' came the only answer.

'Possibly someone called Billy?'

The man frowned. 'I said no.'

'Do you mind if we have a look around?' Sarah asked.

'Yeah, I do mind. This is my farm and I like my privacy. If I need the cops, I'll call you. If someone goes missing, I'll call you. But you can't just turn up here and demand to look around the place. That ain't right.'

'I haven't made any demand, as you put it. I asked.'

'Well, you can ask all you like. It ain't gonna happen.'

Jackie became aware that another man had stepped out of one of the outhouses and was watching them, a heavy spanner in his hand. She began to feel uneasy. Something didn't feel right. This wasn't the same kind of welcome they'd received on other farms.

'There's been a theft of copper wire in the area. Have you experienced anything like that? Any kind of theft from your farm?'

Jackie had to give Sarah credit. Her boss wasn't about to weaken her stance in the face of such obvious intimidation.

'No.'

It was difficult to read anything in the man's implacably expressionless face. It would be a brave thief who tried to steal anything from Greymoor Farm. Jackie suspected that this man wouldn't call the police if it did ever happen. He'd probably administer his own form of justice to anyone found making the attempt. She decided to follow her boss's example and show that intimidation didn't work, not while she was in uniform anyway.

'You don't get any problems from people on that stretch of public footpath crossing your west fields?' she asked.

The man's head swivelled to face her. 'What are you talking about?'

'The map shows a path crossing two of your fields. It drops down from the moor, then across your land. It comes out at the lane, down the track opposite and into the woods. Quite close to where that man's body was found, in fact.'

'People don't use it.'

'I don't see how walkers can avoid it. It's the only official path in the area coming down from the moor. Plenty of hikers must come that way.' Jackie was determined not to give way.

'They stay the other side of the fence.'

'Across Highcroft Farm? Yes, we saw that the Brights had put in a temporary permissive path across their fields. But the official one is on your land. Have you blocked off access?'

He sneered. 'What's it to you? It's not a police matter. It's the council.'

'You're right. But it becomes one if the council put an order on the path, the landowner ignores it, someone protests and there's a breach of the peace.'

'Really? Well, that won't bother me. I'm just the tenant, see.'

'So who is the landowner if it isn't you?'

A flicker of uncertainty crossed his face. 'Why should I tell you?' he said, his face set. 'I've wasted enough time. I've got stuff to do, so you can shove off now.' He turned and went back inside.

Jackie looked again at the upstairs window just in time to see the face turn away and the net curtains sway back into position. She was sure it had been a young woman. They turned and walked back towards their car, still being watched by the tall, thin man from the outhouse doorway.

They climbed back into their car and drove away. Jackie noticed that Sarah's face was set grimly.

'Well, that was interesting and no mistake,' Sarah said.

'You're right. Dealing with Donny Lomax is child's play compared to that guy and his mate.' Sarah flicked through some notes that she had in her bag. 'Bryn Guthrie. I think it might be worth doing some checking when we get back to the station.'

'We were being watched from an upstairs window,' Jackie said. 'I think it was a young woman but can't be sure.'

'In that case, we certainly need to do some checking. And report it to the crime unit. Your pal Polly will be interested.'

'My pal? Is that what you think?' She laughed. 'With her it's all work, Sarah. Plain and simple. I'm not taken in by their friendly manner, her and that chief super.'

Despite her remark, she pulled over and called Polly before turning onto the main road. The boss needed to know about the unwarranted friction shown by that moody farmer.

* * *

Sophie Allen was about to head back to Dorset. 'I'll be back in a couple of days,' she said to Polly, as she headed out of the door. 'Can you get someone to check up on that Babs, the Braycombe housekeeper? Something about her has been niggling me but I just can't think what it is. These two lines of inquiry might be linked in some strange way, though I'm a bit baffled how. Could it be her? And listen, it's probably best to stay at arm's length from Braycombe House until we're sure. People from these old landowning families still carry clout, in ways hidden from us mere mortals. That woman would have been straight on the phone to her lawyer after I left. The old boys' network will have been activated and we need to tread carefully. But there's a secret hidden up there somewhere, I'm sure of it.'

Barely ten minutes after Sophie had left, Polly's laptop pinged to signal the arrival of an email. This turned out to be an important one, from the county pathologist. She called Rae and Ade across to discuss the contents.

'The bruising on the body found in the woods,' she told them. 'The doc's been looking at the scan results and thinks some of it was almost certainly made prior to the road accident. He's confirmed that the victim might well have been seriously assaulted shortly beforehand, maybe earlier that day or the day before. And something else.' She pointed to the relevant line in the email. 'There were faint marks on his leg above his right ankle.'

'I remember a mention of those,' Ade said. 'He put them down to some kind of rash.'

'Well, he's now wondering if they're residual marks from a rope burn. It's possible our victim was tethered just before the accident.'

Rae was thinking hard. 'Do you think he was beaten up, tied up, then escaped somehow? That might explain how he came to be out in the open that night. No one else was. The weather was just dreadful, by all accounts.'

'Donny Lomax was out, too,' Polly pointed out.

CHAPTER 30: ASSAULT ON THE MOOR

Sunday

Justin Penhale was back at Bynehill View, the house on the moor, starting the onerous task of going through his dead uncle's possessions now that the property had been released by the police. Who else was there to do it? His mother's health was deteriorating. Justin's sister lived in New Zealand and hadn't yet managed to arrange a visit to this side of the world. And the police still hadn't traced this missing daughter, Maddy, the young woman with Down's.

He spent the first part of the morning in the ground floor rooms, sorting through papers and documents, most of which could be safely trashed. He then climbed the stairs to the studio, intending another look at his uncle's paintings. How valuable were they? Would a small number be suitable to be retained by family members for sentimental reasons?

He glanced out of the window, the one at the back of the house, and was intrigued to see a short flash of light from a low ridge some half mile from the house. He remembered seeing something similar the day he'd first visited the house, when the police forensic teams had just left. Why would someone be out on the moor at that particular spot? Unless, of course, the place was being watched and someone had moved their binoculars momentarily.

He fixed the location in his mind, then took out his phone to call the police on the number that woman officer, Rae Gregson, had given him. Blast. No signal. It was always erratic up here. He sent her a short text message instead, then headed for the door.

He left via the front of the house, trying, as far as possible, to stay out of sight. Luckily the small orchard provided cover and he dashed from there to a clump of shrubs, then found a dip in the ground which ran east. His plan was to circle around to the ridge and find a way to come upon the suspicious spot from the rear. Would it work? He didn't know. He wasn't a countryman, after all, and he'd never felt at ease when out on moorland like this. There were areas of bog, sporadic pools of black water, strangely shaped hummocks of coarse grass and clumps of heather to impede him. Nevertheless, he made steady progress, working his way slowly anticlockwise in a rough semicircle.

He finally found himself at a point almost due north of the house and about half a mile away. He descended a rise and spotted an old Land Rover parked some twenty yards away. It was empty. Could it be there for a wholly innocent and legitimate reason? A rough track wound away westwards, probably heading towards the road. Maybe the vehicle was owned by a gamekeeper or a wildlife photographer. The flash of light he'd spotted could have been caused as the vehicle turned, catching the sunlight as it did so. Justin took a photo on his phone, then walked past the vehicle.

There didn't seem to be anyone about. He climbed the slope of the low ridge and rounded a rocky outcrop. A man was lying on the ground, a pair of binoculars beside him. As Justin watched, the man picked them up and took a look, seemingly pointing them at the house.

Justin looked around. There was nothing else to look at, not in that southerly direction. The view here was particularly bleak. There were a few trees in the distance that might provide some shelter for birds, but this spot was much too far away to see anything in detail. A legitimate birdwatcher would be much closer to the small copse. Justin took a couple more photos, then pocketed his phone.

'What are you looking at?' he called out.

The effect of his words was startling. The man jerked round, mouth open in astonishment. He rose and his manner quickly changed to being confrontational.

'What's it to you?' he said.

'Well, you appear to be watching my house. I can't see anything else of interest.'

'Your house?' came the reply.

Justin nodded. 'It belonged to my uncle. He's dead. It now belongs to my mother and me.'

The man looked at him, his face a mixture of confusion and mistrust. 'It's open land, this is. I can be here if I fucking want to.'

Justin began to feel uneasy. He hadn't expected such an aggressive manner. Maybe he was just too naive. After all, there was unlikely to be an innocent explanation for this man to be keeping an eye on him while visiting his dead uncle's house.

'My uncle was murdered,' Justin went on. 'The police have only just finished with it. And now you're here, watching it. What am I supposed to think?'

'I'm not watching the house,' the man hissed. 'Just mind your own fucking business.'

Justin decided that there was little point in prolonging the conversation. It could only end in trouble. He turned around and started to walk away, ascending the faint path to the top of the rocky outcrop. He'd just started the descent the other side when he heard a noise behind him. He started to turn but felt a searing pain in his head. The world went black.

* * *

Rae and Tommy had just finished crosschecking the latest batch of records of women with the name of Barbara or Babs when Rae's phone indicated the arrival of a text message. She frowned when she saw who it was from and frowned even more when she saw how long it had taken to arrive. Justin Penhale had included the time he was setting out on foot from the house in the text, along with a few details of what he'd seen and how he planned to check up on the flash of reflected sunlight.

Rae phoned him back but to no avail. She went to find Polly to report the strange message and got the go ahead to check on the man's well-being.

She and Tommy reached Bynehill inside half an hour. Justin's car was parked outside but the place was empty. Rae unlocked the door and dashed up the stairs to the studio.

'I'd guess he was up here when he saw something suspicious,' she said, looking out of the window. 'This is where he said he saw a flash of light. Let's see if he's still out there somewhere.'

She glanced at her watch and frowned. It was more than two hours since he'd sent the message. Surely he should have been back by now? The two detectives hurried out of the house and headed for the distant ridge, picking their way through marshy areas of ground, and trying their best to avoid boggy pools of dank water.

'It's still sopping wet from all that rain a few weeks ago,' she complained. 'It must have been a real deluge up here. We've had some rain since but not enough to make it as wet as this.'

They clambered on, thankful when the boggy heath started to give way to drier and stonier ground. The rocky ridge was steeper than it appeared from a distance, with a few low faces that were almost sheer. As they topped the ridge, they could see a track circling west, leading back to the road. They hurried across and quickly spotted tyre tracks in the gritty surface.

'They're still sharp,' Tommy commented. 'Left not long ago.'

They retraced their steps towards the ridge, but this time kept to the northern side, the edge that faced the coast rather than Carlyon's house.

'Over there,' Tommy said, pointing. 'Look.'

Justin lay near a clump of heather, just below the ridge, his head in a shallow pool of peaty water. It looked as though he'd taken a tumble down the rocky outcrop. Rae felt for a pulse.

'It's there,' she said. 'But it's a bit weak.'

She slipped off her coat and draped it across his body. Tommy already had his police phone out, hoping for a signal. He was in luck. Weak but good enough to log an urgent request for an ambulance.

Polly's frustration was obvious when Rae called her at the same time. 'Bloody hell,' she said. 'Missed the action up there again.'

'Yes, but the chief super will feel even worse when she hears,' Rae responded. 'She's back in Dorset until tomorrow.'

Rae wasn't sure that Polly had caught this last comment. She realised that the phone had gone dead as she finished speaking.

Polly arrived rather sooner than Rae had expected. She must have broken every speed limit on the route, Rae thought, wryly. Those blue lights have their uses, after all.

* * *

'How is he?' Polly asked, when she arrived at Taunton's Musgrove Park Hospital two hours later.

Rae had driven behind the ambulance to provide police attendance should it be needed, and was now waiting in A & E.

'He'll survive, they think. But he's still in a coma. Anything interesting show up at the scene?'

Polly grimaced. 'He was lucky. You probably spotted it yourself when you found him. Left face down and unconscious in a pool of water. What are the chances? He'd be dead if his chin hadn't come to rest on that stone.'

Rae nodded grimly. 'That's what Tommy and I thought too. Someone left him for dead. But why? I just wonder if there's something in the house that might incriminate someone.'

Polly shook her head. 'They'd have taken it by now. They've had ample opportunity. No, my thoughts are that he saw who it was watching the place, and they didn't like that. Two people dead already, so does it matter if there's a third? Not to them. So we need to keep him safe and hope that he comes round and can identify who it was.'

Rae was still not satisfied. 'But there has to be a reason, boss. Why was he there, whoever it was? What was he up to?' She stayed silent for a few seconds, thinking hard. 'None of our lot or the forensic unit reported seeing anything suspicious. It was only Justin who spotted those flashes of sunlight. So maybe they're not there to keep an eye on the house. Maybe they're watching Justin himself.'

'But why? True enough, he stands to inherit. But is that a good enough reason?'

Rae shrugged. 'I don't think we'll know until we find out who assaulted him. It's a real puzzle.'

CHAPTER 31: THEY DON'T PLAY GAMES

Monday, Week 3

Rae didn't feel happy. This investigation was bothering her with its loose ends and its tantalising leads that ended up going nowhere. Surely something must link all of the strands together, if only she could spot what it was.

The team of detectives had just finished reviewing the weekend's events but nothing obvious had jumped out at them. At the end of the briefing, Polly summarised Jackie Spring's findings and something stirred in the back of Rae's brain. She waited until the team members had dispersed to their tasks, then approached Polly.

'Boss, can I go and speak to Jackie? There's something about what she reported that sounded odd, though I can't put my finger on it. I want to see if I can pull her out of her library job for an hour or two and pay a visit back to Carlyon's house. I don't think she's been inside yet, and she seems to be an ideas type of person. Maybe something will strike her.'

'Of course, but be gentle. We don't want to put her library job at risk.'

'Would I ever?' Rae laughed but noticed the worry in Polly's eyes. She must be feeling the pressure. Or was it something else? Polly rarely opened up about her personal life. It was far too easy to forget that senior police officers had their own family and relationship problems, ones that they often tried to hide from work colleagues. Maybe she, Rae, should have a quiet chat with Ade, the unit member who knew the boss best. But would even he have had a chance to get to know her? Probably not. Rae suspected that Polly was the kind of person who kept her worries to herself.

She made her way to the library, almost devoid of visitors this Monday morning, and approached Jackie. She put her suggestion to the woman and waited.

'Maybe I could. It's quiet enough in here to leave it in my colleague's hands for an hour or two. Is it that urgent?'

Rae shrugged. 'I don't know. I just want to take you up to the area around Carlyon's house, just to see if anything occurs to you. It might be a total waste of time, but who knows? You're local. You might see things through a different lens.'

The drive took half an hour, during which the pair chatted about their mutual back stories. The sun was out when they drew up at Carlyon's empty house.

'Just wander through it,' Rae said. 'Take your time. Speak out about anything that occurs to you.'

Jackie gave her a puzzled look. 'I'm no detective,' she said.

'I know you're not,' came the reply. 'But you are local. You might see things from a different angle. I mean in terms of local people, and the communities up here on the moor. Well, really, I don't know what I mean. I just thought it was worth a try.'

'Things aren't coming together very well, I take it?' Jackie was obviously perceptive.

Rae shook her head. 'But we'll keep plugging away.'

The duo wandered through the ground floor rooms, then went upstairs to the bedroom and the studio. Windows in the bedroom gave beautiful views to the south and east. The wide expanse of moorland seemed to glow in the spring sunlight, looking placid, almost welcoming. The studio's window gave a view to the north, although nothing could be seen beyond the ridge.

'It was in here that Justin spotted the reflected sunlight,' Rae said. 'Someone was watching this house from over near that ridge. That was where we found him, badly injured.'

'Can you take me there?' Jackie sounded alert. Had she thought of something?

'Of course.' Rae was intrigued but opted not to probe any further just now. If Jackie had thought of something, she'd tell her in her own good time.

'Can I take the binoculars from downstairs? I spotted them in the living room.'

'I don't see why not. I can't see Justin objecting. Though I do keep a set in the car.'

Jackie was becoming increasingly assertive. 'You might need them for yourself,' she replied. 'Bring them along.'

Rae retraced her steps of the previous day, heading for the ridge north of the house. They climbed the slope, then turned to look at the panorama spread out in front of them, the rear of the Carlyon house in the foreground. Rae swept her binoculars across the view, not sure what she was meant to be looking for. She noticed that Jackie was keeping hers focussed on somewhere due east.

'I thought so,' Jackie said.

'What am I meant to be looking at?' Rae asked.

'Across there, about two or three miles away. Do you see a couple of farms?'

Rae looked carefully. 'Yes.'

'Highcroft and Greymoor. Neighbouring farms, but very different in a lot of ways. Donny Lomax works on Highcroft. It's owned by the farmer, Kevin Bright. Nice person, even though he employs our dubious friend Mr Lomax. But Greymoor is a very different matter. The farmer is a tenant. Nasty bloke. Confrontational. He almost threatened my boss, Sarah, and me on Saturday when we were up there making enquiries. He's blocked off a public footpath that drops down from the moor and across his land. His neighbour's made a temporary permissive path, so people aren't stuck when they come down from the long-distance route from Exmoor. I think it's why that couple who found the second body ended up half lost.'

Rae felt disappointed. She'd been hoping for something a bit more useful than a closed footpath. There was something about the views from Carlyon's house. Something had stirred in her own mind when she'd first come across the solitary building, that day when she'd spotted Justin Penhale halfway up a ladder, trying to break in. But the slight flicker of an idea had never crystallised into something she could hold in her mind and examine. That was why she'd decided to bring Jackie up here, to see if she could spot something key.

'The thing is, if we can see the farms, they can see what's going on up here. They can see Carlyon's house. They can see if a car's parked out front.'

Rae began to see where Jackie was going with this idea. Had it been the lonely and vulnerable position of the house that had wormed its way into her consciousness but then been forgotten?

'So what you're saying is, if they see a car parked here, they might send someone up to have a snoop, to see what they're up to?'

'Exactly. And keep looking. Sweep a bit further east. What do you see?'

Rae did as she was asked. 'I can just make out the edge of Braycombe village, tucked in the valley.'

'Keep going.'

'There's a biggish house half hidden behind some trees. Is that what you mean?'

Jackie nodded. 'Braycombe House. They'd also be able to see what was going on up here.'

'So, we have a kind of triangle? The farms, the big house and Carlyon's house. All able to spot each other in clear weather. Is that what you mean?'

‘Yes. And shall I tell you a few other snippets that have come to light via the local gossip channels? They’ll all need checking, mind.’

Rae laughed. ‘Go on. I’m all ears.’

‘Guess who the landlord is for Greymoor Farm, the one with the prickly tenant?’

Rae’s smile disappeared. ‘Not the Braycombe Estate?’

‘Right first time. Lady Braycombe. And guess what other property, not a million miles from the spot we’re standing on, the estate owned until about six years ago?’

Rae’s jaw dropped. ‘You don’t mean Carlyon’s house, the one in front of us?’

‘Got it in one. Top marks, boss. You’ll go far. Rumour has it that the Braycombe Estate sold it to raise much-needed funds to help them through a cash-flow crisis. Less complimentary gossip claims that Lady Braycombe bought a property in Barbados about the same time.’

‘You know what? You’re wasted as a special constable. You ought to be in our unit.’

‘Well, thank you for the compliment but it’s all circumstance and supposition, isn’t it?’

So do you think someone across there is watching us right now?’

Jackie smiled grimly. ‘Probably. They’ll have spotted your car. But they won’t come and investigate, not after that fiasco yesterday. They’ll keep quiet for a while. That’s my guess.’

‘Well, Jackie, your guesses are obviously worth considering. Of course, we have a justified reason to pay them a visit now. Yesterday’s assault on Justin Penhale is being treated as attempted murder. Polly decided after hearing the doctor’s analysis of his injuries. Hit on the back of the head by a heavy stone. He was lucky to survive.’

‘Hmm. Nasty lot. They don’t play games, do they?’

‘No. And that possible missing farm worker you reported sounds intriguing. What did you say his name was? Billy?’

‘That’s right. But no one’s called it in officially. It’s just some comments made by an odd guy from Greymoor Farm.

Have you found Billy yet? That's what he said. And our friend Donny Lomax said that the self-same bloke had asked about someone called Billy before.'

'Shall we pay them a visit?'

'I'm game. Be prepared for some very unsubtle intimidation, though. The farm manager, a Bryn Guthrie, fancies himself as a bit of a thug. Maybe he is one, for all I know.'

'Right up my street, then. Let's go,' Rae replied.

CHAPTER 32: SHATTERED GLASS

The farmyard area of Greymoor seemed somehow quieter, more serene, than on Jackie's previous visit. She felt the altered atmosphere as soon as she stepped out of the car. No one stalked out of any of the outhouses. No one was lingering in a shadowy doorway, fingering a potential cudgel. Apart from the sound of a few hens clucking as they pecked at seeds scattered across a small patch of scrawny grass beside the flower bed, the place seemed deserted. Except for the house, that is. The sound of music drifted out of an open window beside the door. Probably the kitchen, Jackie thought. Of course, she was in plain clothes today. On her previous visit she'd been in uniform.

'Let me take the lead,' Rae said. 'But feel free to chip in.'

She climbed the two steps and rang the doorbell. It was quickly opened by a short woman with a somewhat round face and wispy hair. Rae frowned momentarily. Had she seen that face somewhere before? She couldn't be sure.

'Good morning. I'm Detective Sergeant Rae Gregson, Wessex Crime Unit. I wonder if I can ask you a few questions? We're trying to trace a missing man and we think he may be from around here.' She paused, waiting for a reply, but none came. The woman looked confused, so Rae took the initiative. 'May we come in?'

The woman stood aside, still looking undecided. Rae stepped inside. A small porch led directly into a large kitchen.

'This is lovely,' Rae said as she glanced around the spacious room. It was well fitted with modern storage units and clean, tidy worktops, in marked contrast to the shambolic state of the outside yard and sheds.

The woman gestured to the large central table, so Rae and Jackie sat down.

'It's Mrs Guthrie, isn't it?' Rae said.

The woman nodded nervously. 'I don't have long. I've got to go to work in another hour.'

'Oh, it won't take that long, I'm sure. It's only a few short, simple questions. Are you here by yourself this morning?'

'My husband is off getting supplies. He does it most Monday mornings.'

Rae noted the cautious way the woman had answered the question. She was picking her words carefully. Rae was also intrigued by the black clothes she was wearing. Didn't most women farmers live in jeans and loose shirts? Somehow this woman didn't fit the bill.

'Where do you work, Mrs Guthrie?'

'At Braycombe House.'

A shiver ran up Rae's spine. 'Does that mean you're the housekeeper there? If so, you met my boss a few days ago.'

'Did I? I don't remember. There are lots of visitors to the hall and my memory isn't what it was.'

Her eyes said different. Her gaze was nervously darting around the room. Rae was on full alert now. She wondered if she should make some excuses and leave in order to report back to Polly and Sophie. They might want to follow a specific strategy in their questioning because of the possible implications. But if she did so, the initiative would be lost. Moreover, the woman's husband would probably be back and would undoubtedly try to intimidate everyone, if Jackie's assessment of him was anything to go by. No. Better to keep going. The music from the radio momentarily ceased because of a gap between songs. Rae heard a creak from upstairs. They weren't alone in the house after all.

'Is your name Barbara? Babs?'

The woman nodded.

Rae suddenly realised why her face seemed familiar. She was the woman whose image had been captured on the hospital CCTV system two weeks earlier, attending with her daughter for a rushed check-up, after the girl had suffered a sexual assault.

Rae needed to think quickly. She realised that the woman was looking increasingly tense, and her expression was hardening into something resembling anger.

'Could I have a drink of water, please, Mrs Guthrie? It was a bit of a trek up from the police station and the sunshine has made me thirsty. Would that be okay?'

Babs stood up and moved to the sink, pulling a tumbler from an overhead cupboard.

Rae looked at Jackie and raised her eyebrows. Her colleague's expression showed that she, too, had realised the importance of the situation. There was a creak as an interior door was pushed open and a figure appeared, peering around the frame.

'Mum?'

It was a young woman with Down's. She had a smooth, pale complexion and extremely attractive almond-shaped eyes. She was wearing fitted jeans and a loose, multi-coloured top, and she glanced nervously at the two strangers. She was the young woman in Carlyon's portrait, beyond any shadow of doubt.

Rae took the bull by the horns. 'Are you Maddy?' she asked.

The young woman looked confused. 'Yes,' she said.

Babs dropped the glass of water that she'd been holding. The sound of the shattering glass echoed around the room.

'How old are you, Maddy?' Rae asked. 'I'd better explain. I'm a police detective.'

'Nineteen. But my birthday's next month. I'll be twenty then and out of my teens. Then the world's my oyster. That's what Billy used to say.'

'Who's Billy?'

'He worked here. He's gone now.'

Her mother hurried across the room and took Maddy by the elbow, as if to push her out of the room.

'Shush!' she said.

Before she could move any further, there was a loud bang as the door from the yard crashed open. Bryn Guthrie stood in the doorway, a tall, thin man behind him.

'What the . . .' Guthrie said, as his head swivelled and he took in the figures in the room. His gaze settled on Jackie. 'You again! Get the hell out,' he shouted, his face red with anger. He lunged forward but stopped as Rae rose and put her hand up, palm out in a pacifying gesture.

'Whatever it was you were thinking of doing, don't, Mr Guthrie. Any assault at this stage would land you in police custody. And then where would your family be? We'll leave and come back later because we have some questions for you, your wife and Maddy. But they can wait a short while.'

The tension in the room was almost unbearable. Maddy was sobbing. She turned away, retreating into the depths of the house. Rae heard stairs creak and assumed the girl was returning to her room. She decided to leave and give the family some time to calm down.

'We'll leave for a short while. But we will need to get to the bottom of some of the issues here. One of us will need to talk to Maddy.'

'She's vulnerable,' Babs said.

'I realise that, Mrs Guthrie. We're not unfeeling monsters, despite what you may think. We'll find a way of having someone she trusts present. That may be you, but the decision will be up to my boss.'

The two police officers left the farmhouse and returned to their car. Rae phoned Polly and reported the morning's events.

'I'll be with you inside half an hour,' Polly said.

In fact, she arrived in just over twenty minutes but was beaten by a large black Mercedes that drove into the yard a couple of minutes before her. A smartly-dressed man climbed out, glanced across at the two cops sitting in their car, and went into the farmhouse. He was carrying an expensive-looking briefcase.

'This is getting interesting,' Rae said to Jackie. 'A lawyer, I bet. And not a cheap one by the looks of things.'

Her guess was right. When Polly arrived and approached the house door, she didn't even need to ring the bell. The door was opened by the smartly-dressed man.

'I'm Paul Cooper, Mr Guthrie's lawyer,' he said. 'All inquiries should come to me from this point on. We're happy to answer any questions but only at meetings arranged by prior appointment at my office in Nether Stowey. Please phone my secretary to arrange a slot.' He handed his card across, went back inside and closed the door.

'Shit,' Polly said. 'Where on earth did he spring from? How can someone like Guthrie afford a top-drawer solicitor like him?'

'He can't,' Rae replied. 'He'll be Lady Braycombe's solicitor. That's my guess. It's getting to be a bit tangled, isn't it?'

'The understatement of the year. Bloody hell.'

'It might be time to play your secret weapon, boss.'

Polly looked puzzled. 'What?'

'The chief super. She eats oily lawyers like him for breakfast. She draws them in by playing it coy, then floors them with a punch to the nose. Proverbially, I mean.'

'I should bloody hope so. Though I wish I could give people like him a real punch on the nose. I'll get to do it one day and probably lose my job as a result.'

CHAPTER 33: WE DO DIGGING AND STUFF

Donny Lomax had a bee in his bonnet and, when that happened, he couldn't let the issue go. What were those two guys from Greymoor Farm up to? He knew they dealt in illegal scrap metal but there must be something beyond that. There were the seven or eight other men who seemed to live on the farm, in those ramshackle caravans. They were the ones he'd seen out searching the farm the previous week, presumably looking for someone called Billy. Donny was now convinced that Billy was the person he'd hit in the van that stormy night. But who was Billy? What was his link to Greymoor Farm? The man's disappearance had clearly created problems on the farm, judging by the effort that had gone into probing every dip, gully and hedgerow. Come to that, who were the people out searching the fields for the missing man? They were a real ragtag group of individuals; scruffily dressed, lean-looking, and somewhat vacant in their expressions. It was all a bit weird.

Although he'd been open with the cops about the collision, he'd steered clear of any mention of his contact with Bryn Guthrie and the other man, Harry, at Greymoor. Guthrie himself was intimidating enough, but Harry was, if anything, even worse. There must be a reason why they acted in that way. Why did they feel the need to scare people away?

What was there to hide? Were they up to something other than farming and the scrap metal business?

These kinds of questions kept turning over in Donny's mind while he was working. He was back in the top field again, tidying up around the rebuilt section of wall. He was pleased with the result of his recent efforts. He wasn't a formally trained drystone-waller, but that new length was bloody good. Even his boss, Kevin, had said so.

'Good work.'

Donny looked up with a start. That odd guy was there again. Gordon. That was his name. Middle-aged but very slow on the uptake.

'Hello, again,' Donny said. 'What are you doing up here?'

'Looking for Billy. I miss him. He's my best friend but he's gone.'

'Where's he gone?'

Gordon shrugged and looked vacant. 'He might not ever come back. It makes me sad.'

'Where do you live, Gordon?'

He pointed down to the farm buildings. 'I've got my own place. I'm really lucky. We're all really lucky. It's 'cos we do good work.'

'What kind of work?'

'We do digging and stuff. We go in a van. It's hard but we do good work.'

'Who tells you that you do good work?'

Gordon frowned. 'Harry and Mr Guthrie. And Mrs Guthrie. She gets our food. Sometimes Maddy brings our food.'

'You're not working today, though.'

Gordon shook his head solemnly. 'I got a leg injury. Then Maddy got hurt. Mr Guthrie's angry. The others are out at work but not me. Harry doesn't make me work as much anymore 'cos of my bad leg. I do some tidying work instead of Maddy and I look out for Billy in case he comes back.'

Donny looked at the strange, forlorn-looking man. 'Well, I've got work to do so I'd better be off. Nice to chat to you, Gordon.'

Gordon looked back at him, then scanned the wall once more.

'Good work.'

Donny finished throwing tools into the back of the pick-up, then climbed into the cab. What on earth was going on in that place? Donny was becoming concerned. He'd never thought of himself as having much of a social conscience, but something wasn't right across on Greymoor. The place was secretive; Guthrie and his foreman, Harry, seemed to be out and out bullies, and the gang of workers looked like zombies. It was an odd set-up and no mistake. But what could he do? He was already on their radar, judging by the threats made against him that time they'd taken the copper he'd nicked. And they knew who he was and where he worked. He needed to keep his head down and hope for the best.

An idea struck him. Was there a way he could get the copper back and return it to the substation? That might get the cops off his back. It was worth thinking about. The stuff might still be lying around in one of Greymoor's sheds. Maybe even the old rickety one he'd been in when he offloaded it. Was it worth having a look-see one quiet night? A bit chancy, so maybe not. One man murdered, another wandering in the woods and probably killed in that collision with his own vehicle, and a third seriously assaulted just yesterday, up near that lonely house on the moor, according to local gossip. They must all be connected somehow. And if he started to poke his nose in too far, he might suffer the same kind of fate. No harm in just watching the place though.

He drove back to Highcroft's farmyard and told Kevin Bright that the wall repair was finished and in good order. He helped with the cows until the end of the day, then wearily climbed into the cab of his old Land Rover and headed home. He couldn't think of a way out of his predicament except for the obvious one. Coming clean to the cops and owning up to the copper theft. Was he ready for the consequences, though? He'd have to make his mind up soon. Those two local women cops, they had him in their sights for sure. They'd made that clear on Saturday. He needed to stay ahead of them and do something before they pulled him in. Things were so bloody depressing.

CHAPTER 34: WIRE CUTTERS AND SHOTGUN

Tuesday, Week 3

Tommy Carter sniffed the air, clean and fresh up here on the Exmoor heights. Benjamin Carlyon must have known what he was doing when he bought this house. On a bright, fresh day like today the views were beautiful and the whole area seemed welcoming. He finished tying the laces of his boots and stood up. He wondered what Rae was doing. She had a mirror in her hand and was using it to reflect sunlight back in a southerly direction. She finally slid it back into the glove pocket of the car, then locked the vehicle.

'Ready?' Rae said, tucking some loose hair under her woolly hat.

Her colleague nodded as he slid the map into his pocket. 'So, we start by walking southwest but then slowly swing round south, then east?'

'That's the plan. We move in a flattened semicircle, keeping to the higher ground. That means Braycombe village should always be below us, in a sort of bowl. If we stay high, we'll be able to swing round behind Highcroft and then Greymoor farms.' She pointed south. 'Over there somewhere we should join one of the main Exmoor footpaths, the one that drops down through Greymoor. Have you got the wire cutters?'

Tommy patted his backpack as he slung it across his shoulders. 'And the twine.'

'Well, time to head off. It's about three miles as the crow flies, so about seven or eight for us. We're rendezvousing with Polly at half past eleven, so no time to waste.'

The two detectives set off, keeping their points of interest in sight. The idea had come from a walking map found in Carlyon's house, this route marked on it in red pen. Polly had speculated that many of Carlyon's landscape paintings had been captured from views on this very set of tracks. Moreover, it ended up at the farm where Maddy, his estranged daughter, lived. That rather peculiar farm by all accounts: Greymoor.

The first section was on a narrow, rough path that meandered slightly uphill, heading for the ridge that carried the long-distance route. The ground underfoot was mostly gritty, with an occasional peatbog blocking the most direct route. Even so, they made good progress. Rae stopped occasionally to take photos, both of views that Carlyon might have painted and of the path ahead, with both Greymoor Farm and Braycombe House in the distance, but creeping closer with every step. At these stops Tommy would flick through a set of images on his phone, taken of the landscapes Carlyon had painted. He was matching them up, working out the artist's exact location when he'd captured each scene.

Once on the ridge, they made more rapid progress. The path here was wider and had a drier base, tramped regularly by large numbers of people trekking across this part of Exmoor. It also sloped slightly downhill, slowly dipping towards the valleys in the east, although they in turn were hemmed in by the distant heights of the Quantock Hills, a hazy blur on the horizon.

Rae glanced at her watch. 'Phew, we're slightly ahead of schedule. Time for a coffee break.'

Tommy looked surprised. 'I only brought water, boss.'

'Craig and I have done enough camping and trekking over the last few years to appreciate a bit of luxury when we're out,' Rae said. 'The kitchen staff at our hotel did it for me. Don't worry, there's enough for two.' She peered inside her bag. 'And they've popped in some flapjack too. The benefits of my charming personality.' She laughed.

'This is beautiful,' Tommy said as they found a nearby rock to sit on.

'Well, don't relax too much. There's likely to be fireworks of some kind when we start down the footpath at Greymoor. Or, I should say, where the official line of the footpath ought to be. Remember, we want any confrontation filmed, so check your bodycam is switched on. By the way, we're now on the path that couple were using. The ones that stumbled on the body in the woods, down below the farm.'

'Do we need to track their route beyond the farm as well?'

Rae shook her head. 'Already done by the local cops.'

'This all seems a bit vague, boss. It's a great way to spend a morning, but how important is it really?'

'Well, we've got it cleared right up to the chief super. After she read the report that I put together with Jackie Spring, she realised the importance of the geographical layout of these three or four places. She wonders if Carlyon made this walk on a regular basis, heading across towards the farm where his daughter lived. That was once he found out about her, though we don't know when that was. Did he find out just recently or was it years ago? Not that we're likely to find the answer to that problem this morning. And it's all coordinated with what Polly and Ade are planning, even the chief super herself. Anyway, why question what we're told to do when it's something as enjoyable as this? We've been slogging our guts out for weeks, Tommy. Let's just count our blessings.' She looked around her as she finished her coffee. 'The path passes by a clump of bushes about half a mile ahead. I'll need a loo stop and that'll be ideal. One of the drawbacks of my surgery. I need to wee a lot.' She laughed. 'Saved my life, though.'

Tommy was curious. He'd never had the nerve to ask Rae for any details about her previous life. 'What do you mean, boss?'

'I couldn't have gone on living the way I was, not really, not as a bloke. Everyone tries to fight it for a while but it's like an emotional avalanche when it finally gets too much. It's either go ahead with the transition or suffer a total breakdown. With me, it was either suicidal madness or do it. No contest, really.' She stood up. 'Time to move.'

The going got easier as they swung further round to the east and slowly descended to lower levels. The landscape around them gradually changed to a less harsh type of environment and the footpath was easier underfoot. They were approaching the outermost field of Greymoor Farm. Ahead lay the original line of the footpath. Tommy looked at the map.

'It ought to be a stile,' he said. 'You can see the location but there's barbed wire across it.'

They could see that the trodden path had been diverted north towards the neighbouring farm. Tommy took out binoculars.

'There's a rough sign next to a stile. Temporary permissive path.'

'That'll be the farmer there. One Kevin Bright. Obviously has a social conscience, unlike this lot.' She took a deep breath. 'Ready? Switch your bodycam on.'

Tommy took out the wire snippers. He twisted the two snipped lengths of wire into coils and tied them to the left post. Once they'd clambered over the wooden struts, they looked around. The half-rotten stumps of the old approach steps for the stile were peeking out from a clump of grass. Presumably they'd been flung there by Guthrie or one of his workers.

Rae held the map out and laid a compass on top of the page. The old path should head directly downhill from here to a gateway. One was still there, permitting access from one field to the next. But there was no discernible path connecting the two points, though there was a slight discoloration on the grassy surface. Presumably a century or more of tramping feet had compressed the underlying soil such that the grass didn't grow quite as well along the line, despite its lack of recent use. A few sheep looked up nervously as they noticed the two unexpected figures making their way across the field.

The duo had managed to cross two more fields before they spotted two men approaching them from the direction of the farmhouse, a tall, thin man who was carrying a shotgun, and a stockier man. Rae checked the compass and the map once again, ensuring they were walking the line of the official path, as registered by the county council. At the same time, Tommy turned so that his back was facing the oncoming men and spoke into his phone. The two detectives then stayed where they were, facing the oncoming duo.

'Get off this land,' the stocky man shouted as he got close. Bryn Guthrie.

'Good morning,' Rae responded. 'It's a lovely day, isn't it?'

She and Tommy kept walking. The men stopped, as if to block their progress. The man with the shotgun was holding it sideways, across his body.

'What the hell do you think you're doing?' Guthrie replied. He was clearly furious. 'This is private land.'

'The land may be private, but a public right of way crosses it,' Rae replied, trying to sound calmer and more confident than she felt. She was choosing her words carefully. 'The landowner is required to keep a one-metre strip free from cultivation, along the length of the path, though that's not been a problem in the fields we've crossed so far because they're all put down to grass for grazing. Would you move aside, please, so we can continue on the correct line.'

The men didn't respond but neither did they move off the path line. Instead, the thinner man with the shotgun shifted it against his shoulder so that it pointed upwards, a move obviously meant to remind them of the threat the firearm held.

'Don't even think of pointing that thing at us,' Rae said. 'The moment you do, you break the law.'

The man sneered. 'Know that particular law, do you?'

'Dead right I do,' Rae said. 'It's my job.'

A frown crossed the stockier man's face, a quick flicker of uncertainty. He glanced at his companion. He's handing over to his boss, Rae thought. That confirms where the power lies.

'You're a long way from the law up here,' the taller man sneered. Even so, Rae felt that there was some bravado, some uncertainty, in his voice.

'I think you'll find that access laws apply everywhere in this country. Distance from a town doesn't matter, not in these days of instant communication and rapid response vehicles.'

She saw Guthrie give both her and Tommy a closer look. He'd probably spot the small bodycam that Tommy was wearing on his collar. And surely he'd recognised her already from the short but intense altercation he'd had with her and Jackie Spring the previous day, even though she was now wearing a hat.

'Footpaths are a council thing, not the police,' Guthrie spat out. So he had finally realised who she was.

'It changes as soon as someone tries to force a confrontation, particularly one with a shotgun,' Rae replied. 'We're causing no harm and no damage, not unless you count the barbed wire that we snipped up at the entry point to your land, though that's still there, neatly coiled back and tied. We even tied a twine barrier across the gap to prevent any of your animals escaping, not that there were any in that field. That was thoughtful of us, don't you think? We didn't have to do it. By the way, who's the legal landowner? I expect you're a tenant farmer, aren't you?'

Guthrie looked at them suspiciously. 'I don't have to tell you that.'

'No, true. But I thought I'd ask anyway. I can find out from the Land Registry.'

'Well, in that case, just do that. You're not getting any information from me.'

Guthrie was looking about him, as if undecided what to do. Rae wanted to prolong the conversation.

'It was a really pleasant morning until we met you two,' she said.

Guthrie narrowed his eyes. 'What's that meant to mean?'

'You know what. I bet you've been tracking us for the past couple of hours, ever since we set out from up there on that ridge to the south, where the old house is. We'd have been visible from your farm all the way.'

Guthrie didn't react but the uneasy look that passed across his colleague's eyes spoke volumes. Tommy realised what Rae had been doing with the mirror, back at their start point. Making their presence obvious. Clever.

'Don't be fucking stupid,' Guthrie said, angrily. 'Are you paranoid? Why'd we be watching a couple of dozy walkers? We've got better things to do. Like now. I can't stand here all morning wasting time on the likes of you. So just get off my land.'

'That's all we want to do,' Rae replied. 'But we'll be using the line of the official footpath.'

Guthrie had a few quiet words with his companion. Tommy strained but couldn't hear what was being said. The taller man quickly walked off down the hill, towards the farmhouse area.

'I've sent him off to check the fences. I don't want any more of my barbed wire cut by amateurs. You've no right. It's criminal damage. You wait here until he gives the all clear.'

Tommy was thinking how strange this whole conversation was. They were up to something, these two confrontational individuals. But what was it? Hiding something that might arouse suspicions? Warning someone else? It was pointless speculating. He just did what his bosses had told him to do: remained silent and kept the bodycam filming going. One thing was for sure, by now Guthrie must have realised he was dealing with police officers on some kind of reconnoitre. Not that any evidence they'd gathered could be used in a court case. They'd deliberately not declared themselves, but that was part of the plan, dubious though it was.

Guthrie, watching both them and the barn area, must have spotted a signal from the man with the shotgun.

'Okay, head straight on down, then follow the farm track out onto the road. But don't come back. Never.'

Rae looked at him coolly. 'I'll come back whenever I feel like it. It's a public right of way. I suggest you tell the landowner that and get that path sorted.'

The man stepped aside, his facial expression venomous, and the two detectives made their way down the slope towards the farmhouse buildings. They could make out a cluster of five or six old caravans grouped together, half hidden by a copse of trees.

'I guess we're still being watched,' Tommy said.

'I'm certain of it, Tommy. From all directions.' Rae had the sudden realisation that she and her bosses may have seriously underestimated the people on this farm. Maybe confrontational violence was the order of the day here. The events of the past twenty minutes or so would certainly indicate so.

CHAPTER 35: MADDY OPENS UP

Polly and Ade had been waiting in their car, parked out of sight a few hundred yards beyond Greymoor Farm. As soon as the short message from Tommy came through, Polly glanced at Ade and nodded. They would only have a short window of opportunity while Bryn Guthrie was engaged elsewhere on the farm, and Polly needed to speak to the daughter without his intimidating presence. Ade started the engine and drove quickly into the farmyard. They hurried out and knocked on the door. It was answered promptly. Babs Guthrie must have been in the kitchen.

'Mrs Guthrie? I'm DCI Polly Nelson. May we come in? I need to speak to Maddy with some urgency. And you too, I expect.'

'I'm not sure I can let you do that. She's vulnerable.'

Polly pushed forward through the doorway, followed by Ade. 'We've scrutinised every single health and care system we can, and Maddy isn't recorded on any of them as a vulnerable adult. We believe she's been the victim of a serious assault and we need to speak to her urgently to check on her well-being. She's nineteen so doesn't need your permission.'

She didn't wait for a response from the girl's mother, instead moving through the doorway to the small hall.

‘Maddy? Maddy? Can you speak to me please?’ Polly was calling loudly but trying not to sound threatening.

She heard footsteps on the stairs, so followed Babs and Ade into the kitchen. She was soon followed by the young woman, who stepped warily into the room.

‘I’m DCI Polly Nelson from the police. We need to talk to you, Maddy. You and your mother. We’ve been searching for you for several weeks, since we learned of a young woman getting treatment for possible rape in the local hospital. You both fit the description of the two women there that day. My officers have been to the hospital and shown the staff pictures of you, and they confirm the likeness to the patient they treated. It’s our duty to talk it over with you and discuss your options, as a possible victim of a serious assault. Do you understand?’

Babs had regained some of her composure. ‘But we don’t want it investigated any further. We’re her parents. She’s vulnerable. We decide things on her behalf. She wants us to, don’t you, Maddy?’

Polly looked steadily at the woman. Why was she pursuing this line? ‘That wasn’t the judgement of the medical staff who treated Maddy on that day. They thought her to be capable of being involved in any decision-making. Medical judgements like that carry a lot of weight, Mrs Guthrie. There’s also the visit made here by members of my team yesterday, when they met Maddy. They judged her to be an intelligent and aware young woman. So we have to seek her account of the events, even if she and you decide not to press charges against the person responsible. That’s your right. But you should only do so from a position of full understanding, not ignorance of the process.’

Babs’ face reflected the confusing mixture of emotions she was obviously feeling. Was she scared of her husband? Polly thought that she looked worried and angry.

‘Maddy, were you the victim of a sexual assault? One that was unwelcome? The hospital staff treated you for injuries that looked, to them, as if they were non-consensual.

They noticed signs of both internal and external bleeding and it worried them. Were you raped?'

Maddy's lip quivered, and her eyes dampened. She nodded slightly. Her words came out as a whisper. 'I think so. I was mixed up. I still am.'

'Who was it? Was it a regular boyfriend?'

'I thought I liked him. We used to chat.'

'Had you had sex with him before?'

Maddy glanced at her mother and then dropped her head, staring at the pine tabletop. Tears dripped onto its scrubbed surface. 'Just once. But I didn't like it very much. So when he asked me again, I said no. But he told me I was his girlfriend and had to do what he said. I tried to get away, but he forced me to stay. I was scared.'

Polly looked at the girl. 'Who was he, Maddy?'

Maddy shook her head. 'No, I can't say.' She glanced at her mother, a look of fear in her eyes.

'Is that why you didn't tell us earlier? You were too scared to?'

The young woman nodded, looking both vulnerable and miserable. Polly, sitting sideways on, could see that her hands, lying in her lap, were constantly twisting, turning and kneading into each other. She looked desperately sad.

'Was it this person Billy? The one who's gone missing?'

Babs looked shocked and Maddy gasped. 'How did you know?' she said.

'He hasn't been reported as a missing person, but we suspect that someone with that name might have gone missing. Does he work on the farm?'

Babs reached across and put a hand on Maddy's arm as if to warn her.

'Sometimes. That's all I know.' She then seemed to close up, as if she realised that she'd told them too much.

Polly turned to the mother, now white-faced. 'Mrs Guthrie, how much did you know of this? Why didn't you take the advice of the medical staff and report it?' Polly was finding it hard to keep her anger in check.

Babs' voice came in a hiss. 'What's the point? What ever gets done? And where on earth would the proof be? Do you think we want to see our Maddy dragged up in court? For everyone to see and goggle at? No way!' She looked as if she was about to add something else but instead bit her lip.

'Where's this Billy?' Polly asked.

Babs shrugged. 'Don't know. Don't care, either.'

'Is he the body that was found in the woods nearby?'

She shrugged but remained tight-lipped. Maddy, though, looked shocked.

'What?' she said, her eyes wide.

'A man's body was found last week. He'd been dead a week or more, so we think he died almost three weeks ago. He'd been badly beaten.'

'Mum,' Maddy wailed. 'You said you wouldn't! You said he'd just move away. He was my friend.'

'Did you have something to do with his death, Mrs Guthrie?' Polly asked.

Babs looked scornfully at the detective. 'Of course not!' she scoffed. 'What happened to him had nothing to do with us.'

'What was his surname?' Polly asked.

The mother remained silent, but Maddy spoke. 'Potter,' she said. 'He was my friend, Billy Potter.'

Polly looked across at Ade, who'd just finished writing in his notebook. He nodded, as if to say, got it all.

'Did he wear a blue scarf?' Polly asked.

Maddy put a hand to her mouth. 'I gave him one for his birthday.'

Polly extracted two contact cards from her bag and passed them to the two women. 'We'll need to see you both again, and soon. Here are my contact details. Please call me if you have a change of mind or need to tell me anything else.'

The two detectives were about to get up and leave but they paused when Maddy spoke. She seemed a little calmer.

'You said you showed them pictures of me, the nurses, I mean. Where did you get them from?'

Polly thought carefully before replying. 'We think that a local artist had painted some portraits of you. Benjamin Carlyon. I'd taken a photo of one of the paintings.'

'In the summer. I wore my prettiest dress. His paintings were lovely. I haven't seen him for a long time. Did he show you the paintings?'

Polly couldn't help but glance at the girl's mother, her hand partly masking the look of angry frustration on her face. Polly felt her own anger rising. Maddy had been deliberately kept in the dark by her mother. Surely Babs knew of the death?

'I'm sorry to have to tell you, Maddy, that Benjamin is dead. We were in his house investigating the nature of his death.'

Now it was time for Maddy to look shocked. 'Oh, no. He was a really nice man. I liked him a lot. How did he die? He was fine before Christmas. He gave me a present.'

It didn't take a genius to identify what the gift had been. Maddy was fingering a gold locket around her neck.

'He died in suspicious circumstances, Maddy. We're convinced he was murdered.'

Maddy shrieked and stepped back, a look of utter shock on her face. 'Oh, no! He was the nicest man I know. Why?'

'That's what we're trying to find out. Who and why. When was the last time you saw him?'

'Last month, I think. He came across on my birthday. He gave me a card and a coloured scarf.' She frowned, her face screwed up in concentration.

'What is it, Maddy? Do you remember something?'

'Dad was angry. He saw Mr Carlyon when he was leaving, out in the yard. He got angry. So did Harry.'

Babs hurriedly interrupted. 'Hush, Maddy. They don't want to know silly things like that.'

'Oh, but we do, Mrs Guthrie. We want to know all about Benjamin Carlyon and the people he knew. The people he cared for. The people he argued with. We have to find who killed him and bring them to justice. He was a good man, was he, Maddy?'

'Oh, yes. He was always so kind to me. He cried sometimes but he wouldn't tell me why. That's when he was painting me at his house, in the upstairs room. He said it was because he was so happy.'

Babs stood up. She was clearly fighting to hold back her fury. 'That's enough, Maddy. I want you to go to your room now.' She straightened herself. 'Go!' she shouted.

Maddy rose and backed away, then fled out of the room.

'How could you do this? Bring news of such bad things here?'

Polly sighed. 'We know, Mrs Guthrie. We know she's Benjamin Carlyon's daughter. Maddy's name might be Guthrie, but Bryn isn't her biological father, is he? Didn't you ever think that she had the right to know? Particularly now, with Carlyon's death. I can't believe you could just keep her in the dark like this.'

'I said, she's vulnerable.'

'She deserves the truth. We all do. After all, what else is there? The alternative is a kind of madness.'

All Polly received in return was a venomous glare.

'We'll be back. We need more information from Maddy. And you. And your husband, by the sound of it.' Polly suddenly stopped. She'd realised the extent of the deceit. 'Does your husband know? He doesn't, does he?'

Babs said nothing but her facial expression spoke for her.

CHAPTER 36: IN THE LION'S DEN

Sophie Allen stood outside the grand front entrance of Braycombe House and glanced once again at her watch. If everything was going to plan, Rae and Tommy would be approaching the top end of Greymoor Farm about now, drawing Bryn Guthrie away from the immediate vicinity of his farmhouse. Polly and Ade would be waiting in their car, ready to move to the house and speak to the girl and her mother. And here was Sophie, the architect of the plan, having fixed an appointment with Lady Braycombe and her highly favoured lawyer, partly to probe rather more deeply into the background of this tangled mess, but also to keep the lawyer occupied and, hopefully, out of contact with the Guthrie duo at the farm.

The door opened. Of course, this time it wasn't Babs Guthrie pulling it ajar. This had all been fixed to coincide with Babs' day off, as part of Sophie's somewhat devious plan.

'Detective Chief Superintendent Sophie Allen,' Sophie said, smiling.

'Lady Braycombe is expecting you,' the woman said. 'She's in the drawing room.'

'Thanks,' Sophie replied. 'Who are you? It was Babs, the last time I came.'

'Julie. I fill in on her days off.'

'Nice to meet you.' Good manners didn't cost anything, and a possible ally could be made in a situation like this. Unlikely, but it was always worth laying a foundation stone for a possible bridge.

Sophie followed her through the house, just as she'd done the previous week with Babs. As she expected, the lawyer, Paul Cooper, was also present, standing with Lady Braycombe in front of the large fireplace. Neither of them smiled as Sophie approached. They looked wary. If they knew what was going on elsewhere, within a couple of miles of this place, they wouldn't just be wary, Sophie thought, they'd probably be speechless with anger.

Lady Braycombe didn't speak but the lawyer took two steps forward and extended his hand a few inches in a nod to etiquette.

'Paul Cooper,' he said. 'I'm the family solicitor.'

Sophie gave him a smile too.

'Detective Chief Superintendent Sophie Allen,' she replied. 'I'm the commanding officer in the Wessex Serious Crimes Unit, WeSCU for short. Lady Braycombe said that you'd be here next time I called. I'm glad, in a way. It puts things on a more formal footing, doesn't it?'

Cooper pointed to a chair set on one side of a low table. He and his client sat on the other side.

'How can we help you?'

'Several things. Let's start with the stolen Gainsborough, the theft I spoke to Lady Braycombe about a few days ago.' Sophie turned to face the woman in question. 'We've discovered that particular painting was sold to a German art collector only a few weeks after it was found following its theft. Which begs the question, which is the real version? The one sold or the version still on display here?'

Lady Braycombe seemed to bristle with outrage and looked as if she was about to speak. The lawyer put a hand on her arm as if to calm her.

'The sold one, of course. Can I point out that no crime has been committed? A painting owned by the family was sold to raise some much-needed cash. An artist was commissioned to produce a likeness for sentimental reasons and for continuity of display here in the hall. As I say, no law has been broken.'

'On that issue, you may be technically right. But Lady Braycombe is guilty of wasting police time. Twenty years ago, when the local CID had a team investigating the theft, and now, during the current investigation. Do you agree with my assessment?'

He nodded. 'It was regrettable and continues to be so. And you are absolutely right. We'd like to come to an arrangement with you and the CPS to prevent this going any further. I can assure you that it was done for the best possible reasons.' He sounded earnest.

Smarmy bastard, Sophie thought. They seem to expect me to make it easy for them. Sod that approach.

'I'll give it my consideration,' she replied. 'The most important factor, though, is that the artist who painted the copy was the man found dead in Watchet harbour two weeks ago. He was murdered. Do you fully understand the seriousness of the situation?'

He slid the palm of his right hand across his hair as if it might be windswept and in need of some serious taming. In fact, Cooper's hair was perfectly coiffured.

Body language is such a giveaway, Sophie thought. He's tense, rattled maybe. He wasn't expecting this. Did he even know about the art switch before this morning?

'Your client lied to me about something else in addition to deliberately misleading me about the art theft.' She didn't explain, merely looking steadily at Lady Braycombe.

There was no response.

'Could you explain?' the lawyer said.

'I don't quite know how to interpret that request,' Sophie retorted. 'Do you mean there have been several such incidents of deliberate deception? The fact that you want further explanation tends to suggest just that. I'll be helpful and start with the deception linked to the art theft. Your client told me clearly that her husband was the art lover, the chair of the local art appreciation group, the organiser of that exhibition where the Gainsborough was supposedly stolen. A complete fabrication. Lord Braycombe was a country squire, interested in running his estate and little else. It was Lady Braycombe herself who formed the close links to the local art group. She organised that exhibition. We've checked the paperwork. Her signature is on all the official documentation.'

'You've been very thorough, I see.'

'That comment is both patronising and condescending. We're investigating a murder, for goodness' sake. Of course we chase everything up carefully. Do you think we're amateurs? What do you take me for?' Sophie's blood was up. 'On second thoughts, keep going in the same vein. It makes things easy for me.'

Cooper was nonplussed. 'Can we make another appointment to continue?'

'No. I'm too busy. Lady Braycombe insisted on a formal appointment with you present. I've gone along with that and here we are. The only alternative is for you both to come in to the local police station. Do you really want that? Does Lady Braycombe? I don't think so. So we keep going until I'm happy with your level of cooperation. Let's continue. I'd like to know about the status of Greymoor Farm.'

Cooper was obviously taken by surprise by the change in subject matter.

'What do you mean?' he said.

'The farmer at Greymoor, Bryn Guthrie, is a tenant. It's owned by the Braycombe Estate. You're his lawyer. Coincidence?'

He frowned. 'Of course.'

Sophie deliberately widened her eyes. Did he somehow still think she was that gullible? 'Really, Mr Cooper? Yet you don't represent any other farmers like Mr Guthrie, certainly not from around here. You specialise in large estate properties such as this one. I'm puzzled.'

Cooper merely shrugged but didn't elaborate.

'So my guess is it's all part of the same contract. The one for Lady Braycombe and this whole estate.'

Another shrug. Sophie decided not to press it further. More background was required. Maybe change tack and throw in a red herring. 'Has someone gone missing from Greymoor Farm? I understand people have been seen searching.'

'I wouldn't know.' Cooper glanced at Lady Braycombe, but she maintained an expressionless look. That in itself was suspicious. If she really knew nothing about the goings-on at Greymoor, she'd have been puzzled by this question and, in all probability, displayed it by a raised eyebrow or a perplexed look. But the woman's face was little more than a mask. Sophie realised that Lady Braycombe must be viewing this interview as a test of her endurance. Maybe it was time to needle her rather more.

'Lady Braycombe, do you deal with your tenant farmers directly or do you use an agency?'

'An agency of course.' The woman almost spat the words out.

'So, no direct contact with them at all? Not even Mr Guthrie?'

'No!'

Sophie nodded her head gently. 'Despite the fact that Babs Guthrie is your housekeeper and has been so for many years?'

'What's that got to do with anything?'

Sophie ignored the question. 'Do you have any contact with the Guthrie daughter, Maddy?'

'I don't get involved in the family issues of my tenants. Why would I? Anyway, what has this to do with anything? Or are you just trying to stir things up and see what happens?'

Well spotted, Sophie thought. You're not stupid and are entirely capable of manipulating people and situations to your own advantage. You might even be capable of murder, planning it even if employing others to carry out the act. Someone killed Benjamin Carlyon, someone from around these parts.

Who had the most to lose if he'd finally decided to spill some secrets? Sophie glanced at the time. Job done. She'd successfully tied up Cooper for nearly half an hour, enough time for Polly and Ade to have got into Greymoor Farmhouse and spoken to mother and daughter, if things had gone well.

She rose. 'Thank you for your time. We'll certainly need to see you again as things develop and we require further information.'

* * *

Rae and Tommy had reached the farmyard area and were about to turn west, through the yard to the public road beyond, as directed by Guthrie. They'd expected the tall man with the shotgun would be waiting to see them off the farm, but they caught sight of him heading back up the hill in a buggy.

Tommy put his hand on Rae's arm.

'Boss,' he said. 'What's up there? It looks like a couple of caravans.'

They paused at the track junction, taking a good look around. There was no one in sight.

'Let's take a peek,' Rae said.

They walked some twenty yards and found themselves approaching a semicircle of five old caravans, set out around a small area of thin grass with a firepit in the middle. Rae couldn't help but notice how secluded the immediate area was. The mobile dwellings were probably all but invisible from most angles of view.

A man was sitting on the step of the nearest caravan, watching them, although he seemed completely unconcerned by their presence. 'Are you looking for Billy?' he asked. 'He's gone. No one can find him.'

'Who's Billy?' Rae asked.

'He's my friend. He was Maddy's friend too. She's still here, in the house. I like Maddy.'

Rae and Tommy stopped in front of the man. 'What's your name, then?' Rae asked.

'I'm Gordon. I do good work.'

'Do you live here, Gordon?' Rae said.

He nodded his head solemnly. 'This one's my home. I share it with Billy, but he's gone. Have you found him yet?'

Rae shook her head. 'I don't think so. Do you have a photo of him?'

Gordon gave them a smile that revealed the gaps in his teeth. He looked delighted. 'I'll get one.' He seemed very willing to please. He hurried up the steps and through the open caravan door. He was back outside within a minute, handing Rae a slightly grubby image of two men standing side-by-side in front of this very caravan.

'That's you, isn't it?' Rae said. 'On the right?'

The look of delight returned to Gordon's face. He nodded enthusiastically. 'Yes! It was in the summer. Maddy took it. On my birthday. It's my best photo. Billy liked it too.'

Rae looked closely at him. 'Can I keep it, Gordon? It might help us to find Billy. We have been looking. What's his full name, Gordon?'

'Billy Potter. He's my best friend.'

Tommy spoke. 'Do you have something that belongs to him? Maybe a comb or a toothbrush?'

The smile stayed on Gordon's face. 'Yeah. He's got a Superman toothbrush. Maddy gave it to him. It was on my birthday. She gave me a Batman one. She didn't want him to feel left out.'

He disappeared back into the caravan interior, then returned clutching the toothbrush. 'Will it really help?'

'Of course,' Tommy replied. 'You see, everyone leaves skin cells on a toothbrush. That can help us to find lost people.'

Gordon's smile faded. 'He might have hurt Maddy,' he whispered, looking around as if for non-existent eavesdroppers. 'He was too rough sometimes.'

Rae realised the importance of Gordon's words. She put a hand on Tommy's arm. 'We'll need to do this formally,' she said quietly. 'He'll need a responsible adult present.' She turned back to Gordon. 'Who lives in these other caravans?'

Gordon looked around him. 'They do good work. They're all out. I used to go out, too. But I hurt my leg and can't work hard anymore.'

He pulled up his trousers and displayed a grubby-looking calf, badly scarred.

'Did you see a doctor when it happened?' Rae asked.

Gordon shook his head. 'Harry fixed it for me. He works with Bryn. He was an army medic. He does good work.' He suddenly looked serious. 'Harry says Bryn might not be able to keep me 'cos I can't work hard any more. I don't want to go.'

'Who is Harry, Gordon? What does he do, here on the farm?'

Gordon looked puzzled. 'He's the gaffer. I thought you knew. He takes the crews out for their work. Not today, though. He left it to one of the others. Don't know why.'

'How long have you been here, Gordon?' Rae asked.

Gordon frowned. 'Since I was young. Since I got out the hostel. It was nasty.'

'I know you all do really good work, Gordon. But what is it you all do? What kind of work?'

Gordon shrugged. He looked so innocent, so trusting. 'Any kind of stuff, really. We do digging. Like foundations and stuff like that. We build barns and walls. Even some painting. That's what I like, painting.'

'So general building and maintenance work?'

'Yeah. But I can't do much of it since I got my injury. Just the painting. I'm a bit scared. What happens if they can't keep me on?'

'Do you get paid?'

'Yeah. Harry gives us twenty-five pounds each.'

'What? Each day?'

Gordon looked at Rae as if she was mad. 'No!' he snorted. 'Course not. Every Friday. It's our pocket money. I'm saving mine up.'

Rae didn't know what to say to him.

'Harry always says we get a home and food. They look after us.'

Rae regained her composure and glanced at her watch. 'We need to go, Gordon. But we'll try to find out what happened to your friend Billy. And we'll come back to see you again soon. Is that alright?'

The man smiled. 'Yeah. I like you. You're nice, like Maddy.'

'That's good. Better if you don't mention this chat with anyone else. But I promise we'll be back soon. Maybe we'll have news of Billy. What's your last name, by the way?'

'Binnie.'

'Thanks, Gordon.' They turned and walked away.

Tommy shared his thoughts. 'That photo, boss. It looks like the man whose body was in the woods. It's his friend, Billy. And isn't what he said really suspicious? What are they doing here?'

'It's what the super says, Tommy. It might look as though it's a tangled mess but keep picking and it'll all come apart sooner or later. I just thought that you and I were bit-part players in this morning's scheme. But here we are, having found who our second body is. And a lot more besides. It sounds like there's some serious exploitation going on here. I think we've stumbled on a perfect example of modern slavery. It's really worrying and kind of complicates things a bit. We'll need to see what the boss says. We need her lawyer's brain.'

CHAPTER 37: DECISION TIME

The team was assembled around a table in the incident room in Watchet. It was early afternoon. Outside, the weather seemed to be undergoing a change. The recent fine spell was coming to an end, with rain and gusty winds forecast for the evening and overnight. The atmosphere inside the room was muted, thoughtful even.

'It's a lot for us to take in,' Polly said. 'I expected to get something out of the morning's efforts, but not this much. In a way, we all struck gold. We now have a name for our second body, Billy Potter. We also know Maddy Guthrie was the rape victim and that her parents have been trying to keep it hushed up. Billy Potter was the rapist, but Maddy was fond of him. We know Lady Braycombe's been lying to us and that she's more closely involved than we suspected. All that information is more than we expected to get, to be honest. But on top of that, we know that some kind of modern slavery is going on at Greymoor Farm. Sophie? Anything to add?'

'Of course. Well done, everyone. It was a bit of a hair-brained scheme to be honest, but it worked a treat. We have to move fast on this slavery business. That Gordon Binnie will probably give the game away in some way, and sooner rather than later. It looks as though you've got a plan, Ade. Care to enlighten us?'

Ade had worked fast on the suspicions about the probably illegal work gang based at the farm.

'I took your advice, ma'am,' he said to Sophie. 'There's a dedicated unit in Bristol looking into this kind of thing, covering the region. It ties in with what they suspect, that a labour gang of exploited men has been operating in this area of Somerset and into Devon for some time. They want us to keep them informed but don't have anyone free to visit us until tomorrow.'

Sophie frowned. 'We can't wait until then. If Binnie lets something slip, they'll clean the place up fast and shift the men out. Maybe even tonight. We need to move now. Any chance of getting your local snatch squad involved?'

She looked at Polly, but it was Ade who answered. He shook his head. 'There's a big organised-crime operation going on in Bath this evening. A lot of them are being used. I checked. The most we could get is about five or six.'

'We should manage with that,' Sophie said. 'We're all here, after all.'

Polly agreed. 'Can you get it sorted, Ade? Meanwhile, I think we've reached the point where it's realistic for us to consider who's in the frame for Ben Carlyon's murder. Possibly even our body in the woods, too, considering he was badly beaten before being hit by a vehicle of some type. Lining up our ducks in a row, as it were. We have three strong contenders, as far as I see it. Bryn Guthrie, if he's always assumed Maddy was his child. He might have killed Carlyon in a fit of rage if he found out the truth. Thoughts, anyone?'

'Well, he's got the temper for it,' Rae said. 'Nasty piece of work. My guess is that he enjoys intimidating people. He tried it with us this morning, didn't he, Tommy? He probably has that family of his right under his thumb. Learning Maddy isn't his will have come as a real shock to him. Maybe he reacted violently and went after her biological father.'

Polly frowned. 'Could be. But we don't know when he found out the truth. It's possible Babs was honest with him right from the start. If that was the case, why would he kill Carlyon now?'

Tommy spoke up. 'Maybe Carlyon found something out, like this slave work gang Guthrie seems to be running. If Guthrie found out that Carlyon suspected something, he might have decided to kill two birds with one stone, as it were.'

'Plausible,' Polly said. 'And the forensics seem to point to Carlyon being killed in almost a frenzy. That might tie in with Guthrie's violent temper, as you and Jackie Spring described it, Rae.'

Ade had been listening carefully. 'I'd certainly pencil him in as the front runner for Billy Potter being beaten up. If he found out that Potter was the man who raped Maddy, it would be right in character for him to react that way.'

'Anything else about Guthrie before we move on?' Polly asked.

'Don't leave out his foreman, Harry,' Rae added. 'He's also an intimidating individual cut from the same cloth. He had a shotgun with him this morning and I had to warn him about where he was pointing it. The two of them might have worked together.'

'Point taken. So, let's consider Babs Guthrie. Is she a strong candidate?'

Sophie fidgeted in her seat. 'I've got mixed thoughts,' she said. 'On paper, she's a front runner. Surely she must have known that Carlyon was living nearby. Maybe she found out that he was painting Maddy. They both had a hand in that art theft from years ago. His reappearance must have upset the fragile understanding that had existed for many years between the people involved in that little escapade. He knew too much. The other thing to remember about her is that she's the link between all these strands. A fling with Carlyon, with Maddy as the result. She was involved with that art exhibition and the theft. She's obviously Maddy's main emotional support and took her to the clinic. She'd have reacted badly to discovering that her daughter had been abused like that. I can fully understand her wish for revenge on the man who raped Maddy, this Billy Potter. The thing I have difficulty with, though, is her small size. How would she be able to get the best of our two victims? Carlyon was a fairly hefty bloke, as was Potter. Her husband has the physique to overcome each of them. She doesn't. The other guy, this Harry bloke, could. If it's her, she was working with someone else who had the muscle.'

Polly was nodding. 'My thoughts exactly. And the same thing applies to our last suspect, Lady Braycombe. She's got the motive to silence Carlyon, particularly if he was thinking of blackmailing her over the art theft. But it's unlikely she was the person who actually killed either of them. That would be difficult, by herself anyway. I think we're looking at Guthrie or his foreman Harry, either working alone or as the muscle for one of the women. And I don't think the two deaths are directly linked, even if they were the work of the same person. Billy Potter was beaten in a fit of rage, possibly caused by the attack on Maddy. It's probably not linked to Carlyon's murder.' She sighed. 'It's what you say, Sophie. We've got to pull the tangled threads apart and look at them singly.'

* * *

As the weather forecast had predicted, the wind had picked up somewhat by the time the various units arrived at Greymoor Farm and moved to their pre-planned locations. Several social support staff were waiting in a car parked outside, in the lane.

Polly, with Sophie and snatch-squad leader Greg by her side, rapped hard on the door to the farmhouse. It was quickly opened by Bryn Guthrie.

'I thought I told you lot to—'

Polly deliberately ignored what he was saying and held out the warrant. 'Mr Guthrie, I have here a warrant issued in accordance with section one of the Modern Slavery Act, 2015. We have reason to believe that vulnerable people are detained here, not of their own free will, and that this constitutes modern slavery. We will be searching the farm and the buildings on it. Please gather your family and remain in the kitchen. Do not leave that room. If you attempt to do so, my officers will arrest you immediately. I'll be back to talk to you directly.'

She turned to the team waiting behind her. Sophie, Ade and a member of the snatch squad pushed their way through the doorway and into the kitchen, where Babs and Maddy sat open-mouthed at the table. Greg glared at Guthrie for a few seconds until the farmer did as he'd been told and entered the kitchen, then Greg and Polly returned to the group outside.

Greg led the way up the track past the barn towards the cluster of half-hidden, rust-streaked caravans. He was followed by Polly, Sophie, Rae and Tommy, along with the remaining members of the squad. They spread out as they reached the clearing with the ramshackle mobile dwellings. Anxious-looking faces started to appear at dirt-streaked windows.

'Where are the rest?' the unit leader asked Rae. Only four of the caravans had been occupied, yet the others showed signs of having been vacated in a rushed way earlier in the evening. Kettles were still warm, and plates had relatively fresh food residues stuck to their surfaces. Six confused-looking men sat with Gordon, watching the activities of the police officers.

She shrugged her shoulders. 'Let me ask Gordon.' She walked across to the nervous man sitting on the step outside his dilapidated home and watching everything that was going on.

'We don't think everyone is here, Gordon. Did some go out again this evening, even though they'd done a day's work?'

'Think so.' Even Gordon looked worried, his thin face lined with anxiety. 'Harry took them.'

'Why?'

He shrugged. 'Dunno. He was shouting and swearing.'

'Has he ever done that before?'

Gordon shook his head. 'No. They always do good work. We always have, all of us. He was angry. They went in the old van. We're scared.'

It seemed likely that the group had become used to the regularity of a daily routine, and that had been upset today. The men looked bewildered. Polly approached.

'The place is secure,' she said. 'I'll get the social team in to look after them. I guess they'll all need a medical check, judging by the dirty conditions they've been living in. Don't they have showers here?'

Rae looked back at Gordon, who'd heard the comments. 'Fridays,' he said. 'We get a shower on a Friday after dinner if we want one. Harry says it saves money if we don't.'

Polly shook her head in exasperation. 'Unbelievable.'

She walked through the yard to the lane and called to the social support team, then explained what they'd found. 'It's over to you now. But we think four of the men are missing. A group left about an hour ago with the foreman. We don't know why.'

Rae and Polly went into the farm kitchen, joining Sophie and Ade, already there. Polly had a quiet word with Sophie about what they'd found, watched all the time by Bryn Guthrie. He seemed somehow muted. The intimidating manner he'd displayed during their earlier visits was almost completely absent.

The seven men from the caravans were judged by the social services team to be adequately nourished but poorly cared for. They were driven off for more detailed assessment, first at a local clinic, looking for potential health problems, and then for social issues. Rae and Tommy went with them, partly to provide some reassurance to Gordon Binnie, now terrified that he might fall foul of some form of violent retaliation from Bryn or Harry.

The question facing the police was this. Where were Harry and the missing men? The general consensus was that he'd somehow got wind of the conversation between Gordon and the detective duo of Rae and Tommy. He and Bryn had probably made the decision to ship the men out quickly but had only just left with the first vehicle load. So where had he taken them and were they in danger?

CHAPTER 38: GENTLE PROBING

Wednesday, Week 3

There were mixed feelings among the members of the crime team the next morning. Satisfaction at the outcome of the raid and the rescue of the seven modern-day slaves. Disappointment that four of their number had somehow been spirited away. Satisfaction that Bryn Guthrie was currently in custody awaiting interview, but disappointment that Harry Campion was still at large.

Ade had discovered Harry's full name on looking through some letters on a shelf in the farmhouse's kitchen. He'd been given the task of finding out more about him, so got started as soon as he could the next morning. It didn't take long for information to build up, including some items that caused his eyes to widen and his jaw to drop. He hurried across to speak to Sophie, who was planning the next stage of the investigation. The other more junior members of the team were out trying to trace the whereabouts of the missing men.

'Harry Campion,' he said, rather breathlessly. 'He was the thief who stole the paintings from the art exhibition here in Watchet twenty years ago. Because he returned them undamaged, he just got a fine and a suspended sentence.'

Sophie sat back in her chair, her brow furrowed in concentration. 'So if the whole thing was rigged, which is what seems to be the case, he must have known both Babs Guthrie, or Rogers as she was then, and Lady Braycombe. This just gets more and more intriguing, doesn't it?'

'But there's more. Before coming to Somerset, he lived in Croydon. This was when he was a young man. I found an old address for him. Croydon rang a bell in my brain. It was when I was looking into the art theft, last week. The insurance brokers who provided the cover for that stolen painting were based there, so I did some checking. You won't believe this. He lived in a flat above the row of shops and offices. Not directly above the broker's but only a couple of doors away. Didn't you say that Lady Braycombe used to work in insurance? Could there be a link?'

'Great work! This opens up all kinds of things for us, Ade. First thing, go back and do a bit of searching about her ladyship. Her previous name was Sharon Billings. That was before she married our local aristocrat. Thinking about it, she told me she met him because of some insurance he needed. The implication was that she was arranging it. Get Tommy involved once he's back and Rae when she's finished at the hospital. This could be the first big crack in the armour they've put in place. I'd usually hug you at this point but there's no chaperone-type person present.'

He laughed. 'I don't mind.'

He'd heard about these displays of over-enthusiastic congratulations from the chief. Sophie gave him a quick embrace, then stood back. 'You deserved it. Now let's get back to work. I need to rethink things in light of what you've found out. I'll call Polly.'

* * *

Polly was visiting Justin Penhale in hospital in Taunton. She'd been contacted because he'd come out of his coma the previous evening and would be able to receive short visits.

He was propped up in bed, his head heavily bandaged. Polly deposited the bag of grapes she'd brought along onto a dish that sat on the bedside locker.

'I never know whether grapes are a good idea or not,' she said. 'But take them as a peace offering. I feel that we didn't protect you very well.'

'I didn't realise I was in any danger of being attacked,' he replied, his voice weak. 'I don't expect you did, either.'

'No. You're right. Things did escalate rather quickly and the attack on you was the first sign of that. If it's any reassurance, we think it showed that they were starting to panic. Of course, we weren't aware of that.'

'What's been happening?' Justin shifted slightly against the pillows piled behind him, a movement that caused him to wince.

'A lot. But I can't go into any details. Not at present. I've come along to find out how you are and to see if you've remembered anything about the attack.'

Justin grimaced. 'It's all a bit hazy, still. I was in the house, starting to check through my uncle's paperwork. I remember seeing something flashing in the sunlight, a few hundred metres away, out the back. I went to investigate what it was. That's all I remember for sure. I think I remember speaking to someone but can't recall what I said. One of the doctors said that my memory of what happened is likely to come back bit by bit. I wish it would hurry up.'

'Don't push yourself, Justin. Other people with the same level of head injury as you have sometimes said that the recollections come back when they're most relaxed and not trying to push their memory. Just take your time. Here, have a grape. It might help.' Polly paused. 'There is one thing you can help us with. It's possible that the house was owned by the Braycombe Estate sometime in the past. Have you ever spotted anything that supports that idea?'

Justin shook his head, albeit very gently. 'I guess there must be deeds somewhere, but I haven't found them. The place is well over a hundred years old. It must have quite a history.'

'Were you planning to keep it?'

'I can't see how I can. It needs some work doing to it. Anyway, what would I use it for? I work in Exeter. It's too far to commute. It's not my kind of place anyway. I'm more of a townie. I like people around me and a bit of social life.'

'Were you aware of your uncle having any children?'

'Not until you mentioned it a few days ago.'

'Well, I need to tell you we've been speaking to her. She's nineteen, and is the young woman in the portraits in your uncle's studio. She's his daughter but probably didn't know it. It's possible that he didn't know about her until fairly recently.'

'So, she'd be my cousin? And she'd inherit the house?'

'It looks like it. It might explain some of the animosity that's surfaced.'

'That's a lot to take in. Does she know about me?'

'Not yet, as far as we know. It'll be up to her mother to explain things. As far as we know, she hasn't even broached the fact that her father isn't who she thinks he is, not as of last night. But we've told her it has to be done. The young woman is nearly twenty. I think I mentioned previously that she has Down's.'

'I can see the problem, then.'

Polly shrugged. 'I don't think there is one. She's by no means stupid and I'm sure she'll cope fine.' She glanced at the time. 'I'd better be off. Contact me when you start remembering things.'

Her phone rang before she could leave the bedside. She glanced at the caller display and saw it was the boss, Sophie Allen. What now?

* * *

Tommy and Rae were interviewing the men rescued from the squalor of their rundown homes on Greymoor Farm. They'd been found provisional accommodation in a hostel that was temporarily closed for a refit. A uniformed police officer was on duty in the foyer as a precaution against attempts to intimidate or even abduct any of the men. None of the seven seemed able to help by suggesting possible locations where Harry might have gone with the missing four. The two detectives found the experience of talking to the erstwhile prisoners chastening. They were hollow-eyed and seemed bereft, as if they were somehow lost.

'In a way they are lost,' Rae said quietly to Tommy. 'The one thing they had while being kept closely guarded up at Greymoor was a strange kind of stability. It sounds as though each day was predictable and like any other. They were told what to do, all the time. No opportunity to develop a sense of self-reliance. But no decisions that might cause anxieties.'

She shook her head in exasperation. The only member of the group who opened up to them in any substantial way was Gordon, probably because he'd talked to them before, but even he didn't seem to fully comprehend the nature of their lives on Greymoor Farm, that they were, in reality, slaves or prisoners. It became clear to the two detectives that the only person who'd shown any real kindness to the men was Maddy. Every single one of the seven mentioned how caring the young woman had been. Which, of course, begged the question: had she been aware of the crimes that were being committed by keeping the men at the farm and forcing them to work in the way the Guthries had?

Rae and Tommy probed them gently about their memories of Billy Potter and possible reasons for him going missing. They picked up on an awkwardness in the responses. Somehow, Billy had broken a taboo of some type by becoming too friendly with Maddy. Billy had been the youngest of the group, possibly only a decade or so older than the young woman. It also became clear that Billy was probably the brightest of them. He could read faster than the others. He could write more clearly and would sometimes write notes and messages on behalf of the others. And, most damning, he'd sometimes walk back to the farmhouse with Maddy, carrying empty pots and pans. Weekend food was provided from the farmhouse and carried across to the caravans in large pots. These communal meals were the high point of the men's lives, an opportunity to chat and mix in a relaxed way. It was on one of these occasions that Billy had said to Gordon that he loved Maddy and wanted to be with her. The two detectives wondered if things had quickly deteriorated from that point. The Guthries might not have been best pleased if this had been reported back to them. In all probability, Billy had gone several steps too far, his own limited intellect incapable of treating his relationship with Maddy with sufficient sensitivity when she rebuffed his second set of advances. Double tragedy had followed. The rape and the subsequent punishment beating. Then the probable escape on that dark and stormy night, an escape which had only led him as far as the nearby lane and a collision with an as-yet unknown vehicle, though Jackie Spring, the local special constable, had already expressed her views on the possible identity of the driver who was involved in that particular incident.

Despite the slowness of the dialogue with the men, Rae felt that a number of important pieces of information were forthcoming. It was when the individual contributions were put together that an interesting picture began to emerge.

They returned to the incident room to report to Sophie and Polly.

CHAPTER 39: WE KNOW WHERE YOU LIVE

Meanwhile Jackie Spring and her boss, PC Sarah Levy, took the opportunity to have a quick look around Greymoor Farm. They joined one of the police teams searching the fields and outhouses. Nothing much had shown up in any of the buildings with only one old barn left to inspect, the one situated in the corner of the yard, furthest away from the farmhouse. It was locked.

'Curious,' Sarah said. 'None of the others were locked like this. Our friend Bryn Guthrie has been surprisingly cooperative and opened everything up for us. Let's go and see him.'

They walked across the yard to the house and rapped on the door. Guthrie was a changed man. He looked sunken, defeated. His demeanour lacked the challenge of their earlier encounters. He just looked at them sullenly.

'What now?'

'That shed in the far corner, Mr Guthrie. It's padlocked. I can't get in. The key, please?'

'It's only old feedstuff,' he said. 'Nothing of any use to you in there.'

'I'll be the judge of that. The key, please.' Sarah held out her hand.

He disappeared into the house for a minute or two then returned with a key. He handed it over without comment, but his facial expression spoke volumes. He was seriously worried.

The two uniformed officers walked back across the yard to the locked shed.

'It's a proper high-quality padlock,' Sarah said. 'The locks on all the other outbuildings aren't as good as this. A bit suspicious in itself.'

She unlocked the door, pulling it open as wide as she could. The interior was only dimly lit but she spotted a nearby light switch. The lights weren't bright, but they permitted the two officers to see that the layout and contents were very different to the other outbuildings. Small pens were set against the walls, all covered with roughly spread tarpaulins. They pulled on latex forensic gloves and took a closer look, lifting the covers from a number of the small enclosures.

'Do you think these were pig sties at one time?' Jackie asked.

'Could be,' came the reply. 'Whoa. Look here.'

Sarah had lifted one corner of the tarpaulin on the nearest pen, revealing a neatly set out spread of what looked to be antiques. They lifted nearby covers and found similar collections of other semi-valuable objects such as small items of furniture, porcelain and chinaware. One pen contained trays of jewellery.

'Stolen, I expect,' she said.

Jackie walked across the floor to the other side and pulled back some covers. Here the enclosures seemed to contain items of metal scrap, carefully separated by type.

The second in the row had sections of copper pipe and, against one low wall, two reels of copper cable.

'Well, well,' she said. 'Looks like we've found our stolen copper. Maybe it wasn't Donnie Lomax after all.'

It looked as though a small shelf at the far end held a couple of folders, so Sarah moved down and flicked one open.

Among some loose-leaf paper was a notebook. She extracted it and glanced through the pages. One of the final handwritten entries told them what they needed to know. *Donny Lomax. 2 reels copper. £600.* It also noted a phone number.

'No. You were right first time, Jackie. His name's down here. It looks as though our Mr Guthrie was operating a big fencing operation, moving on stolen goods. No wonder he didn't have to put a lot of effort into his farming. Handling this stuff probably made him a lot more money. Along with the labour gang.' She turned and moved back to the door. 'Let's secure the place and tell the boss and the forensic team. I think the Guthries need to be moved out while this stuff is examined by experts. We need to get back to him pronto. He's probably on the phone right now warning people. Let's lift him for handling stolen property. We've got the evidence and we can keep him out of contact with whoever's pulling his strings.'

Bryn Guthrie proved to be surprisingly acquiescent. It was almost as though he'd come to terms with the inevitability of his demise. When Sarah made the arrest statement he merely shrugged.

'Okay. Just get on with it,' he said, before turning to Babs.

'Get the lawyer,' were the only words he spoke to her. No endearments, no statements of affection.

What an odd couple, Jackie thought.

* * *

After delivering Guthrie to the area police station, Sarah and Jackie were asked to return to Exmoor. In the light of their discovery of the stolen copper, another visit to Donny Lomax was required.

He was in the yard at the neighbouring Highcroft Farm, tidying tools away, when the two uniformed officers appeared in their car. They spotted him immediately and noted the worried look on his face as they approached him.

'It's a nice day, Mr Lomax,' Sarah said.

The worried look remained. 'Mr Bright is out in the fields,' Donny said. 'He probably won't be long.'

Sarah smiled. 'It's you we've come to see, Mr Lomax. We want to talk about copper with you. Specifically, the two reels of copper cable that went missing from outside the substation on the night of the big storm. Do you remember we spoke about them a couple of days ago?'

She waited until he nodded in agreement.

'Well, there's some good news. We've found them. Along at Greymoor Farm, carefully locked in a shed. We're wondering how they got there. Any comments?'

He shook his head.

'Well, here's the thing, Mr Lomax. We have evidence to suggest that you were involved in the theft. Quite a lot of evidence, to be precise. And you've already admitted that you were out on the road that night. Any comment now?'

Donny's face had paled somewhat, and he was clearly thinking hard.

Sarah continued. 'If you're worried about possible revenge if you tell us the truth about the stolen copper, then there's little chance of that happening. You must have seen all the police and forensic activity at Greymoor since yesterday evening. We'll be charging the farm owner and managers with a range of offences including modern slavery. Receiving stolen goods will be the least of his worries. Happier now?'

He sighed. 'Okay. I admit it. And I've been worried sick about it ever since. It's not something I make a habit of doing, pinching stuff. But it was just sat there on the verge when I passed at the end of the afternoon. I thought I'd go back for another look, later on. That's why I was out in that storm. I wish I hadn't. I've been scared about it ever since. I sold it on to Bryn Guthrie a few days later, when I found out he could dispose of loads of different stuff.'

'Six hundred pounds. That's what you got for it, wasn't it? See, I wasn't tricking you. We don't tell porky pies, Mr Lomax. Not the police. Well, not me or Special Constable

Spring, here. We're as honest as the day is long. So, do you want to come down to the station, make a statement and get it all off your chest? That would be the easiest way. It saves having to make a scene. Your employer's wife is watching us right now, out of one of the house windows, and we don't really want to upset her by taking you away in handcuffs. You'd probably end up losing your job, wouldn't you?'

'That might happen anyway,' he said. He looked despondent.

'Well, that's up to them. The story will get out sooner or later. Just now the bigger picture is those poor guys forced to work on that farm for a pittance. I think you got to know one of them, didn't you? Tell Mrs Bright you're making a statement about it. We won't say any different in the short term if you convince us you're a reformed character. But I need to warn you that your statement has to be full and detailed. My colleague, Special Constable Spring, is a hard person to convince. I think you know that already. I'll trust to her judgement over what you say. Understood?'

He nodded. 'I've been regretting it since I nabbed it. And since I sold it on to Guthrie. Him and that helper of his, Harry whatever, they really scared me.'

'Put it all in your statement, Mr Lomax. We'll expect you down in Watchet in an hour. Don't make us come looking for you. We know where you live, remember.'

His relief was clear to see. The police duo returned to their car and waited until they were clear of the farm before dissolving into laughter.

'We know where you live?' Jackie chortled. 'You total rascal, Sarah Levy. You sounded like a mafia heavy.'

'Well, it worked, didn't it? He looked suitably worried, which is what we want. Let's head back and report to your friend, the DCI. She might want to speak to Donny Lomax herself.'

CHAPTER 40: THE FINAL SEARCH BEGINS

'Twenty-five years ago. That's when they married, Lord Anthony Braycombe and Sharon Billings. It's in the parish records.' Ade had been busy, trying to build up a picture of the current Lady Braycombe. 'Harry Campion was one of the witnesses and signed the official record in the church. I can't really get my head round it. Why him? He was a Londoner, for goodness' sake. It seems odd.'

'It means he was involved right from the very start,' Polly said. 'You said he lived very close to the insurance office in Croydon where Sharon worked. My guess is that they knew each other, maybe really well. When she came to Braycombe to sort out his lordship's insurance, she might well have hit on the poor guy. You know, used her charms to seduce him. Am I being too cynical here?'

Sophie shook her head. 'We've all seen it before. It's not a certainty, but it's an obvious possibility.'

Polly continued. 'So she could have wangled her way into the life of our lonely, possibly sex-starved, aristocrat. Marriage was the next step. Then she arranges a job for Harry in the area. That needs checking, guys. Can you get onto it, Ade? The problem is, none of this helps us find those four missing men.'

'Maybe that's not strictly true, Polly. Where we find him, we're likely to find them. I wonder if he's in hiding somewhere on Braycombe Estate land. That includes part of the moor.'

'True. He certainly seems to know his way around, up on the moor. I've found out why Bryn Guthrie seems so crushed, by the way. He didn't know that Maddy wasn't his daughter. Babs only told him yesterday evening, just before we raided the place. No wonder he seemed down. He was probably still getting to grips with the news.'

Sophie was thinking hard. 'That removes his possible motive for killing Carlyon. We were thinking hot-headed revenge when he found out Carlyon was Maddy's father, but it now seems he didn't know it at the time the man was murdered. Does he still have a motive?'

She glanced around at the team. They were all shaking their heads. 'Can't think of one,' Rae said.

'So we're left with Harry Campion and Lady Braycombe. Working in league, maybe? Motive?'

'Blackmail over the art theft,' Polly replied. 'We've already identified it as a possibility. It's looking stronger now. By the way, Babs also told Maddy about Bryn not being her father. Maybe we should speak to her again. See what she can tell us about Harry. But our main focus has to be finding those missing men. They could be in serious danger.'

Sophie spoke. 'Let's swamp the Braycombe Estate with everything we've got. Search every nook and cranny, every outhouse. Time's ticking by and, as you say, those men are at risk.'

'That's just what I wanted you to say. So, do we have the go ahead?'

'Absolutely. But I'll just be in the way, Polly. You've done enough searches like this. You don't need me there. Shall I visit Greymoor and interview Maddy again? We need to get her take on things.'

'Fine by me.' Polly looked almost relieved.

The areas of land owned by the Braycombe Estate could be divided into three. The house and surrounding parkland, two local farms worked by tenants that butted up against the park, and, finally, several square miles of windswept moorland that stretched west from the lonely house that had been owned by Benjamin Carlyon. They had most of the local police force at their disposal, so divided them into three groups, each with an assigned search area and with an accompanying WeSCU detective. Polly led the group searching Braycombe House and its immediate surroundings, Ade was with the team checking the two neighbouring farms, and Rae, accompanied by Tommy, drove back to the high moor and the area around Carlyon's empty house.

* * *

The old house on the moor looked as desolate as ever, perched by itself beside the narrow road snaking uphill towards the distant heights. No windows were open, and no vehicles were parked nearby. There were no signs of life in any direction. Rae still couldn't fully comprehend why anyone would want to live in such a lonely spot, but then she was no emotionally tangled artist specialising in brooding landscapes.

Rae and Tommy unlocked the door and went in, quickly scanning through each room. Nothing. They checked the old rickety garage and the shed that had given them an early lead in the form of the spilled tar wash on the hard floor. Still nothing. They hurried to the nearby high point where Justin Penhale had been assaulted but to no avail. The moorland looked calm and serene as far as the eye could see.

Rae checked her detailed walkers' map, looking for signs of farm buildings of any type. It looked as though there was a rough track leading to some kind of byre set back almost a mile from the road.

'We'll need to give it the once-over,' she said to Tommy. She looked at her small, low-slung sports car. 'Not sure how we'll get on but it's the only car we've got with us, so it'll have to do. It's got new tyres, though.'

They headed west, climbing as they went, and reached the rough sidetrack a couple of miles further on. Rae took her car up the trail as fast as she dare, sliding around several corners on the rough gravel and constantly wondering how much damage was being done to the underside by the constant spray of stones flung up from the skidding tyres. Tommy was holding on to the side of his seat to prevent himself being thrown about too much.

Finally, the car slid to a halt in front of an old timber shed that had clearly seen better days. Tommy and Rae hurried out and approached the building. Nothing. It was both empty and semi-derelict. They hurried to a nearby high point. Tommy used his binoculars to check all around but could see no other buildings or shelters.

'No,' Rae said. 'We've drawn a blank up here. If they're still somewhere local, it must be lower down, around Braycombe itself. Let's head back and join the others.' Just then her phone rang.

'Rae, I need you,' came Sophie's breathless voice. 'I'm on the path down to Watchet, in pursuit. Can you tell Polly? She must be in a signal blackspot.'

Just then her voice faded as the connection dropped out.

'She was in a panic,' Rae said. 'Let's move.'

* * *

Ade's team made short work of visiting the two farms that neighboured Braycombe House. Both of them were very different from Greymoor, perched as it was on the edge of the bleak upland plateau. These two, despite being less than four miles away, were in the valley, with its richer soils and rather gentler climate. They were both well-maintained, with neat and tidy buildings. Both sets of tenant farmers were happy to help and accompanied the police groups on their searches. Nothing suspicious showed up so Ade spent some time questioning the farmers about their dealings with Lady Braycombe, the landlord. He sensed some reticence on their part. Both farmers claimed the relationship to be a positive one, but he remained unconvinced by their words. They admitted that they rarely saw her in the flesh. Routine matters were usually dealt with by the estate manager, a certain Harry Campion.

Ade called Polly to report his findings, then scanned the outer extremities of the second farm using binoculars. There, seemingly on the edge of the farm, was an old outbuilding near a clump of tall trees. He turned to the farmer.

'That shed in the distance,' he said. 'Why wasn't it on your list? I said we need to check everything.'

The woman beside him followed the line of his outstretched arm.

'That's not ours,' she replied. 'It's across the boundary, inside the parkland grounds. Maybe you can't see the boundary wall clearly.'

Ade adjusted the binoculars a fraction. Sure enough, he could now make out the drystone boundary wall just in front of the shed. The timber building looked in reasonably good condition. Could it be a store for hay or some other crop? Maybe he'd better phone Polly again and let her know of its existence within the grounds of the main house. It might be difficult to spot from the house itself. Even from this angle it was half hidden by a clump of trees.

As he looked, he spotted a thin haziness above the building. It coalesced into something more tangible. Smoke.

'It's on fire,' he gasped. 'Let's get across there!'

He spoke hurriedly into his radio as he and the team ran swiftly to their vehicles.

* * *

Polly had made little headway in her search of Braycombe House. A hope that she might be able to speak to the current Lady Braycombe was frustrated before it began when it became clear that Sharon wasn't at home. The only person around was a late-middle-aged gardener, spreading manure around the bushes in the ornamental rose bed. In one aspect they were in luck. He had access to a house key so could let them in to the main building. Not without protest, though. He examined the search warrant suspiciously, as if he was inspecting every word for signs of possible forgery.

Polly's team spread through the silent house, quickly checking every corridor, every stairwell and every room. A group of three officers concentrated on the cellars, vast caverns of dust and musty smells. The officers involved reported back to Polly that they felt disappointed at the emptiness. They'd expected well-stocked wine cellars at the very least. They'd found the wine cellar, complete with racks, but it was devoid of bottles.

'It's like a ghost house,' the lead officer had reported to Polly.

So where was Lady Braycombe? Polly sighed in frustration but was disturbed by the sound of her radio unit buzzing into life. She listened to Ade's hurried voice reporting the signs of a fire in a barn situated just inside the Braycombe House boundary wall. She hurried outside, calling her team together. They peered eastwards, looking across the green meadow spread in front of them, past a small copse in the distance. One of the officers pointed.

'There!'

A small plume of smoke could be seen rising from an area to one side of the copse. The squad hurried towards their vehicles and headed across the parkland as fast as the rough terrain would permit.

They arrived only a minute or two after Ade's team, already clustered around the timber building. Flames had just broken through the roof and were beginning to stretch skywards in the middle of the rapidly darkening smoke. Shouts could be heard coming from inside the barn.

'Get them out, quick,' Polly ordered.

'The door's padlocked,' Ade replied. 'Someone wasn't taking any chances of them escaping. But to set fire to it? That's inhuman.' He was scanning around, looking for a possible alternative entry to the burning building.

One of the search team, a burly man wearing black fatigues, was hammering at the hasp of the lock with a large stone that he'd found nearby. He was quickly joined by another, wielding a wheel brace that he'd pulled from the tool rack of a police minibus. The first man stepped aside, having loosened the hasp slightly from its mountings in the timber upright. The brace was inserted, and the officer leaned on it with as much body weight as he could bring to bear. For a moment nothing happened, then a cracking noise accompanied the tearing of the lock system away from its mount.

The two officers flung the door wide, and four men staggered out coughing, with tears streaming down their cheeks. They were raggedly dressed, their eyes wide in panic.

One of them launched himself at the last to come out. 'I fucking told you not to smoke in there,' he shouted. 'You fucking moron. You nearly killed us.'

Several squad members pulled them apart.

Ade approached Polly. 'We were only just in time. It's already an inferno inside. We'd better move back.'

'You sure there's no one left inside?' she asked.

'Pretty sure. The two guys who opened the door had a chance to look around. They said, no.'

'So where are Lady Braycombe and her friend Harry? Shit. Have we lost them, Ade?'

'We got the men out, boss. Surely that was our main aim?'

Polly merely scowled. Anything she was planning to say was interrupted as her radio buzzed into life. She listened intently then turned back to Ade.

'It's Rae,' she said. 'Apparently the super's in trouble. Does that mean she's stumbled across them somewhere? Bloody hell. Why her?' She glanced around. 'You stay here and do what you can. I'll head off and see what the hell is going on. From what she said, there's been some kind of incident on the back road down into Watchet.'

She ran towards her car.

CHAPTER 41: CAR CHASE

Sophie was, at heart, feeling slightly despondent. It wasn't this case or its slow progress. She was used to that, having dealt with many tricky murder investigations over the years that had proved slow to disentangle. It wasn't the area, either. Watchet and Exmoor were beautiful places, stuffed full of quirky buildings and interesting characters. The fact was that she missed Barry Marsh, her usual number two. Polly was good at her job and had always been the obvious choice for her role in WeSCU. But their personalities didn't mesh in quite the same way that hers and Barry's did. That special aspect, their unspoken understanding, was missing. She'd built up the original Dorset murder team herself, with hand-picked members. And they'd all gelled in a totally unexpected way that, at times, had seemed almost supernatural. And that included past members who had left for new roles in the county force, like Lydia Pillay and Jimmy Melsom. Was it because Polly was another go-getting person? But that couldn't be true. Sophie had several close women friends who could be described in that way. She was on first-name terms with the Home Secretary, for goodness' sake, and you couldn't find anyone more go-getting than Yauvani Anand. She was the epitome of womanpower. But she,

Sophie, could share her somewhat offbeat sense of humour with Yauvani. Could she do the same with Polly? Not really. Polly was extremely guarded and very cautious in her interactions with her fellow officers. Was there something in her past? Impossible to say. Anyway, feeling maudlin like this wasn't productive. Barry was due back from his honeymoon next week. Not that he was likely to be involved in this case. She knew that people often thought of Rae Gregson as her protégée. Only partly true. Really, it was Barry.

She shook herself. She shouldn't be feeling this way. The case was drawing to a close. She could feel it in her bones, that sixth sense that things were starting to point one way, towards an obvious suspect. Or, in this case, two. Sharon Billings and Harry Campion. She needed to find out more about Campion's character. He was the great unknown in all of this. That was why she was on her way to Greymoor Farm. She was hoping that Maddy Guthrie and her mother, Babs, could supply some information about him.

She drew into Greymoor Farm and parked close to the house. She half-expected the yard to be deserted, but spotted Maddy spreading chicken feed to a cluster of squawking hens. The young woman looked up as Sophie clambered out of her car and waved. She waved back and walked across.

'Hello, Maddy. How are you feeling today?'

Maddy frowned. 'Tired. I didn't sleep proper last night. I'm worried at it all. I don't understand anything. I'm scared.'

'That's to be expected. We have people who can help, Maddy. They listen to problems and suggest ways of making things easier. Let me know and I can contact them.'

Maddy nodded solemnly. 'Everything's upset. I don't know what's what anymore. If I think about it too much, it makes me feel sick.'

'It'll get better, though. Is your mum in?'

The young woman nodded. 'In the kitchen. She's not talking much.'

Sophie followed her inside. Babs was sitting at the table, elbows on the surface and head in hands. She looked up at the detective through red-rimmed eyes. 'I'm worried about Bryn,' she said. 'What has all this done to him? He'll think he's lost everything. I can't cope without him, not really. I thought I could, but I can't.'

Sophie tried to look sympathetic, despite feeling that this woman had brought so many of her troubles on herself. Why hadn't she been open with her husband and daughter years earlier?

'If he's cooperative and wasn't involved in the deaths, he might get bail and be back here in a few days. That depends on us finding the missing men, though. Do you know where they could be?'

The two Guthrie women shook their heads. Babs kept glancing towards the window and door.

'I tried to look after them,' Maddy said. 'Then it all went wrong. Billy got jealous when I was being painted. He thought Mr Carlyon was trying to steal me away.' She looked at the floor.

Sophie suddenly came fully alert. This was not on their list of possible motives for Carlyon's murder. They'd pretty well settled on some kind of blackmail over the historic art theft as the motive, with Sharon, Lady Braycombe, being the main driving force and one of the men carrying it out. Could they have got it totally wrong? Could this man Billy have murdered Carlyon, then got badly beaten himself by Bryn for Maddy's rape, and finally come a cropper out on the road that stormy night? It all fitted. The problem was, other scenarios fitted just as well. It ought to be followed up with some urgency, but first she needed to probe Maddy's memory.

'You're aware, Maddy, that Billy Potter's body was found in the woods last week. It looks very likely that he was hit by a car out on the lane on the night of the big storm. I think the DCI told you this a day or two ago. What I want to know is, what happened to Billy before then. He was badly beaten up. We're trying to find who did it. Do you know?'

Maddy looked tearful. No wonder, Sophie thought. Recent events were enough to shock anybody. But Maddy, with her difficulties and her sheltered, almost claustrophobic background would be reeling from the jarring emotional fallout from the violence.

'I've been really worried about it. I talked to Gordon and the others. They said it was in the tractor shed. They heard it. They could hear him shouting to stop it. Someone was hitting him with a stick.'

'Do you know who, Maddy?'

She dropped her eyes and shook her head. Sophie glanced at Babs, gripping the edge of the table as if she was about to fall.

'Was it Bryn? As a punishment for Billy's attack on you? And was Harry Campion there?'

Neither of them answered but their facial expressions said it all. Correct on both counts. Babs was looking particularly tense, again glancing at the door. Was she expecting a visit from someone?

'I need to check in with the forensic team up at the caravans,' she said to the two women. 'By the way, did either of you do any unusual laundry for Billy before he went missing?'

They both shook their heads, looking puzzled. They were probably unaware of the blood loss that would have accompanied Carlyon's murder. The assailant's clothes would have been soaked with the stuff.

'What can you tell me about Harry, Babs? He's the big unknown in this.'

Babs shrugged. 'He's always worked for Lady Braycombe. For years. Even Bryn's scared of him.' She looked at Sophie. 'Bryn's a good man really. Underneath it all.'

The implication was there, in those few words. Babs was implying that Harry was the driving force behind the violence and intimidation. But was she just trying to protect her husband, currently languishing in a cell in the local custody suite?

Sophie went outside and made her way up the track to the semicircle of old caravans. The forensic team were still working on the middle vans and probably wouldn't get to

Billy's before the end of the day, particularly with it recently being unoccupied. She clambered inside a nylon forensic suit and entered the mobile dwelling. The air smelled damp and musty. What was she looking for? Bloodstained clothing or shoes, evidence that the occupant might have been involved in a vicious assault. She began peering into the few cupboards and storage units in the caravan, not a pleasant task. Everything seemed threadbare and grubby but there were no sets of bloodstained clothes anywhere to be found. She stepped back and happened to take a glance out of the window, where she spotted a slight movement in the line of trees that separated the caravan area from the lane. She heard an engine start, a car door slam and the sound of a vehicle accelerating away. Someone must have been watching the forensic search, checking up on progress.

Sophie hurried outside, discarding her overall, and ran to her car. She set off in pursuit, trying to spot the vehicle that had been lurking in the narrow roadway. She saw nothing for a few minutes, even though she was driving as fast as safety permitted. Then, as she slowed slightly to enter Braycombe village, she spotted a car ahead overtaking a slower vehicle on a narrow section of the High Street. Someone was in an almighty hurry. She quickly decided that a high-speed chase might not be the best option open to her. The car in question looked to be a powerful Mercedes and would be difficult to force into a stop on this narrow road. Better to hang back and follow, trying to disguise the fact that she was in pursuit. She remained behind the slower vehicle for a short distance and was thankful when it turned into a driveway. She picked up speed and, on a long bend, spotted her quarry well ahead. It was slowing. Maybe the occupants thought that they had succeeded in getting away without being spotted. But what, exactly, had they been up to? And who were they?

She stayed well back, content with just the occasional glimpse of her quarry. They were driving mostly downhill, at a quick but safe pace. Would the driver notice her at some point? Surely they were bound to? She thought that the car probably held two occupants but couldn't be sure. The local comms signal was weak again, fading in and out. Had her report of the pursuit got through or was she on her own? No one had got back to her, so it might well be that the Exmoor police-radio gremlin was active again.

Sophie was right in her guess that she would be spotted at some point. It happened once they reached the main road, the A39, running east-west a few miles inland from the coastline. Unlike the country lanes, it was busy with traffic and Sophie was forced to move closer to her quarry, overtaking several times. This must have caught the attention of the Mercedes driver. The car took the local road down towards Watchet, then accelerated hard, speeding off at a dangerous rate. Sophie tried her best to follow but the occasional tourist vehicle got in her way. She lost sight of the target car completely. Finally, she came round the long bend near Saint Decuman's church and realised that traffic was at a standstill in front of her. She braked hard and came to a juddering stop. The Mercedes was a few cars in front, having skidded across the grass verge into a hedge near a junction, in order to avoid a tractor that had been coming up the hill. As she watched, the car reversed noisily then shot left along the narrow side lane, probably in an attempt to avoid the clog-up on the Watchet Road.

Sophie glanced at her satnav display. The lane was a dead end, going no further than the nearby church. Hadn't the driver realised? She followed carefully and soon came across the Mercedes, stationary in the road, its doors open. It had been abandoned. But where were the occupants? Sophie looked again at the electronic map on the dashboard. There was a footpath, leading down the steep hill into Watchet, maybe half a mile in length. She got out of her car and took a look, catching sight of two people hurrying down the path. It was partly obscured by high hedges, trees and shrubs, looked steep and seemed very quiet. What to do?

She tried to contact Polly directly but had no success. In the end she reported her situation to the central control room on her police radio, hoping that there was some kind of connection, then rang Rae's phone. Glory be! The signal was weak, but she heard Rae's voice answering.

'Rae, I need you,' she said. 'I'm on the path down to Watchet, in pursuit. Can you tell Polly? She must be in a signal blackspot.'

The signal died. Had Rae heard? Sophie glanced around. The two figures had vanished from view. If she let them get away now, they might never be traced or identified.

She set off in pursuit.

CHAPTER 42: CONFRONTATION

The steep path had a tarmac surface, indicating continued heavy and regular use, probably by dog-walkers and tourists. Sophie imagined that it had once been busy with local parishioners, struggling uphill from Watchet to the ancient church on the hilltop, though she couldn't take the time to note the niceties this morning. She had to keep her eyes peeled for signs of movement ahead. Ruins of an old building appeared beyond the bushes to her left. This must be the site of the old paper mill. She suddenly slowed. There was a dark tunnel ahead, presumably where the path ran under an old road or railway siding. Was it safe? She ventured in with trepidation, creeping along its length as quietly as she could, ears fully alert for any sound. Nothing. As she approached the exit, she backed against one wall and moved along it slowly, senses primed. Again, nothing. It was a relief to come out into the bright daylight. She should be coming into Watchet very soon, downhill another couple of hundred yards, beyond the dense bank of trees and undergrowth.

She stopped. Could she hear voices, speaking quietly? There were signs that someone had pushed through the greenery, and very recently: a couple of broken branches and crushed leaves on the left side of the path. There were no more sounds, so she followed, trying to remain as quiet as possible. She found herself behind a set of derelict buildings, looking across an area of weed-infested wasteland. That must be the Washford River across on the far side, and this was probably where Carlyon's body had been dumped into the fast-flowing water, to be carried down to the harbour area by the current. She rounded the corner of the ramshackle building and suddenly stopped. Two people were in front, and both turned to face her. Sharon Billings, or Lady Braycombe, as she'd been in recent decades, and Harry Campion, wearing a cloth cap. They must have known she was following. The man was carrying a solid-looking stick. The woman bent down and picked up an old metal bar that was on the ground near her feet.

'Don't do anything stupid,' Sophie said. 'I have people with me.'

She glanced quickly around, looking for something that she could use as a defensive weapon. Nothing.

'Really?' Sharon mocked. 'You have people with you? And where are they, then?'

Her carefully structured accent had gone, replaced by a broad south London inflection. She cocked a hand to her ear in a scornful gesture. 'I hear nothing.' She lifted her hand above her eyes and melodramatically looked around. 'I see no one.' She returned her gaze to Sophie. 'We were okay 'til you lot arrived on the scene. We had everything planned out. It was all running *tickety-boo*.'

Sophie couldn't help but respond. 'What? A man murdered, another badly beaten, a young woman raped and a group of people living in slavery? You call that tickety-boo? You're deranged.' She was edging slowly back towards the gap in the hedge.

'Watch her, Harry. She's thinking of making a run for it.' Sharon gently swung the metal bar in her hand as the duo cut off Sophie's main escape route.

Sophie didn't wait. She ran the opposite way as fast as she could, past the last of the derelict buildings and across the open expanse of pitted, cracked concrete. Maybe the river was fordable. She reached it, panting hard, Harry only a few steps behind. Her last hope was dashed. The river was running high from the heavy rain of recent nights. She looked around in panic. Was there a way out? It didn't look like it. She turned to face her pursuers and dodged sideways as Harry swung his stick at her. Then she felt a crushing pain to her right leg and started to fall, catching sight of Sharon still swinging the bar she held in her hand. Sophie tried to twist again but her leg was in agony, and she saw the ground rising up as she tumbled. She hit the ground with a thud that nearly knocked all the breath from her body. But she deliberately kept rolling and entered the fast-flowing water with a splash. The cold liquid closed over her head as she rolled again.

On the bank, Sharon turned to Harry. 'That's her a goner. We'd better be out of here pretty quick. Otherwise there'll be all hell to pay.'

CHAPTER 43: RUSHING WATER

Rae and Tommy were the first to arrive at the road junction near Watchet. The skid marks were clearly visible, showing that a vehicle had recently ended up on the verge. Muddy tyre tracks led along the narrow lane to the church where a car sat, abandoned in the road. Sophie's car was behind it. Tommy had been studying the local map closely.

'There's a path down from an old church towards the town centre,' he said. 'I can't see any other that makes sense. She definitely said "path"?'

'Yes.' Rae slewed her car to a stop. Decision time. 'That was twenty minutes ago. They might be down at the bottom by now.' She paused, thinking hard. 'I'll take the car down.'

She turned the small sports car as rapidly as she could, then raced back to the junction, taking the winding main road down towards the town. Tommy was on the phone to the local police.

'I've got a bad feeling about this,' Rae said.

'But she of all people knows the procedure,' Tommy replied. 'Wait for support.'

Rae slewed the car sharp left along an approach road to an old industrial area. 'This is the boss we're talking about. I know the way she thinks. She'll have gone after them.'

Her car screamed across the rough ground, sending clouds of dust and debris into the air.

'There!' she shouted.

Three figures were moving on the bank of the river, one swinging some kind of rod or bar. The two detectives watched in horror as the further figure slumped to the ground and toppled into the water.

'It's the boss!' Tommy cried.

Rae drove directly at the other two people and flung her car door open as she reached them, the car still moving. The edge of the door caught the man on the side of his body, and he tumbled to the ground. Rae slewed the car round in a circle, brought it to a standstill and launched herself out. The woman was still on her feet and running, but Rae was fitter, faster and younger. She launched herself forward and pushed her quarry to the ground. The woman had a metal bar in her hand and started to swing it. Rae kicked her in the midriff and the rod fell out of her hand.

The woman was crouching on her knees and groaned. 'Christ. That hurt.'

Rae punched her in the face, hard. She looked up in time to see a police squad car approach. Sarah Levy and Jackie Spring jumped out.

'We got your message,' Sarah said.

'No time,' Rae gasped. 'The chief super went into the river. These two assaulted her. Where will the water take her?'

Jackie spoke. 'She'll either come back up right here, or down in the town centre.' She looked horrified. 'It goes through a couple of culverts further down.'

'Tommy, get these two cuffed then look around here with Sarah.' She turned to Jackie. 'We'll head downriver. Tell me where to go.'

Rae took the car out of the old mill area as fast as she dare, then accelerated downhill into the town centre, her hand on the horn.

'Where?' she said. 'Tell me.'

'Keep going. Down by the Star Inn. The tide's out. There's a wide area where the river gets shallow. If she's not there, then God knows.'

The car screamed around several bends and ended up in the busy centre of Watchet. Rae raced through the streets following Jackie's directions and finally slewed to a halt in a narrow approach road to the white-painted pub. The two officers flung their doors open and rushed to the low wall, scanning the river, much wider and shallower here.

Jackie pointed. 'There!'

A hunched form was sprawled in the water at the point where the river suddenly widened. Rae desperately looked around, seeking an easy way down. There wasn't one.

She looked at the wall in front of her.

'I'm going down here,' she said. 'You'll need to balance yourself, grab my arms and lower me. I'll drop the last couple of feet.'

'You might break your legs,' Jackie said.

Rae turned to face her. 'Do I care? Let's move.'

Rae was down at water level within a few seconds, and still upright. She rushed through the water to Sophie's prone body and pulled it a few feet to a drier area. Rae couldn't feel a pulse. She tipped Sophie onto her back and started mouth to mouth CPR. She'd counted to eight when Sophie made a choking noise and a gush of fluid escaped from her mouth. Her eyes fluttered as she started to breathe again.

'Thank God,' Rae muttered. 'Bloody hell. Thank God.'

CHAPTER 44: HOSPITAL

Thursday

Rae was dozing in her seat in a corner of the waiting area but looked up when she heard footsteps approaching. It was Barry Marsh, WeSCU's DI. She'd completely forgotten that he'd been due to return from honeymoon the previous day. She was about to utter a few words of welcome but decided against it when he got closer. Despite being tanned, his face was almost white with anger, his eyes fierce in the intensity of his gaze.

'For God's sake,' he hissed. 'Tell me she'll be alright, Rae.'

'She's got a fighting chance of pulling through. That's all they'll say. They've put her in an induced coma because she hit her head badly when she fell. And she's got a fractured femur from where she was hit by an iron bar. The problem is, they don't know how long she was under water for. They're worried about possible brain damage.' Rae paused for a few seconds, her eyes on Barry's face. 'I can guess what you're thinking but you'd be wrong. We did all the planning by the book. We think she spotted someone or something and decided on a quick look-see by herself. You know what she's like. Added to which, the comms in that area were all over the place yesterday. Things must have escalated badly at some point. Honestly, Barry, I got there as fast as I could.'

Barry shook his head from side to side, muttering to himself. He looked as if he wanted to punch someone or something, hard. She knew that feeling. Hadn't she done exactly the same on the previous day when she'd caught that twisted woman, Sharon Billings? Better keep Barry away from the two people who'd assaulted the boss. He looked as though he'd tear them apart, limb from limb.

At last he spoke again. 'Martin's been in, then? Has he been looked after properly?'

'Of course. Polly's been good, Barry. She's no empty head. Martin, Jade and Hannah are in the room with the boss at the moment.'

He still looked distraught. 'Should I disturb them? Christ, Rae, I don't know what to do, or say. Or even think. I mean, this is unthinkable. It can't be happening.'

Rae stayed silent for a few moments. What could she say? She hadn't slept last night, and her brain was all over the place. She decided to switch tack.

'Polly, Ade and Tommy are dealing with the interviews. I don't want to go near the people who did it. You should stay away too. It's too raw for us, Barry. But I think it'll be okay for you to pop your head in her room. Maybe Martin and the girls need a break. Do you want me there?'

'Not at first. Give me a few minutes, will you?'

He left the waiting area and moved into the ward proper.

* * *

Barry tapped on the door and opened it a few inches. Martin was at the bedside and looked up, as did his daughters, Hannah and Jade.

'Barry! You're back from your honeymoon! Maybe things are looking up, after all.'

Martin stood up and came across to the detective, embracing him.

'I can't believe this, Martin.' Barry sounded choked up.

'No. None of us can. But it's happened, and here we are. And things could be worse, couldn't they? She could be dead. Do you want a few moments? We could do with a coffee break, to be honest.'

'That would be good.'

Jade spoke as she stood up to leave. He hadn't seen her for a while and his thoughts flickered through the history of their encounters, from her as a prickly, mischievous teenager to the beautiful young woman she was now, in training to be a doctor. 'She's stable, Barry. And there are optimistic signs. Don't squeeze her hand too hard, will you?' She gave him a hug.

He sat down in one of the bedside chairs, reached across and took Sophie's hand. 'It's me, Barry,' he murmured in her ear. 'I think I've got here just in time. I'm Mr Jump-Start, arrived to get those circuits moving again. We need to get you sorted, Sophie. Martin and the girls. Me and Rae. I think Lydia's trying to rearrange things to get across from Bournemouth as soon as she can. You've got the whole team around you. You can pull through, we know you can.'

He squeezed her hand gently. Was that a slight twitch of a reply or just his imagination?

Rae came in and scanned the display screens on the equipment beside her bed. 'Not much change since an hour ago,' she said. 'Remember she's in an induced coma. They're talking about bringing her out of it tomorrow, but I don't think the final decision's been made yet.'

So that twitch had just been his imagination, then. Wishful thinking on his part.

'Can you take me through what happened, Rae? I've calmed down a bit now, I think.'

Rae didn't think he looked any calmer but decided not to point it out.

'The crazy thing is, the boss had the least problematic task. We were all kitted up, searching for these missing men and the duo we thought had them hidden and were probably behind the murder. The boss volunteered to visit a nineteen-year-old woman with Down's, along with her mother, on their farm, just to get their take on things. It should have been a walk in the park in comparison. Apparently, she spoke to them, toddled off to see the forensic team working through a group of caravans, then had a look in one of the vans. She was then seen moving to her car in a bit of a hurry. That's it. She must have caught sight of the two thugs and gone off in pursuit. We think she tried to call it in but, as I said, comms were messy at the time. And here we are.'

Barry didn't say anything. He looked as though he was thinking things through, so Rae continued.

'You're my boss, Barry. I can't tell you what to do. But I can guess what you're thinking. That you'll come back a few days early, maybe even tomorrow. Please, check with Polly first. I'll let her know you've called in here, at the hospital. If she wants you back in, then fine. But she's as devastated as we are. And she's nervy about it. The last thing she needs is to find you trying to muscle in, making her insecurities worse. I'm sure she's got it all under control. Trust me.'

Barry looked at her steadily. She was right, of course. He knew nothing of the sequence of events that had led to this point, nor of the protagonists involved. If he turned up now, trying to throw his weight around, he'd just end up making things worse and putting his own future in jeopardy. Polly was his senior, after all.

'What about if I just offer my services?' he replied. 'There must be something I can help with, surely.'

Rae pondered. 'Probably. I'll call Polly, then let you know.' She put her arms around him. 'Don't you think you should just go home? I can talk to Polly and let her know you were here. And I'll let you know what she says, I promise. Trust me?'

'Yeah, of course I do. But it's not that simple, Rae. The boss means everything to me. I don't think I can sit idly by. It would drive me nuts.'

He sat back down at Sophie's bedside for a few more minutes, pondering on what Rae had said. Her advice sounded right, but this was the boss they were talking about, and an attempt on her life. He gave Sophie's hand another squeeze before leaving.

Once Barry had gone, Rae wondered again at the exact nature of the relationship between Barry and Sophie. Had she somehow become a substitute mother for him in the years following the death of his real mother?

She waited until Martin, Hannah and Jade returned, had a long conversation with them, then left too. There was a lot of work still to be done.

CHAPTER 45: ACUTE STRESS

Polly was feeling acutely stressed. She now had four distinct crimes to probe, each with its own sequence of events, and each with its own cast list, even though there was obviously some overlap of personalities. It was like a set of Venn diagrams from school maths lessons in which she had to wrestle with the problem of identifying which individual was involved with each of the four strands. The murder of Benjamin Carlyon; the assault on, and subsequent death of, Billy Potter; the slavery-style conditions under which the group of men were kept and worked; and, finally, the attempted murder of her own boss, Sophie Allen. Then the side issues. The historic art theft, if one had actually occurred; the rape of the girl, Maddy Guthrie; the assault on Carlyon's nephew, Justin Penhale. The strands were all connected, but needed separate investigation records and methodologies, just to keep the legal aspects clearly identifiable, ready for the CPS. At least she'd been promised a modern slavery expert to deal with that particular strand because of the specialist knowledge required, although they weren't due to arrive for another day. It was the absence of her own boss, Sophie Allen, that she felt most keenly. At a stroke she'd lost the person who would be the greatest use in a complex situation like this. Someone from whom she could seek advice and guidance. Or, in more simple terms, someone with whom she could bounce ideas around.

She heard the office door open and looked up to see a familiar figure walking towards her.

'Barry!' she cried. 'Rae called and let me know you were back. You must think I've made a shambles of this whole case.' She put a hand to her head. What on earth would he be thinking? Could she go through yet another lengthy, emotion-wrenching explanation?

He gave her a weak smile. 'Rae's filled me in on the details. She said it was probably better for me to stay away for a day or two until my official leave is over.' He looked Polly in the eye. 'I can't. I'd never forgive myself. Have you got a job for me, boss?'

Polly realised that his last word said it all. He was reassuring her that nothing had changed, that he'd got over any initial sense of frustrated anger in which he might lash out at his colleagues.

She smiled grimly. 'Of course. In fact, you're a blessing in disguise. I can give you one of the cases, of course I can. But what I really need is someone to bounce ideas off. You know what I mean, don't you?'

'Course I do,' he nodded, then waited for a few seconds. 'There's a big vacuum, isn't there? That's what I feel. An emptiness.'

'Too bloody right. And thanks, I'm feeling better already. But remember, Barry. She's not dead yet. Isn't she meant to be as tough as old boot leather? You must know better than anyone.'

He opted not to answer and Polly decided not to probe more deeply. Maybe, over the years he'd worked for Sophie Allen, he'd seen below the surface more than most. And this wasn't the time to ask.

'Can I read through the case details? Rae gave me a quick summary back at the hospital.' He was obviously changing the subject.

'Of course. Then maybe we could put our heads together. What do you say?'

'Glad to help.'

'We've been using a local special constable in an investigative support role, Barry, and she's been brilliant. Her name's Jackie Spring. She's a local librarian but she's worried that her library job might disappear. I wonder if we can use her in WeSCU somehow? Have a chat with her if you can and tell me what you think. Get Rae's thoughts as well. I don't really want to say it, but it might be me and you running the unit for some time. We need to plan ahead.'

Barry frowned and merely nodded.

* * *

The plan the two senior officers came up with was this, as explained to the rest of the team by Polly and Barry at the late-morning briefing. Barry would take over questioning about the murder of Carlyon and the assault on his nephew, Justin Penhale, now recovering rapidly from the effects of his head injury. Justin's memory of the attack was coming back, so there was hope that this part of the investigation could be wrapped up quickly. More forensic evidence was accumulating from the scene of Carlyon's murder, so hopes were high of a breakthrough, and the photos Justin had taken just before he was knocked unconscious were proving to be invaluable. The old Land Rover he'd spotted was registered to the Braycombe Estate, and the man sprawled on the ground watching his house looked to be Harry Campion, though there was no frontal view of him in the photos.

Rae and Tommy were to lead the group looking into the rape of Maddy Guthrie and the subsequent attack on Billy Potter. Meanwhile, Ade would be working with Bristol-based DS Charlie Keen, who'd arrived to help with the modern slavery angle.

This left Polly free to pursue the attempted murder charges against Lady Braycombe and Harry Campion, for their vicious assault on the chief super, Sophie Allen, still lying in her hospital bed in a coma.

All the suspects were in custody. The WeSCU team only had two days left to work their way through the accumulated evidence and try to disentangle who did what, and why. They needed clarity into the complex sequence of events. Murder, rape, brutality, intimidation, assault. It was all there but mixed up in a shadowy muddle.

'Realistically, we have little more than a day and a half if we want them charged before our three-day window runs out,' Polly said. 'Let's get moving.'

* * *

Both Polly and Barry felt that the obvious weak link they could exploit was with the men who'd lived in the caravans on Greymoor. They'd need to be handled with care, with an appropriate adult present during their interviews because of their cognitive difficulties. Nevertheless, Ade's careful questioning technique should yield much useful information about events at Greymoor. He and Charlie Keen interviewed the men one by one, starting gently with questions about their day-to-day life before moving to more specific probing, focussed on relationships at the farm: Billy Potter, the Guthrie trio and, most of all, Harry Campion.

Gordon Binnie was less guarded than the others, maybe because of his recent chats with workers on neighbouring farms when he'd asked about the missing man, Billy Potter. The detectives learned that Billy could be hot-headed, that he'd been sweet on Maddy, that a secret romance had developed between the two, that they'd fallen out after Billy had hurt the young woman during sex, and that Maddy's parents were furious when they found out. Others among the men confirmed Gordon's account that Billy had been severely punished for his treatment of Maddy, and that he'd subsequently disappeared. One of the men could also remember the evening the beating had occurred as being the same night as the big storm.

'Bryn and Harry had to go out to fix some covers,' the man said. 'That's when Billy got away.'

Once Ade felt that he'd got the information he wanted, he allowed his colleague to take over. The line of questioning shifted to their own working and living conditions. Their lives were lived completely under the thumbs of Bryn Guthrie and Harry Campion, with Babs playing the part of cook and nurse. They had enough to eat but the food they were given was nutritionally poor and unappealing. If they complained, they were locked in a tiny wooden shed for a day without access to water or hygiene facilities. And a picture began to emerge that was less than flattering towards Babs Guthrie.

She'd presented herself as a browbeaten bystander, forced into her role by her bullying husband. Ade and Charlie realised that this was somewhat false. Most of the men, despite their initial reluctance to speak out fully, were beginning to paint a different portrait of her, one that showed cruelty and a willingness to indulge in the humiliation of these men. It forced Ade to rethink some of the assumptions the detectives had made. He messaged Polly with the news.

* * *

Barry called in to see Jackie Spring in the tiny police station at Watchet. Polly and Rae were right. She impressed him with her deep understanding of the case. He then went to visit Justin Penhale before the man was discharged from hospital. He'd been given a clean bill of health, and just as importantly, his memory of the attack had returned. Barry showed him a series of photos of the men they had in custody, including the caravan dwellers.

Justin looked at them all carefully, then returned to the second in the sequence.

'That's him,' he said. 'No doubt in my mind. He was the one watching the house.'

The photo he'd selected was of Harry Campion.

Barry was puzzled. Why would Campion have been keeping a watch on the house? It didn't make much sense. Polly and Rae were both of the opinion that the murder of Justin's uncle in the shed was the work of either Bryn Guthrie or Harry Campion, with the latter as the favoured killer. If Carlyon had started to blackmail Lady Braycombe about the art theft two decades earlier, then she would want the man silenced. That was understandable. But once the murder had been carried out, surely the killer wouldn't keep returning to the scene, watching the comings and goings? Unless there was something at the house that might prove incriminating in some way.

'Are you going straight back to Exeter?' Barry asked.

'I guess so. But my car is still up at my uncle's house. I'll probably sleep over there tonight and go home tomorrow.'

'I'll drive you up there. I'd like to take a look around and get a feel for the place. I expect Forensics have gone through it with a fine-tooth comb.'

'That's what I've been told,' Justin replied. 'And I'd be grateful for a lift.'

In truth, Barry was still feeling edgy and wanted to skewer his niggling worries about this whole case. He had no doubts that Polly and the team had the right people under lock and key. He knew full well how good the WeSCU team of detectives were. But they'd all been involved right from the start and that had shaped the way their ideas had evolved. His own late arrival had given him a slightly different perspective, and there were a couple of things that niggled him, the main one being Babs Guthrie. After all, she'd been present, or could have been present, at all the major incidents in the case. The art theft, the affair with Carlyon that had resulted in the birth of the girl with Down's, close involvement with the workmen who had been little more than slaves, the beating of the man Billy, access to Braycombe House because of her role there. Maybe he could call into Greymoor Farm and speak to her briefly, once he'd visited the lonely house on the moor. But what exactly would he be looking for? He didn't know. He suspected that his worries were just the outward manifestations of his shock and frustration over the assault on his boss and the desperate state of her health.

His phone beeped and he glanced at the message. It was an observation from Ade that Babs Guthrie might be more involved in the intimidation of the slavery victims than the team had thought. He smiled wryly. Maybe he hadn't lost his touch after all.

CHAPTER 46: GINGER HAIR

The descriptions had been right. Barry stepped out of the car and followed Justin Penhale across the gravel path to the front door of the remote building. Windswept. Rainlashed. Brooding. Who on earth would want to live here? But at that very moment the rain stopped falling and a shaft of golden sunlight swept across the moorland, causing the grey walls of the house to gleam. It was transformed into a building of beauty. The change had happened in less than a minute. No wonder Justin's uncle had decided to settle here. That sudden change in appearance Barry had witnessed would inspire any artist.

He followed Justin inside, then wandered around the rooms for a few minutes, not knowing exactly what he was seeking. All his colleagues had been up here at one time or another. Even the boss herself, Sophie Allen, had been inside, poking through the rooms, and Rae had been the first to see the upstairs studio and had discovered the portrait of the girl with Down's. Did he really think he was likely to spot something that they'd overlooked? Get real, he told himself.

Barry looked at that painting now. So, this was the young woman who lived on Greymoor Farm. He studied it carefully. Despite what Rae had said, he thought it was an outstanding piece of art. He thought that there was real feeling conveyed by the composition of the work. He knew he was no expert but, to him, the painting showed happiness in the eyes of the subject and, more subtly, signs of pleasure from the artist.

Barry looked up to see Justin watching him.

'It doesn't alter things,' he finally said. 'To be honest, it was a real positive, to learn that I had a cousin I never knew existed. I realised that this house would go to her, when I was told.'

Barry nodded. 'I'm going there next. Do you want me to ask if she wants to meet you?'

'Of course. As long as it doesn't upset things.'

'I'll use my judgement on that. Don't get your hopes up too much.'

'What makes you think she'll open up to you?' Justin sounded puzzled.

Barry laughed. 'Look at the painting. Ginger hair. How could I fail?' He scratched his head to draw attention to his own dark ginger hair colour.

He left Justin at the house and drove the three miles to Greymoor Farm, looking at the scenery with interest. This was his first visit to the area, and he needed to get a feel for the key locations and their relative positions. His role in the wrapping-up stage of the investigation was a little hazy, but he guessed what he'd want if his and Polly's roles were reversed. Someone who could take a step back and view things dispassionately. Hah! How likely was that, with the chief super in a hospital bed, at death's door?

He drew into the farmyard and parked beside a squad car that was already there. A young woman was throwing corn feed to a group of clucking hens. The scene brought back memories of his own childhood growing up on a small farm, albeit one in a rather more benign location than this. She looked across at him as he climbed out of the car. It was her, the subject of the painting, Maddy. He smiled and raised his hand in a wave.

'I'm with the police,' he said.

'Mum's inside,' she replied, jerking her head towards the farmhouse door.

'It's actually you I've come to see,' he said. 'Well, your mother as well, at some point. You're Maddy, I expect. You look just like that painting of you, across at the old house.'

She frowned, her face darkening and her eyes crinkling up. 'It brought trouble. Too much. All this hate.'

By now Barry was by her side. 'I grew up on a farm. This reminds me so much of my childhood. Can I help?'

She nodded, so he scooped a handful of meal and scattered it in front of the chickens.

'Whereabouts?' Maddy asked.

'In Dorset, near Swanage. It was one of the happiest times of my life. Helping my parents. Feeding the animals. I'll never forget it. Do you feel the same?'

She seemed to relax a little. 'Yeah. It's all gone stupid now, though. I feel sick with worry. I didn't sleep much last night. Nothing is what I thought it was.'

'No, I can imagine. Things changed for me when my father was killed in an accident on the farm. It was never the same afterwards. We had to move out.'

She shielded her eyes from the glare of the spring sun as she looked at him. 'How old were you?'

'Fourteen. We moved down into the town and my mum opened a café. It's what she'd always wanted to do. It was okay for me, I suppose, but it wasn't the same as living on the farm.' He paused for a few seconds. 'Is that how you feel?'

'Yeah. I dunno if we can stay here. Mum's acting up. I knows things are going on, but they won't tell me anything. They all treat me like an idiot, but I'm not.'

'How did you meet the artist, Mr Carlyon?'

'You mean Ben? See, that's something else. He's meant to be my real dad, but they won't say nothing. They think I'm a kid and won't understand. But I'm not.'

Barry merely nodded.

She sighed. 'It were the year before last. I was walking back from the village and he was down in the dip by the stream, painting. I ain't ever seen that before. I stopped to look. He gave me a biscuit. We got chatting.'

'When did he suggest painting you?'

'Oh, that were a lot later. See, I shouldn't have been seeing him. Mum was okay at first when I told her. But she saw him and that's when it changed. She told me to stay away. She got really angry. I dunno why, 'cos he was really nice. He gave me this.' Maddy fingered a gold locket that was hanging around her neck. It was the one in the painting. She looked sad. 'He must've found out about me, that I was his daughter. He didn't tell me, though. No one did. Mum always knew. That's what I reckon.'

She gave Barry a piercing look.

'Did Dad kill him? When he found out? Is that what happened?'

'We can't be sure, not yet, Maddy. There could be other reasons. Other people. That's what we're trying to discover. We've got everyone in custody though, so we'll get whoever did it, I'm sure.'

'That's what you think. But you ain't got everyone, have you? Mum's still up here, ain't she? Even though you've taken Uncle Harry in.'

Barry frowned. What was this? 'Uncle Harry? What do you mean?'

'He's Mum's brother. Or half-brother really. I've never liked him. But he's shacked up with Auntie Sharon, and she's got all the money. That's what Mum says. Dad does everything Uncle Harry tells him.' Her blue eyes focussed on him even more intensely. 'Are we gonna lose the farm?'

'I don't know, Maddy. But as Benjamin Carlyon's daughter, you stand a good chance of inheriting his house, across on the moor. Everyone thought it would go to his nephew. That's all changed since we discovered you. He'd be your cousin.'

Her frown disappeared. 'So, I've found someone else?'

Barry smiled back. 'We all think he's a nice guy, and he's very happy that you've been found. He's across at the house now. Would you like to meet him later?'

'Sure.'

'He's got ginger hair, too.' Barry couldn't help but grin.

Maddy laughed. 'All the best people do. That's what Ben said.'

He called Polly and exchanged a few words, then turned towards the farmhouse, knocked on the door and went in, nodding to the uniformed constable who was there on duty.

Maddy's mother, Babs, had obviously been watching his conversation with her daughter from the kitchen window. Her anger was evident from the expression on her face.

'You shouldn't be talking to Maddy. Not without me there.' Her voice was almost a snarl.

'She's an adult, Mrs Guthrie. She's intelligent. I have a cousin with Down's. He struggles more than your Maddy does, yet he lives independently. Take it as a positive judgement on Maddy's upbringing, that she copes so well. I'd better introduce myself. I'm DI Barry Marsh, part of the WeSCU team. I know your husband is under arrest and being questioned, but he hasn't been charged yet. It was decided to leave you here with Maddy, but that decision has changed. I'd like you to come in for further questioning. I'll leave an FLO here on the farm to keep an eye on Maddy.'

He had a few words with the duty constable, waited for the arrival of another squad car, then led the unhappy Babs outside to the vehicle. Barry could see that she was still muttering angrily to the officers in the car as it drove away.

Barry returned to Maddy. 'Do you want to meet your cousin now? He's keen to see you.'

She replied nervously. 'S'pose so. Dad always says, no time like the present.'

The comment made Barry wonder about the character of Bryn Guthrie. Was he really the confrontational thug that the rest of the team thought, or had he found himself pushed into that role by his wife and her brother? Time would tell.

'Okay. Let's go. He's across at Benjamin's house, doing a bit of last-minute tidying before he returns to Exeter. He's been in hospital, recovering from concussion. I can't tell you more.'

'Was it Uncle Harry?' Maddy asked, quite openly. 'He used to hit the workmen. I hated it.'

Barry didn't comment. He'd need an official interview and statement from her, probably with an appropriate adult present.

When they arrived at the house on the moor just a few minutes later, Barry stood back as the newlyfound cousins greeted each other, quite formally at first. That formality lasted only until Justin took Maddy up to the studio and she spotted the painting. She looked at it for several minutes while fingering her gold locket, then started crying. Justin put an arm around her shoulder.

'He was lovely,' she explained. 'He was kind and thoughtful. I love this painting.'

'It's yours, Maddy. Along with everything else in the house. And the house too. Bynehill View.' Justin paused. 'Uncle Ben kept a notebook. He used it to jot down ideas and locations for possible paintings. I found this written in it.'

He opened a small, scruffy notebook that had been lying on a work top in the studio, then passed it over.

This is wonderful. I have a daughter! Her name's Maddy. She doesn't know who I am yet. What a lovely personality, despite her difficulties and the parents she has. She positively glows when she sits for me. How do I go about telling her? I'll need to find a way to approach Babs about it, though the thought worries me. Her temper hasn't improved over the decades. If anything, it's got worse. God bless the day I came across the girl when I was painting near their farm.

CHAPTER 47: LUCKY CHARM?

When Barry returned to the incident room after dropping Maddy back at Greymoor and checking that an FLO was in place, he noticed a more upbeat atmosphere.

'Bryn Guthrie has broken ranks,' Polly explained. 'He's started to open up.'

'It fits with some of the things Maddy told me. Or, I should say, didn't tell me, but were there between the lines. I'd guess that she was closer to Bryn than to her mum. Of course, she thought he was her birth father and I guess he did too. According to her, Harry was the hard man. And he was Babs' half-brother. Do you think they were working in league?'

Polly shrugged. 'We'll see what they both have to say. We've just finished round one with Bryn. If what he says is true, he was only guilty of aiding and abetting. But we'd expect him to say that, wouldn't we? Anyone in his position would claim they were innocent of anything serious. It's par for the course. But Harry isn't the brains behind what's been going on. And I don't think Babs is, either.'

'The other woman? Lady whatever her name is?' Barry suggested.

'That's what we're beginning to think. Sharon Billings, as she was several decades ago. Lady Braycombe, as she is now. There's little doubt that she was the brains behind the art-swap business when her husband was still alive. A Gainsborough expert had a look late yesterday at the one in the house and thinks it's a fake. She's a clever cookie, is our Sharon. Whether it was an actual theft would hinge on whether her late husband was aware of the switch, but he's not here to tell us. The real one probably did get sold abroad, by the way. Which opens up another charge for us to use. You can't ship a Gainsborough abroad without a proper licence. But it's small fry, really. Compared to what they did to the boss. We found an independent witness, by the way. A guy was fishing illegally, half hidden in the trees on the other side of the river. He saw the whole thing and he'll testify if we don't prosecute him for poaching. We'll go for attempted murder. Hopefully.'

Barry knew what was meant by that final word. The hope that it wouldn't turn into actual murder.

'How's the modern slavery angle progressing?'

'Good, so far. Those men forced to live and work on that farm aren't criminal thugs. They're simple souls, really. A bit lost. Ade and his buddy just ask them what their days were like, and it all comes spilling out. The punishment beatings, the poor diets, the appalling living conditions, the so-called pocket money they earned. God, it's bloody awful.' She shook her head in disgust. 'Some of them had lash marks on their backs. Can you believe it, in this day and age? They got beaten if their work was poor. The only person who showed them any kindness was the girl, Maddy. She'd come across and put antiseptic on their wounds. It makes me sick with anger. Good job it's Ade and Charlie Keen doing the interviews. If it was me, I'd feel like running out and throttling those four sick-minded brutes.'

'Rae and Tommy?'

'All good. They're pretty certain Maddy's story stands up to scrutiny. It was the dead man, Billy Potter, who raped her. It all checks out, though we're still waiting for DNA confirmation. The clinic had kept several swabs from when she and her mum visited for the check-up the next morning. We're hopeful.'

'So, why was Carlyon killed? That's what I still can't see clearly.'

'Think about it, Barry. It was in everyone's interest. All four of them. Babs was furious that he'd reappeared and got to know Maddy. We think Bryn began to have his doubts about being Maddy's father, even though he claims otherwise. Maybe he guessed more than Maddy herself. Then there's Sharon, who would have spotted Carlyon around and realised that he could spill the beans and ruin their nice little set-up. Carlyon would have kept quiet at first, but once he discovered Maddy, who knows what might have happened? But the real clincher comes from a couple of the men. They said that when Maddy stumbled back to the farmhouse after being raped by Potter, Bryn got the wrong idea. He went straight out in a van with Harry, looking for someone to take out his rage on. He thought it was Carlyon that attacked her. It wasn't until the next day that he realised the mistake and did the same to the real culprit.'

'It makes sense, two of them. Carlyon was a big bloke, according to what's on the incident board.'

'The forensic evidence is there. A couple of specks of tar wash on the foot pedals in Guthrie's Land Rover. And the footprint in the spilled tar wash up in Carlyon's shed matches the tread pattern on one of Harry Campion's boots. And it was Sharon and him who decided to keep a watch on the comings and goings at Carlyon's house. He and Babs took it in turns from an upstairs window at their farmhouse. If they saw activity up there, Harry would pay a visit to watch from the back.' She stopped for a few moments. 'You're like a lucky charm, Barry. We slog away for weeks getting next to nowhere, then you appear just at the time everything falls into place.'

Barry's face was sombre. 'I didn't come across for that reason.' He paused. 'I see what you mean about Jackie Spring. Let's think about it a bit more.'

He was interrupted by the sound of his phone ringing. He glanced at the caller display, then rushed outside.

CHAPTER 48: DORSET GOLD

Rae drove as fast as she could up the motorway to Taunton, with Barry in the passenger seat. It was heart-in-mouth time.

She slewed the car into the closest available parking space and they both raced towards the hospital entrance, nearly cannoning into a familiar figure standing in front of the reception desk. It was Lydia Pillay, Sophie and Barry's ex-colleague and close friend, looking frustrated as the receptionist tried to find the information about Sophie's precise location.

'Come with us,' Barry said hurriedly, grabbing Lydia by the arm. 'She's in the acute medical unit.'

The trio hurried along the corridor and into the ward. Sophie was in the same room as before, with the row of complex monitoring equipment still wired up to her body, beeping gently. Their view was blocked by the family group settled around the bed, today joined by Jade's boyfriend, George Warrander, also a Dorset cop.

Barry looked questioningly at Martin, who gave a weak smile in return. He looked exhausted and relieved at the same time. He moved to one side, giving the trio of detectives a glimpse of Sophie, laying with her head propped against the pillows, her eyes open but fluttering, her face grey.

'What have you been doing to yourself?' Lydia asked. 'You're not getting any younger, boss. You need to leave the fisticuffs to those of us still young enough to cope. Anything we can get you?'

'Dorset Gold,' Sophie whispered. 'Pint.'

'You were lucky, you know.'

'No. Managed to take a deep breath before I went in the river. Just remembered.'

She glanced tiredly at Barry. 'Knew you'd be here, Barry,' she gasped, then closed her eyes.

THE END

ACKNOWLEDGEMENTS

I want to take this opportunity to thank all the staff at Joffe Books for their help, particularly the editorial team for working on my original text so thoroughly. They always do a great job. Any errors are mine, though. If you spot a typo, please email Joffe Books and they'll do their best to correct it.

Special thanks to Kate Lyall Grant and Emma Grundy Haigh. Also to Rachel Malig for her thoughtful and detailed editing. I also want to mention Jasmine Callaghan, a project editor at Joffe, for her enthusiasm when interviewing me about Pride Month. I am a firm supporter of LGBTQ+ Pride events. I also support the aims of the Me Too movement, Black Lives Matter and Disability Rights.

Thanks are also due to my fellow Joffe authors; they're a great bunch and they use social media much more proficiently than me. Janice Frost, Joy Ellis, Helen Durrant, Charlie Gallagher, Judi Daykin, Tania Crosse and the rest: I love, respect and admire you all.

The biggest thanks go to the boss, Jasper Joffe, to whom I owe so much.

I need to own up to the fact that I really dislike social media, the misuse of which causes so much harm to so many people. I like email, though, and I'd like to reassure readers that if they email me direct, at michael@michaelhambling.co.uk, I will always respond as quickly as I can. Please visit my website at www.michaelhambling.co.uk. It went through a bit of an overhaul earlier this year, though I need to remember to post stuff on it more regularly! It does carry relevant information and a selection of free-to-read short stories.

You may like to read the novels I've started writing for young teenagers, the Misfit books. The stories are about a small group of unorthodox young people in Dorset who try to solve low-level, anti-social crimes that have a habit of escalating into something more serious. Rae Gregson, who appears in the Sophie Allen novels, tries to keep an eye on the group in her spare moments, and acts as an unofficial adviser. Available from Amazon.

AUTHOR'S NOTES

LOCATION

The area described in this novel is well worth a visit. Watchet, Dunster and Exmoor are ideal walking locations if you like exploring the UK's countryside. Dunster Castle is owned by the National Trust.

Watchet's Star Inn does exist, exactly in the location described. The manager and the owner gave me permission to make good literary use of their lovely pub when I told them I was planning to write a novel set in Watchet. Please pay them a visit; you won't be disappointed.

Likewise for the Georgian House B&B in Watchet, a really lovely place to stay. Alternatively, consider staying in nearby Dunster.

DORSET GOLD

Dorset Gold is a high-class real ale brewed by Palmers, a brewery in Bridport that has been operating since 1794. As its name implies, it's a golden beer, relatively lightly hopped. I love it, as do Sophie and Martin Allen. If you're looking for the perfect place in which to try a pint of it on hand-pump, there can be few better than the Seventh Wave café/restaurant at Durlston Castle country park, near Swanage. On a pleasant day, you may be able to find a table out on the terrace, with its spectacular views of the coast.

GLOSSARY

A & E: Accident and Emergency Unit in a hospital.
AMU: Acute Medical Unit in a hospital.
CPS: the Crown Prosecution Service, the official body that carries out court prosecutions in England.
Down's (or Down) Syndrome: Typically, a baby is born with 46 chromosomes. Babies with Down's syndrome have an extra copy of chromosome 21. This extra copy changes how the baby's body and brain develop, which can cause both mental and physical challenges.
FLO: Family Liaison Officer; a police officer who stays with a family after a trauma to both support the family and help to gather information from them.
Home Office: a ministerial department in the UK Government, responsible for immigration, security and law & order.

UK Police Ranks (in descending order of seniority)
Chief Constable (or Commissioner in London's Metropolitan Police force)
Deputy CC (Deputy Commissioner in London)
Assistant CC (Assistant Commissioner in London)
Chief Superintendent
Superintendent
Chief Inspector
Inspector
Sergeant
Constable

Detectives hold the same ranks but with a prefix before the name (DC, DS etc.) There is sometimes career movement back and forth between detectives and uniformed ranks.

THE JOFFE BOOKS STORY

We began in 2014 when Jasper agreed to publish his mum's much-rejected romance novel and it became a bestseller.

Since then we've grown into the largest independent publisher in the UK. We're extremely proud to publish some of the very best writers in the world, including Joy Ellis, Faith Martin, Caro Ramsay, Helen Forrester, Simon Brett and Robert Goddard. Everyone at Joffe Books loves reading and we never forget that it all begins with the magic of an author telling a story.

We are proud to publish talented first-time authors, as well as established writers whose books we love introducing to a new generation of readers.

We have been shortlisted for Independent Publisher of the Year at the British Book Awards three times, in 2020, 2021 and 2022, and for the Diversity and Inclusivity Award at the Independent Publishing Awards in 2022.

We built this company with your help, and we love to hear from you, so please email us about absolutely anything bookish at feedback@joffebooks.com

If you want to receive free books every Friday and hear about all our new releases, join our mailing list: www.joffebooks.com/contact

And when you tell your friends about us, just remember: it's pronounced Joffe as in coffee or toffee!

ALSO BY MICHAEL HAMBLING

THE SOPHIE ALLEN BOOKS

Book 1: DARK CRIMES
Book 2: DEADLY CRIMES
Book 3: SECRET CRIMES
Book 4: BURIED CRIMES
Book 5: TWISTED CRIMES
Book 6: EVIL CRIMES
Book 7: SHADOW CRIMES
Book 8: SILENT CRIMES
Book 9: RUTHLESS CRIMES
Book 10: BRUTAL CRIMES
Book 11: HIDDEN CRIMES
Book 12: VICIOUS CRIMES

Printed in Great Britain
by Amazon

34957220R00169